Sarah Champion

Sarah Champion edited the best-selling fiction anthologies, *Disco Biscuits* and *Disco 2000*.

Donal Scannell

Donal Scannell runs Dublin's Stereophonic and Quadrophonic club nights/record labels.

SCEPTRE
LIR

Also edited by Sarah Champion and available from Sceptre

Disco Biscuits
Disco 2000

Shenanigans

edited by
SARAH CHAMPION &
DONAL SCANNELL

SCEPTRE
LIR

Introduction and compilation © 1999 Sarah Champion & Donal Scannell

First published in 1999 by Hodder and Stoughton
A division of Hodder Headline PLC
A Sceptre Paperback

10 9 8 7 6 5 4 3 2 1

British Library C.I.P.
A CIP catalogue record for this title is availble from the British Library

ISBN 0 340 71269 4

Typeset by Palimpsest Book Production Limited,
Polmont, Stirlingshire
Printed and bound in Great Britain by
Clays Ltd, St Ives plc

Hodder and Stoughton
A division of Hodder Headline PLC
338 Euston Road
London NW1 3BH

Pronunciation: she-nan-i-gan
Function: noun
Etymology: origin unknown
Date: 1855
high-spirited or mischievous activity — usually
used in plural

Contents

Introduction

This book is something that just had to happen.

Regardless of what you're used to hearing about our fabled Celtic Tiger very little has changed in Ireland. The old guard still rule our roost economically, politically and culturally. Whilst we have hordes of frequently praised and displayed 'cultural ambassadors' those outside Ireland get a particularly distorted view of what's really making this new Ireland tick. This book is in many ways dedicated to every hapless foreign journalist who arrives in Ireland to document the 'hippest country in Europe' and never leaves our cultural theme park of Temple Bar in Dublin.

There is no young literati in Ireland, they don't hang out, do lunches, write newspaper columns about who they sniff what with.

There does exist this underbelly; the obsessed, the diligent, the inspired who clatter away unnoticed and produce the sort of fiction that made us want to do Shenanigans. Many of those featured have never been published before and you'll notice an immediate distinction between what we feel is exciting about Irish fiction now and what writing is traditionally associated with Ireland. On the other hand if you're looking for unifying themes one thing which doesn't appear to have changed is our penchant for dark, twisted, sordid humour. Don't expect a thesis on the alleged Irish psychosis to follow, but when a lot of these stories make you laugh it's normally for the sickest reasons.

Enjoy this collection and accept it for its variety. If everybody liked every story we'd have completed our task poorly. This is a true cross-section of our bizarre island which has been shaped forever because we had the fortune/misfortune to have English as one of our two languages.

Speaking our larger neighbour's language has given Ireland a status well beyond our size, it's far easier for us to demand the spotlight and it's an advantage we've never been shy to capitalise on.

So read up, enjoy and spread the word.

Donal Scannell

Bridget O'Connor

'THE ALIEN INVASION'

'And that is why the lights on video recorders are the same colour as stars. I now believe the lights on video recorders are there for a purpose. We are guided by electricity, by the foreign language of stars' Malcolm

At night I am transported back in time to the General Accident and Emergency Unit on the mainland. My head is clearing from the anaesthetic plunged into my arm three hours before, and through the pain heat-haze, which is pink-tinged, the colour of a little blood in water, I see my Macy for the first time, dressed in her out-sized porter's uniform, standing on a sea of dirty brown linoleum, tentatively holding out a hanky for me to wipe away my tears.

She'd been slopping disinfectant under the bed when she heard me snivel.

'I would never hurt you like that,' she said, later, when I told her my story, how I'd *stumbled* in . . . my wife, Al . . . and Macy's little face, with the fresh scar cut vividly into her cheek, frowned with such . . . a battered *energy*, I believed her.

This woman could not hurt a fly.

Dimly I heard her mop and bucket clank away across the hospital ward.

'You make me feel safe, Malcolm,' she said, the day we ran away together. Ireland. Her home. Where 'himself', as she called him, would never think to find her. 'So safe'. And, when I woke crying, as I often did in those first few months, with my bad memories in the night, she'd say 'Malcolm, *I'll* never hurt you.' And, 'Malcolm. You're safe here too, lover. Go to sleep.' And I did.

I went to sleep for four years.

One day, returning from the fun factory, I woke up. It was as though I'd been jolted from sleep at the edge of a precipice. I saw, through the white insect-spray on a windscreen, two people sitting together in the shadows of an elderly, scarlet Jag. Idly, attracted by something, their ... languor in the traffic, the tinted glass ... I peered in. Their heads were joining together at the mouth. Lovers. I smiled. They were kissing. It was, I saw, with a sudden flash of recognition, old Mr O'Keefe. With my Macy. Her hands pulling his glasses from his ears.

'Oh Malcolm, I love *you*,' I mouthed, backing onto the pavement, hearing my Macy's voice in my head ... soft, the way she said it in the morning, bringing me my tea and toast just the way I like them, and, when she called me at work for idle chit-chat purposes, what did she say? Oh Lover something ... 'Oh Lover, come home!'

I was right past the Jag before the truth hit me. When was the last time Macy had called me at work? And when was the last time she'd said 'I love you, lover'?

The truth was it was months ago, a year.

Eileen, my ex-wife used to say — and this was before she ran off with Al, my best mate: 'You can't see the nose on your face, Malcolm.' And, 'You're in your own boring tiny world. TV,' she said, 'food,' and although there is no need to go into that particular relationship here, she was, essentially, right. If anyone needed to look more outside themselves, to look up every now and again, it was me.

When Macy came home an hour later, I thought — who *are* you? She looked the same. She's small, has a sprout of rough red hair, a milky-pale skin (the scar still plump on her cheek like an extra purse-lipped mouth), but her eyes, as she smiled at me across the formica, they were ... *lying eyes*. To be honest, I was in shock.

That evening she cooked my dinner as usual and kept up a chatter about her day and who had come into the dry cleaners where she works and what particular stains are hardest to get rid of (oil, blood), and what she'd found in the pockets (an English pound coin, 'a ladies' she said, giggling, 'instrument of the night'). Normally, at dinner, I'd make noises like this — 'u-huh', and 'yup' — while turning the pages of the the Irish *Sun*, catching the soaps, planning my route to midnight, but that evening it was as though my hands and feet had turned to lead. I felt far worse than I'd felt over Eileen and far worse than I'd felt on the day preceding my accident. By the time we were lying in bed watching TV, I was so churned and nauseous Macy had to fetch me a hot water bottle. Eventually I took two of my sleeping pills and fell, not into sleep but into … this large, grey sheet of blotting paper. Through it I could hear Macy's breathing. But, there was something … not quite … It had a different rhythm, a deeper burr. 'I love you, Macy,' I said during that long night, but I said this to the green lights of the video recorder blinking at me across the room.

'I will never hurt you,' Macy had said, pressing mop heads of yellow shine into that filthy brown linoleum. And I'd believed her. I still do.

The more I thought about it, and I thought about it till the blackbirds were stencilled onto the curtains, the more I knew this Macy, this small, sleeping woman beside me, was not *my* Macy.

The next morning I followed her. I called out 'bye love' and slammed the front door. Then I ran straight into our local park and hid myself in the laurel bush by the swings. I watched Macy leave the house. She was carrying a large object wrapped in brown paper and string. It was a dull morning, full of scudding clouds, but the dye in Macy's hair snagged at the light. And I followed it, ducking and diving in the traffic, through the market place, to the dry cleaners where Mr O'Keefe, her boss, was standing waiting for her. At the sight of him on the pavement, jangling his keys, comically tapping his watch, I felt a roar building so … *powerfully* in me I had to bite into my hand. Suddenly I saw my ex-wife and

Al superimposed on the moment — exactly as I'd caught them that afternoon in the bathroom, so long ago. Taking the parcel from her, Mr O'Keefe led the way inside, and as the door closed I had an image of the two of them cavorting, stripping each other naked in the fume-filled back room, all the coats, in their soft blue fuggy wrappers, beginning to crowd together, then spin around the carousals. The heady whine of machinery. Fast. Faster.

I had to remind myself, firmly, that this Macy was not *my* Macy.

Sweating, I went to the library in my lunch hour and down-loaded information on the internet. I down-loaded 'Transformations', 'Impostors'. Then, feeling my fingers tingle, 'Alien invasions'.

The next night, as instructed by the 'net, I dropped a sleeping pill into Macy's cocoa. When her breathing had deepened, I pulled the bed covers back and examined her feet. She had lovely feet, dainty, pearlized, (the only parts of her body left un-scarred by 'himself'), and for a moment I hesitated. The moon had dipped in through a gap in the curtains and Macy was being, so gently, tracked by the green lights of the video recorder.

A tear ran off my face. I fetched my key ring — it has a pencil torch attached and a small blade — and holding Macy's feet down, I chipped away at the polish on her big toes. Under the polish her toe-nails were ... I had to lie back on the pillow, breathing with some difficulty — her toe-nails *were* ridged and ever so slightly green.

It was as I'd suspected. Macy was being stolen from me. Siphoned away.

I didn't bother pulling the sheets back to cover her as she was, I realised, *a stranger to me now.*

A few days later at the Fun Factory, Peeps, the foreman, asked me into the Head Office. Unbeknownst to me I had been crying quite openly as I slit grooves into cardboard boxes or queued in the canteen for lunch. Peeps said he did not mind employing my type but I was to pull myself together. It was bad enough the way the women cried every month without pre-menstrual tension spreading to the men. He was right. My face was wet Monday to Friday. Nine-to-Five. The strange thing was it stopped right on the dot of five. My tears ducts dried in time for me to sit clear-eyed outside Mr O'Keefe's house.

Macy visited Mr O'Keefe's house three times a week. I'd watch her sneak in. The O'Keefe's lived in a large, detached, white house surrounded by cars and fruit trees. After Mrs O'Keefe had jogged out to her car for her aerobic session, almost the *second* she left, the floral curtains would swish together on their fancy electrics, and Macy, wearing heavy black glasses, appeared on the steps. She'd always leave an hour later carrying a bulky parcel wrapped up in brown paper and string.

I had to take the breakfast duty upon myself. Macy, after her pill-induced sleep, was a little heavy-headed in the mornings; grumpy on the pillow. Feeding her toast I'd say, 'Oh, I love you, girl', and after a moment Macy would reply, 'I love you too, lover', or some such combination including the love word. But I was not fooled.

For a while I thought I could draw the old Macy back. Perhaps there was enough human left in her? I set simple tests, asked for the basic domestic information every woman should know. Where are the table mats, Macy? I said. The juice extractor? The hoover bags? But Macy no longer knew.

I could not sleep. After the nightly toe-scrape, I'd pace the carpet for a while but always found myself gravitating to the window. I looked up at the sky and stared without blinking. I had to learn to look through light pollution, which is the colour of bad eye-sight, a blur that never ends. I noticed, on some nights, the stars blinked with the same green light as my video recorder.

It didn't take long for me to read Macy's name written in star language. All I had to do was join certain large and asterisk-like stars, the stars which pulsed with the same frequency as my video recorder lights, and MACY was written above our house, clear as day.

7

It was a signal. They'd be — I scanned the skies, and at this thought I felt my eyes burn — coming for her soon.

I kept watch. What else could I do? I climbed into the back yard of O'Keefe's Dry Cleaners, balanced myself on his overflowing aluminium bins, and looked through the cobwebbed layers of grime on the back window. I could see past a hill of dark lumpy objects wrapped in brown paper and string, right through to the counter and the lozenge of pale-yellow watery daylight. Macy and Mr O'Keefe were sitting blackly silhouetted on high kitchen stools, facing outwards, holding hands beneath the counter. Other than that they did not communicate. They were waiting, scanning the street with jerky neck movements. They were, I realised, keeping watch too!

At home I looked at my hands; they were shaking quite independently of me. I had to hold them under the taps — cold water helped. Then I stuffed them into my pockets, where they beat weakly at my trouser legs. I had to sit on them all during that evening's viewing. Macy didn't appear to notice. Just before we went to bed I stuck them under the tap again for ten minutes, enough time for my own sleeping pill to take effect.

I had dreams. I dreamt my name was being written up in the sky; the stars were forming the letters in beautiful glittery sweeps, like bright green scarves. I always woke on the last M for Malcolm.

I couldn't resist testing Macy further. Where was the canteen of cutlery? The ironing board? The silver tea pot? The egg cups? But Macy brushed me away.

She wore bed socks now. She stopped drinking her cocoa, even when I stirred in chocolate buttons, her favourite. I could only check her nail polish about once a week, after I'd managed to grind a pill down into her dinner; and when I looked I saw that the Aliens were taking her rapidly. Her nails were completely ridged.

Then, one morning, opening a drawer, I found a pile of new lingerie; scarlet and yellow, the colour of football kits. When I questioned Macy with my eyebrow she blushed. That night she wore it — some kind of basque with boned ribs down the side, hard yellow lace that scratched at my chest when she straddled me. When I reached up to tentatively touch her breasts, Macy began to cry.

At the fun factory my hands shook and my tear ducts wept. My cardboard boxes were crooked and as often as not, sodden. Peeps took me to one side and gave me the pencil test. I failed. I could not write my name. I could not eat soup. The collars of my uniform were grey, as if smeared with newsprint. 'See a doctor, Malcolm,' Peeps said. 'Get a sick note or you're out.'

At the doctor's I kept my symptoms to the minimum. I'd iced my hands in a picnic cooler I kept in the car. I still managed to extract a hefty load of tranquillisers, sleeping pills and a week's sick leave.

All day Macy and Mr O'Keefe stared out at the traffic of people on the pavement. When a customer opened the door, a bell would ring and Mr O'Keefe and Macy would slide the garment along a rack, set the dry-cleaning machine in motion and then return to their vigil, trailing a little thick blue smoke. They did not speak. Sometimes Mr O'Keefe would switch on a CD player and, dimly, I'd hear Frank Sinatra seeping through the cracks in the dirty window and Macy and Mr O'Keefe would take each other by the shoulders and slowly dance around the hills of objects covered in brown paper and string, like figurines in an old music box. I watched for hours. My hands danced along the window-sill.

I was returning from the fun factory when a woman wearing a lime-green tracksuit under a long fur coat stepped from a car. It was Mrs O'Keefe. She was a dark woman with small features unpleasantly, even monkeyishly, bunched beneath an extremely low forehead. I kept looking at the low forehead as she spoke to me. Under it she was crying. Things were going missing from her house, she said. She kept talking and touching my arms. She'd found a pair of scarlet and yellow panties under her bed. At the word 'panties' (the word hurt), I turned on my heel. Then I turned back. She was still there. I said, very clearly, so that she would understand, 'They are gone from us already.' And, 'Watch the skies.'

When I got home I stood looking around as though for the very first time. Pictures were gone from the walls. The umbrella stand was missing. Whole racks of dresses were gone. My left cheek began to spasm, pulling my lip up as it did so, as if it were being stitched.

The drinks cabinet and the portable telly from the back-room were also gone. I tried to be generous. Macy and Mr O'Keefe would need them in Space. I had read books on the subject. From what I could gather some abductees needed a sense of place, of home. I saw Macy and Mr O'Keefe sitting, plugging in the iron, watching it steam while Galaxies whizzed past the windows. Or when they were being operated on and being, for example, implanted with Alien seed, it might keep them calm to see the TV or the Persian rug Mrs O'Keefe had said were missing from her home.

I came home early. It was, as I recall, an unusual evening. There was a red stain on the horizon where the sun had just been, and a sliver of moon. Early stars were beginning to pock the navy-blue sky. The house was empty. The Aliens had taken everything but the three piece suite and the bed and wardrobe. Every knick-knack. Even the fridge was gone. My eyes, hands and cheek activated. In the hallway I let my body have its way.

I was still shaking in the back yard when Mrs O'Keefe ran through the house like it was a public alley. 'They've taken everything.' She sobbed, 'I'm alone.' Her monkey-face crumpled.

I pointed up at the shining night sky.

I joined the dots for her and showed her where her husband's name was writ large. Where MACY had formed like a giant banner over by the docks. Where my own name, MALCOL-, was being written even as I spoke in long neon loops and shooting stars. They'd be, I swallowed, coming for me soon.

Mrs O'Keefe pushed her face up into mine. I looked at her forehead.

'You . . .' she hissed, and I shifted my gaze to her mouth.

'You . . . *fool*. They're living in fucking Cork.'

But I knew she was wrong. Up in the sky a new language was

being written. 'And that is why the lights on video recorders are the same colour as stars,' I said. 'I now believe the lights on video recorders are there for a purpose. We are guided by electricity, by the foreign language of stars.' But I was talking to myself.

When I turned round Mrs O'Keefe had gone.

Mike McCormack

'THE STAINED GLASS
VIOLATIONS'

Meats for the belly and the belly for meats; but God shall destroy both it and them. I Corinthians 6:13.

Oh, my mother, not again, Tell me it is not my time come round again. Tell me that I can stay here within you, cowering down, letting the whole thing pass over my head. Tell me you will protect and instruct me, bring me news about the world, its trials and convulsions. Tell me you will keep it at a distance from me, something abstract and objectified, never allowing it to touch me. That would make me happy. This time, all seeing, I would be the perfect spectator, casting a cold eye from the margins, suffering none of its humiliations and pains. Yes, that is the way I want it this time.

Oh, Mother, tell me it is a mistake, a momentary flaw in the structure of things. Tell me that if I close my eyes and hold my breath time will pass me over it and I will be able to consign it to those black pits of memory where we keep those dark and unspeakable things. And tell me also, Mother, that for fear of waking it we would never speak of it again.

Oh, my God, who am I trying to fool?

She knows that if she can eat the Christ Child this terrible obsession will be at an end. That is why, in the darkness and humidity of this summer's night, she is up on the western nave of the cathedral, next to the canal, working on the window with her pliers. This is her second time here this night. On her first visit her nerve failed her and she was afraid to touch the Christ Child. She took instead a few of the pieces that surrounded Joseph and Mary, featureless squares that were tight up to the stonework. They were background pieces without detail and when she returned home with them, she knew that they would be useless; there would be no fulfilment in them. So now she has returned again and this time she knows that she will have to prise the infant from Joseph's arms.

Already she is nearly done. The seven white and amber pieces that make up the image of the Child have been worked from the lead strips and she has now only to crawl along the ledge, climb down and walk home. Her thin body is vibrating from within with the energy of neurosis and starvation. On the ground, in the shadow of the buttress, she hunkers down like an animal to collect herself. Despite the narrowness of her obsession she has been careful. She has worn dark clothes and has kept to the shadows. She has made sure to wear something with pockets; she can hear the broken image rattle around in it now. She has been careful in her choice of pliers: it has long jaws like a surgical instrument, its inner surfaces have been milled for grip. Some of this knowledge she has researched — the pliers for instance and the structure of stained glass windows. But other details — the dark clothes, the pockets and, oddest of all, the ability to climb the down-pipe on the cathedral wall — have been pure inspiration. She knows now that this is the knowledge of the violated — one part received wisdom and two parts black inspiration. She gathers herself now to walk homewards through the still city, hands deep in her pockets. She takes one last look up at the window and she sees that Joseph is left clutchng a dark hole in his abdomen where once was the Child. Dimly, she remembers a biblical text: *whosoever eats of the flesh of the lamb will have eternal life*. In the darkness she is not too sure why she should remember it and less sure what it means.

Walking through the silent city she remembers how this horror began one week earlier. At lunch hour that day she had walked into the city square already looking like a maimed thing. She had

16

crossed the grass towards the one vacant bench that faced directly into the sun. She moved cautiously but with speed, threading her way among the coiled lovers who lay on the warm grass.

Already she was beginning to regret having come here. The whole place, the sun, the grass and especially the lovers made her feel alone. She reached the bench and sank into it with a feeling of relief. This too was a mistake. The sun, so bright, seemed to have singled out this one bench for special attention, falling upon it like a white blade. She would have liked to move but there was no other bench free.

All dowdy looks and no confidence, she had neither the nerve nor the style to sit and eat on the grass. And she knew it too. She was now on the verge of tears and she felt bad enough without blighting the air, filling up the beautiful day with the grey substance of her loneliness. My God, she thought, why does it always have to be like this? Once, just once couldn't it be different?

She started. A thin man had loomed up before her. She hadn't seen him arrive.

'Greetings, favoured one,' he said.

Greetings. What a strange word, she thought. He placed his thin frame on the bench beside her and she appraised him. He was a startling old man, thin beyond belief and even on this hot day he carried a beige mac draped over his shoulders. But what was really amazing was that although he was undeniably there beside her with his legs stretched out before him, he projected not the clear lineaments of an identity but the mobile and blurred contours of a confusion; he looked like someone whose true identity had one day been smudged. She thought she could dimly make out a clean-shaven hawk-like face with pointed features but she could not be sure. She felt that maybe deep within him there was some truer and stronger identity with sharper delineation biding its time until it saw the moment to come forth. He was a man who gave the impression of looking unlike himself, not out of some perverse desire to deceive but simply because this projected confusion was itself his true and inscrutable identity. Despite all this and the added fact that his presence beside her was a negative one, an absence, like a vacuum scooped out of the air, she was not afraid. She suspected he was one of the many vagrants about the city, one who at any moment was going to tell her that he was down on his luck, going through a rough patch, and had she a pound to spare to get him a cup of tea.

'Today is a beautiful day,' he continued. 'The sort of day which justifies the world.'

She persevered with the smile.

'I suppose you're on lunch-break,' he said.

'Yes,' she replied, 'I'm a librarian. I have to return at two.'

'Nice work I'd say, clean work. I haven't worked myself in twenty years.' He was grinning now, well pleased with himself. 'Imagine that, twenty years and I haven't done a stroke.'

She liked him now and was well glad that he had sat down beside her. She flourished one of her sandwiches but he waved it aside.

'No thanks. A man of my age need only eat a couple of times a week. You're a growing girl, eat up.'

She liked him now and she relaxed. 'What did you work at?' she asked.

'I worked in a circus,' he said proudly. 'Was born into it and worked in it for the best part of thirty years.'

She remembered the circuses of her childhood and her interest quickened.

'What did you work at? I'll bet it was the trapeze; you're very thin.'

'No, not the trapeze, I had no head for heights. Guess again.'

'Clown?'

'No.'

'Ringmaster?'

'No.'

'Knife thrower or animal tamer. They were my favourites.'

'No, none of those.'

He was smiling at her now, having teased her along like a

18

favourite child. In all this there was something benign, something protective about him.

'I give up,' she said. She had enjoyed the little game.

'Well,' he began, 'it was very strange. I was the only act of my kind in the whole of Ireland. England too if I'm not mistaken. I used to eat things.'

'Everything,' he grinned, springing his surprise. 'Bars of soap, small toys, metal, glass, timber, anything.'

'Anything?'

'Yes, anything. Oh, it's not unheard of. People eat swords, frogs and so on. I'm even told that in England there is a man who over the space of a lifetime ate a small aircraft. Still, though, the range of my consumption was something else. There was nothing I could not digest. Can you believe that towards the end of my career I was working on a way to eat a house?'

It may have been all a joke but she doubted it. He was too earnest, too obviously proud of his amazing craft.

'How did you start?'

He threw up his hands in a gesture of unknowing.

'I don't know. How does anyone start anything? One day you're here and the next you find yourself in the middle of something else. I remember thinking as a child that it was strange and funny that people should limit their intake to simple foodstuffs. I knew that the world was full of things waiting to be eaten. So I asked myself what would happen if I tried some of those other things. One day I sat down to a piece of timber, a piece of softwood. I wanted this first piece to be something organic, something that would not be too much of a shock to the system. I remember it well. I can see myself to this day under the caravan, tearing strips out of that piece of timber with my teeth like it was a piece of meat. Three days it took me to finish it. But I kept it down and I knew then that my vocation had presented itself. I progressed on to metal then, small kitchen utensils that I sawed into little, chewable pieces. It took me two weeks to eat my first saucepan and a further two months to digest it. But again I held it down. It was then that I set my sight on glass. You see, there is a precedent for eating metal. Copper and iron are part of our make-up. But glass is different, glass is taboo. Glass is a killing substance, not for internal consumption. I felt therefore that if I could consume glass I would be at the peak of my craft. Glass was to me what Everest was to Hillary. But first I had to prepare my constitution, toughen it up so to speak. It was at this time that my act became part of the circus repertoire: bleach, soap, timber, metal, that sort of thing. "The Rubbish Man", that's how I was billed. People flocked to see me. But in all that time I was only in training. I never once lost sight of my true goal — glass.

'One evening when I felt that my system had been toughened up enough I took a small piece of glass and ground it up real fine, like talc, and spooned it down with a glass of milk. I walked around with it for a few hours and then put my fingers to the back of my throat to see if I was bleeding. My vomit was streaked slightly with blood but not to a worrying degree. I was pleased. However, the trick was no used as it stood. Spooning down a white dust in the middle of a three-ring circus at thirty yards would never work, it lacked spectacle. So I had to work at consuming bigger and bigger pieces so that it would have the necessary visual impact. When the trick was finally unveiled I had graduated to the point where I could eat a four-by-eight-inch piece of unlaminated glass in under two minutes. People were amazed and shocked. In a few towns I was not allowed to perform. Priests denounced me from the pulpit and so on.'

He raised a forefinger into the sunlight and began to hack the air like a zealot. 'In the words of the Old Testament — in body and in Spirit and in the image of God was man created. Therefore it behoves us to act as God himself would have us act towards that which is his temple. Such mutilation is contrary to God's will.' He lowered his hand and continued. 'You know, even when I thought those Bible bashers were right my audience never failed me. Night after night they turned up to see me. People seem to find gratification in other people eating shite.'

He suddenly brightened.

'Do you know that over the whole of my career I calculate that I have eaten enough glass to build a good-sized glasshouse?'

She would be late for work, very late. But it did not matter. She was now in thrall to this strange man and his extraordinary story. She wanted to take him home and listen to his tale forever, this tale which she was sure was for her and her alone.

The sunlight lay on them now like a dome and the day was so bright it seemed as if through some magic the air itself was polished. Already the square was emptying of people like herself who had to return to work. High on the side of the cathedral, prising out the infant Jesus, she would remember this as the moment when she should have said goodbye and walked away. She could have walked away and been saved, retaining nothing of this incident but the memory of a strange old man with an extraordinary story. But she did not move. Instead she turned to him.

'So what happened? What do you do now?'

'Well,' he continued, 'audiences fell away in the seventies — television and all that. Our circus broke up in the mid-seventies and we all went our separate ways. Some even went as far as Eastern Europe; circus is a recognised and subsidised art form there. But I was too old so I drifted from town to town getting menial work, living hand to mouth. By then, I was in my sixties so it was difficult to get work; there is not much call for a redundant glass eater. One day I was sitting here on this very bench, no work and sleeping rough, when a young man who recognised me came over and started talking. I told him my story, that I was out of work and so on. He told me to hang around the city for a few days till he saw if there was anything he could do. He was a student and the upshot was that I was offered a job by the university as a resident guinea-pig. The university is contracted by pharmaceutical firms to carry out tests on drugs and other substances. Sometimes they find it hard to get volunteers for the more dangerous experiments. So that's where I come in. Seemingly I have built up an almost total resistance to poisons. I've even become an object of study myself.

Sometimes they cut out parts of my stomach and digestive tract for examination. And,' he held up his hands in another gesture of resignation 'that is how I get by.'

This was strange testimony and she felt weird hearing it. She had the eerie feeling also that it was meant especially for her. She imagined that this old man had held his tongue for the whole of his life until this day when he had walked into the square and saw her, the perfect listener, the perfect receptacle for his story. For a short moment she thought about returning to work; the square was by now almost totally deserted. But she wanted to know more, she was convinced there were things she should know before she left. It would not do to leave with just a partial image of this old man. She turned to him again.

'So what's it like?' she asked. 'Eating glass?'

'It's difficult to say. It's dangerous if you haven't got a vocation for it. It can cut up your stomach as easy as that and you won't feel a thing. One moment you're walking around and the next you feel light-headed and sit down. Then you keel over dead. You've been bleeding away internally all the time, unknown to yourself. Therefore any nourishment you gain from it is offset by the danger and poison of the thing. In short it's not much fun. I myself had to go through a long training before I could eventually handle it. Many a bottle of bleach and bar of soap I had to eat and puke up before I could handle it. It's like some sort of spiritual training, I suppose.

He was obviously struck by the clarity and truth of this last formulation and he furrowed his brow, presumably to make certain that he was not deluded. He seemed satisfied.

'Yes, that's what it's like — like doing some sort of penance or spiritual training that leaves you in a condition where you are capable of experiencing something momentous. But the experience is a dangerous one. If you survive it you know you have arrived at some limit within yourself and are almost God-like. But if you fail, it brings death and disaster and you are as well never to have started. I doubt that there are too many people in the world who would be able to survive it. It's a real discipline, an affliction, a thing of inspiration.'

It made her smile to hear the old man explain his gruesome talent in such mystical terms. Did he truly believe that this was what lay at the centre of his craft? She did not dare ask. Now that he had found sense and reason in it, it would be nothing short of wanton vandalism for a complete stranger like her to start picking holes in it. If he was happy with his explanation, and it seemed that he was, then so be it. Suddenly the old man seemed flustered. He began doing something complicated with the hem of his coat. She wondered had he forgotten something, had he told her the full story? Was there one more detail to reveal, probably a shameful one, before the story was complete? He rose up to look at her and he was very agitated, wringing his hands.

'I am sorry,' he stammered. 'I am sorry but I could not help it.'

She was startled. A premonition rose within her that a pleasant experience was going eerily wrong. If it was going wrong then something of it had to be rescued so it could be remembered with joy.

'Don't say sorry,' she pleaded. 'I've enjoyed myself. Don't let it end like this.'

He nodded his head with what seemed to her an odd type of respect and turned to make his way over the grass. She followed his thin back with her eyes until it disappeared off the grass and around a corner into a side street.

That night, for the first of many nights, her dreams were covered, structured and dominated by glass. Beneath her feet the ground had the cold, intractable feel of a synthetic surface. Overhead the sky curved like a piece of engineering and her cries bounced back from it without release. Food was placed in her mouth but it splintered and crackled treacherously. It made her mouth bleed and the droplets fell and clicked onto the ground as beads. But what terrified most was the feeling that she herself was made of glass, a glass that was warm and molten and pliable and that would continue that way until the day of her death when it would solidify and she would be struck rigid in that unyielding and unchanging topography.

She woke the next morning exhausted from a profitless sleep and when she faced her breakfast her whole being baulked in revulsion. At work, the nausea continued all through the morning and at midday on the bench she gagged on the first mouthful of her sandwich. When evening came she pushed away her plate in disgust and decided to go to bed. A twenty-four-hour bug; come the morning it would be gone.

That night her dreams were more complex. Some of the fragmented images from the night before had coalesced into a decipherable narrative. She was attending some religious ceremony in a church which had the polished sheen of obsidian. A priest of some persuasion was berating his congregation from a pulpit, exhorting them to recognise the sacred in all about them and in the least among them. He harangued his congregation on this theme for a while and when the Eucharist came he raised the flesh of Christ into the air not as unleavened bread but as a scarlet disc of stained glass. He put it in his mouth and brought his teeth down hard to fragment it. He raised his head to the roof while swallowing. He then distributed similar discs to the faithful who came to the rails to receive the flesh of our Lord. All of them returned from the rails with blood seeping between their lips or trickling down their chins. When it came to her turn to receive, the priest bent over her and told her in blood-flecked words tht it was not for him to give her anything. She would receive in another way and when she did it would be not just for herself but for the whole world.

Next morning, after refusing her breakfast again she made her way along by the canal to work. So early in the morning it seemed as if the colours and textures of her dream had carried over into the morning light. The sky was streaked with vermilion and the gold of the early sun was giving way to an all-pervasive blue. Passing by the cathedral she was struck by how queerly it was lit at this time of day. It seemed lit from within by some numinous presence and the light fell from its windows in great shafts which seemed to converge upon her. She wondered how the windows of the western nave seemed to be suspended there in the morning light, standing out from the stone structure, vibrant like elongated stars. She could see the Christ Child, the Virgin and Joseph. The Child seemed to luminesce there in the silence with a life of its own. It seemed to reach out to her with some command, some imperative that would brook no avoidance. With an effort she wrenched herself from the spot but for the rest of the day she was haunted by that image of the infant saviour. It seemed to have scorched itself so deeply on the front of her mind that she could not get a focus on any of her work. Her indexing went badly. Nothing she touched fell into alignment and her mind wandered so much it was a relief when the day ended. But before leaving, on a dark intuition, she went to the reference section and took down a book, *The History and Origins of Glass*. She flicked through it and read how stained glass was manufactured and installed. She read for an hour and on her way home bought a hammer, a pliers, a mortar and pestle.

That evening, for the second day, her body refused food. Looking in her cabinets at the boxes of food a nausea rose within her and she had barely enough time to make it to the sink. Her stomach was so empty she suffered acute agony in retching. She sank to the floor in a foetal position, lathered in sweat. It was at this moment that an awareness formed that she was suffering from some sort of inverse inspiration. She could feel a hollow running the length of her whole being, waiting to be filled. Two days without food and she could already feel her strength ebbing from her, a tide that would leave her stranded like a dried fish if it continued. She would have to do something fast or she would be soon totally lost to this hunger.

She rose from the floor like one who had been felled, and gathered up her coat and tools and made her way into the night. She reeled through the streets like a drunkard until she came to the cathedral. In the grey streetlight coming off the nearby bridge she saw Joseph in the stained glass window offering out the Child to her with both hands.

She would have to be quick. Cars whizzed by on the bridge and it would be disastrous to draw their attention. How could she explain this excruciating hunger that had her refusing food and craving something fatal. She grabbed a down-pipe that ran in the shadow of a buttress, offered up an abortive prayer for its solidity and began to climb up hand over hand. It was easier than she had imagined and she knew instantly that this new-found agility was part of the whole neurosis. In the darkness and her heightened condition she moved confidently, hand over hand, finding toe-holds in the sheer limestone wall. She stopped for a moment on the ledge to draw breath and then moved at a crouch over to the window. She straightened up and was at last faced with the Child. It seemed now that in climbing the drainpipe, the concentration and physical effort had sapped away an essential part of her resolve. Either that or it was just shameful awe in the sight of the Child's gaze that persuaded her to avoid Him totally and remove marginal pieces instead, doing as little damage as possible to the window. She took our her pliers and began to prise out the lead strip from the framework close to the stone. Once she had a grip on the lead it tore out easily and she quickly managed to remove four lozenge-shaped pieces. Through the hole she could see into the dark interior of the church where the red sanctuary lamp glowed and the faint aura of the tabernacle door. But she did not wait, her hunger was crying out. Feeling the eyes of the infant on her back, burning his rebuke, she moved over the ledge and with the glass and pliers pocketed, shinned down the pipe to the ground. Once hitting the ground she loped homewards like a released animal.

In her kitchen she laid out the pieces on the table. They were all one colour and shape and with a scream surfacing within her she knew they were not what she needed. She swept them from the table in a quick frenzy, dashing them against the wall, and set out again into the night. This time, in front of the Child, she did not flinch. She set the pliers into Joseph's abdomen, gripped the lead and prised it out carefully, trying not to let any of the Child fall to the ground — she felt bad enough violating the window without committing needless vandalism. Eventually, through the sweat that had begun to sting her eyes, she saw that she had wrung the Child totally from Joseph's grasp. All he had left now was a gaping hole in his abdomen and the lead came like dried veins curving outwards from it. For the second time that night she pocketed the glass and the pliers and crawled along the ledge to the down-pipe. At the base of the cathedral she was consumed by a shaking fit. She squatted down in the shadows with her arms wrapped about her, flicking the darkness with her eyes as she tried to get a hold of herself. She saw the bridge opposite her and the cars upon it, ploughing on into the night, and she wondered about the drivers. Did any of them suspect that so close by there was someone strung out on such an obsession? If one of them knew would they try to help? Would one of those drivers walk over to her in the darkness and say, it's OK, I'm your friend and I am here to help. Come with me and you will come to no harm. She continued to speculate like this until she felt steady enough to move off.

She is at home now, in her kitchen, and she is tempted to lay the glass pieces on the table and spend a few moments rearranging them into the image of the Child. But she cannot bear to look the Child in the eye. Besides, her body senses a nearness and has begun to cry out. She knows what she has to do. She empties the pieces into the dishcloth, lays it on the floor and begins to hammer it methodically until she has a crude multicoloured rubble. She turns the little pile into her mortar and grinds the debris until it is as fine as talc. It is difficult. Despite its lowly origins and ubiquity, glass is one of our more intractable materials. By the time she finishes her arm aches and her brow is sheened with sweat. She now has a little pile of powder in the mortar that looks for all the world like one of those similarly illicit powders that can be had for a price in the underbelly of any city in the world, patented for people like herself who have been ignored, cast out, shortchanged or are just plain unable to cope. Somewhere within herself she can hear a counterpoint to this errant thought; yes, but this is the flesh of the Saviour, the divine fix, the high without comedown. She lifts a spoonful to her mouth and something within her rises greedily to it. With a jerk of her throat it is gone. She spoons back the rest of it hurriedly and washes it down with milk. She stands still, waiting for some reaction. It does not come. She walks to her room and all the exhaustion of the evening comes to rest upon her. She falls face downwards on her bed fully clothed and already she is asleep.

In the morning she wakes ravenous. In a gluttonous frenzy she hunches over a bowl of cereal and sloughs it back greedily. She thinks of animals and eats four bowls in succession with bread and an apple and a bar of chocolate. For the first time in three days she holds the food down. It is warm and weighs like ballast in her stomach and she walks to work with a solid step. Her fellow workers comment that she is looking much better; there is a bloom on her cheeks and she smiles shyly in return.

'I haven't been feeling well these last few days,' she says. 'Some kind of bug.'

In the bathroom she checks to see if she is bleeding but there are no traces. Outside the sun is shining and for the first time in ages she feels a kind of happiness. At lunchtime she returns to the bench in the hope of seeing the old man but he isn't there. She eats with comfort and knows now that her obsession is at an end. She feels also that there has been a shift in the disposition of the world towards her. Several of her colleagues have come to her during the day and engaged her in jokes and silly games. She has laughed a lot, clasping her hand over her mouth like some shy schoolgirl caught in mischief. Even the sun has lost its oppression. It lies upon her now like a comforter, warming her, making her glow.

*　　*　　*

The days which follow are the happiest of her life. She begins to enjoy her work and it seems that a genuine friendship blossoms between herself and her workmates. She goes for drinks after work with them to a little pub where she is shy at first but where the barman gradually comes to recognise her when it is her round. She goes to the cinema and one night at a club one of her colleagues kisses her, and tells her that now, when he has finally got to know her, he thinks she is great.

The next morning she wakes in her flat and rushes to the toilet, throwing up. On her knees she grips the toilet bowl trying to hold down the panic that is threatening to make her scream. Please, oh please, she cries. It is midday before she can hold down any food. And it is the same the following day and the day after that and the day after that again; sick and frail in the morning with her hand clasped over her stomach until the light midday meal that carries her over till the evening. And it is in these morning hours also that she is stricken with the crazed urge to eat things. In her flat she has to remove the detergents, the soaps and even her bathroom sponge from out of her sight. At work she has her desk cleared of ink, correction fluid and her eraser. And one morning in her nausea and weakness she realises that her period, normally like clockwork, is three weeks overdue. She thinks of the days without food and the days of nausea and the glass, and wonders has all of this thrown her biology out of alignment. She waits another week, then two more, and at the end of four weeks she visits her doctor.

Her doctor is a kindly, middle-aged man who listens with his head inclined to his left side, a man hearing signals from a distant planet. He hears her list of symptoms and finally asks her does she herself have any idea what it would be. She skirts around the obvious shaking her head, not wanting to face the incredible. He asks her about her love life and she tells him shamefaced that she has no partner, she is still a virgin. He shakes his head in mystification and tells her he will do a pregnancy test, otherwise he has no clue what it could be. Five minutes later she finds out that she is pregnant.

She remonstrates. 'How can that be, I'm still a virgin?'

'It's very strange,' he tells her. 'I never thought in all my days of practice I would come upon such a case. It is a condition that is very rare, one in a million if I can remember the statistics correctly. There is no medical explanation which covers the case entirely. Its a form of parthenogenesis. What happens is that . . .'

He seems awed by her presence and he moves about the room giddily as he talks, keeping his distance and erecting a barrier of technical language between them.

'I find it unbelievable,' he concludes, 'totally unbelievable.'

'Well,' she counters, 'it's happening, whether you believe it or not.'

'It's not that,' he says. 'I've seen that. It's just that you're one in a million, one in ten million.' He looks at her suddenly. 'You are going to keep the child?' It sounds like an accusation, not the question it is meant to be.

She spreads her hands. 'I don't know. This is such a surprise, such a shock. I hadn't thought about it.'

He sits on his desk, making an effort to bring the situation under control. Despite the lack of frenzy and raised voices there is no doubt that the room has been visited by some disaster. He clasps his hands before his face in the manner of a penitent and seeks inspiration in the ceiling.

'All right,' he says. He has finally come to some decision. 'There really is nothing I can do for you at the moment. I could give you something for the nausea and vomiting but that is not the issue. What I suggest is that you go home, think about it for a while and come back to me with your decision. Think it over. There are other options, things to be done and so on.'

He is becoming flustered, his sentences are beginning to ramble. She unsettles him with her thin face and her eyes continually focused in her hands. He repeats himself again, almost pleadingly.

'There really is nothing I can do for you now. Call back in a few weeks when you have a decision.'

She is glad to leave the room. She has difficulty in breathing there, the air seems filled with smoke. Outside in the sunlight she braces herself and it works its way into her, warming her chilled bones. She is marooned now, at a loss where to go. It strikes her that this world is stranger than she can ever imagine. She wonders is it always going to be like this, will there always be this cruelty at the heart of things. Will the world keep offering up jagged pieces of itself, not as a means to enlightenment but as a reminder that it will always have the upper hand? One moment it will seem solved, comprehensible and full of sense, the next it will have heaved beneath her feet throwing up shapes and configurations without precedent, filled with terrors. She walks carefully through the streets now, unsure of her footing. People look strange, their skins have a funny pallor: she can see their veins. She fears that at every corner someone with a clown's grin will draw her aside and show her some new atrocity. She finds herself walking towards the canal and has to suppress an urge to stretch her arms ahead of her like a blind person. She feels like prey.

In the cathedral car-park there is a crowd. Busy mothers and fathers fuss over children, straightening ties and fixing veils over angelic faces. Today is Confirmation day and these kids have come here to sign up as soldiers of Christ, new recruits in His massive conscript army serving under assumed names. Standing on the edge of the crowd she notices that the Christ Child in the window has not been replaced. Part of the window has been blocked up with plywood from within. Earlier in the week she read in the local newspaper how the police are mystified by the breakage and how they have no clue whatsoever. She remembers the lines — *At this time we have neither suspect nor motive and we are led to believe that it was an act of wanton vandalism. We are looking for anyone with information, no matter how small, to please come forward.*

She stands in the car-park long into the evening and long after the crowd has gone, her hands clasped over her stomach. She has the same wish for herself; would someone with some information please, please come forward.

I would like to think that from the beginning I put up a fight. Not some token gesture of disaffection with my terrible predicament but a full-blooded resistance. I picture myself rising to my knees in the afterbirth, eyes open and sharp — there is nothing of the doe-eyed lamb about me this time — my nose sniffing the air. And do I imagine it or is my slimy hand already reaching out to grasp some weapon? I see myself dark and primitive, grasping it by the hilt and marking a slow watchful retreat. I am not so much a child as a beleaguered rat. But my mother's legs are closed now and I am cut off, left stranded. Alone again. Just for that I wish my entrance had been marked by some carnage. I would give much to be able to say that on entering the world I killed my mother. But I cannot. Therefore did I hang my head and weep in despair. I did not. I filled the room with curses, dark occult sounds that shrieked out at the wretchedness and misery of it all.

Of course it was nothing like that. Instead, I lay stranded on my back choking in the amniotic fluid, my hands rising to my eyes to fend off the light. A nurse upended me with a quick slap across the arse and I drew some foreign but dimly remembered element into my chest, something upon which my young lungs scrabbled for foothold and having found it I rose quickly into myself with a wail. I was immediately aware of the hostile atmosphere, the uniforms, the searing lights, the physical abuse. Oh yes, there is not much difference between birth and interrogation — both are issues of truth and identity.

I am young, very young, but I have the memory of eons. I can remember clearly the last time and all I can say is that father's work or no father's work I am not going to let it happen like that again. This time it will be different. The world will be given an even chance this time and no more.

I am young and I am willing to admit that I am not in full possession of the facts. Maybe there are mitigating details that I cannot remember but I doubt it. Therefore my plan is simple. Bide my time quietly and keep my ear close to the ground, my eyes open and my mouth shut. I will hoard up knowledge. I have got a good thirty years before I make my entrance proper so I will be circumspect. But I do know a few things; I am and I have memory and this time it is going to be different.

Julian Gough

'THE BEST TIPPERARY HAS TO OFFER'

I. *Christmas lights*

We stepped off the bus outside Kavanagh's Hotel. The street was crossed by a couple of dozen thin strands of Christmas lights. The Christmases of one's childhood are traditionally bigger and brighter than whatever Christmas you're enduring as an adult, but in my case I could quantify the decline. I remembered the Christmas the town council first hung Christmas lights across O'Connell Street, our unimaginatively named main thoroughfare. I was five, and there were thirty strands, of mixed red, yellow, green and blue bulbs. I counted them every time I walked down the street with my mother and Juno that Christmas, walking with my head back and our mother scolding me for not looking where I was going, and me not answering for fear I'd forget the number. Thirty strands, with forty and sometimes forty-one bulbs in each strand. As the years went by, bulbs broke or failed and went unreplaced, and entire strands would suffer mysterious disasters and go dead, not to reappear the next year. Now there were twenty-three strands, all with an assortment of bulbs missing and others gone for some reason dim. I counted the strands as we walked to the top of O'Connell Street before turning right, into the narrower Well Street at the end of which lay our family's home. Well Street was dark, with few streetlights, and our bags were heavy and it was cold. We didn't talk till we reached the front door, when Juno said abruptly, 'We'll have to get presents tomorrow.' I put down my bag and found my key. 'Oh my God, yes. Never entered my head.'

The door swung open as my key approached the lock.

'Paul!' we said and embraced him enthusiastically.

'My beautiful sisters,' he said. 'My God, you look wonderful. You're not little girls anymore. I'll have to burn the Barbie dolls I brought you.'

We laughed and jumped around him and pretended to be babies while he picked up our bags with exaggerated groans and carried them into the living room.

'Look what I found,' he said.

Our father grunted from his armchair. 'Oh, more mouths to feed. I thought we were rid of ye.'

I gritted my teeth a little but I was too pleased at seeing Paul to let my father spoil it.

'Paul, Paul, give me my present, I want to weigh it,' a reference to an old family joke about the value of presents, dating from when Juno and I used to weigh each other's presents on the kitchen scales as they arrived in the week before Christmas, as a poor substitute for opening them, which was forbidden until after dinner on Christmas Day. Whoever had the lightest presents would often end up in tears. One year my father gave Juno two bricks among her other presents, to annoy me. I cried when she weighed them, on Christmas Eve, but Juno cried when she opened them on Christmas Day, and our mother stood up and swore at him in front of us all, which was very unusual and silenced everyone for hours after. That was back when he still drank, and thought things like that were funny.

Paul lifted me up in the air and then lifted Juno up in the air.

'Presents of great worth,' he said. 'Oh, valuable presents these two. Who are they for?'

'No-one,' I said, blushing.

'Ah! You're blushing!! You *are* somebody's present!' But he saw I wasn't enjoying the game and didn't pursue it.

'Where's mum?' I said.

'She's gone out,' said my father.

'I *know* she's out, where's she gone to?'

'She's out visiting the Brownes and trying not to get given one of their terrible cakes.'

The Brownes were friends of our mother. Mrs Browne had a love affair with cookery that wasn't reciprocated, and a number of distant, half-remembered Christmases had run aground on the rock of Mrs Browne's Christmas cake. Eventually a rebellion of our brothers had led to a compromise. Now every year Mrs Browne gave our mother a Christmas cake as a present, and every year our mother brought the cake home and put it in the dustbin with much swearing of the family to secrecy, and everyone was happy. I liked all these rituals.

Juno went to put on the kettle. There was a turf fire in the livingroom, and a small, real tree with the familiar decorations, dented silver balls with frosted top halves, and silver and red streamers of tinsel, moulted in places till you could see the string. The fairy on the top of the tree, a baby-doll in a white dress our mother had made out of cardboard and a strip of net curtain, sat at the familiar uncomfortable angle, the glue that held on her head old and yellow and visible through the mesh of her net ruff.

Juno swung open the kitchen door to ask who wanted tea and a small gust of turf-smoke came into the room and suddenly, and just in time, it felt like Christmas.

II. *The Best Tipperary has to Offer*

That night Paul, Juno and I took in the best Tipperary had to offer and went to Connollys Hotel, Bar and Disco.

'Let's take in the best Tipperary has to offer' said Paul, and off we went.

It had been Connollys unfortunate slogan on their local radio ad for years, dating back to the days of the pirates, and a source of unending joy and sarcasm to Paul, William and Jason. Paul and William in particular. They used to roar it, rolling home drunk together at half two in the morning after an evening in Connollys Bar, followed by a night in Connollys Disco, and a shared bag of chips from Connollys Illegal Chip-Van in Connollys Famous Carpark, the Biggest in the South. You'd never catch an apostrophe off a Connolly. A good Tipp hurling family, no time for soccer, the Devil, the Brits or punctuation.

'The *best*,' Paul and William would bellow in accents made even more English by drink, 'the BEST Tipperary has to offer . . . take in the fucking BEST . . .' And sometimes their friend Aengus Cleary would be with them, singing along in his broad Tipperary brogue, 'deh *BESHT*'.

I'd hear them shushing each other below at the front door, dropping the key, entering the house with elaborate care, closing the door as quietly as they could, going into the living-room and turning on the radio full blast for thirty seconds before they could get it together to find the volume control and turn it down, 'Shush!' 'SHUSH!' '*Jesus*, the parents . . .'

If our parents woke, they never did anything about it. I don't think Juno ever heard the boys come home. She slept a lot deeper than I did, but I was sensitive to their coming home, I liked to hear it, I wanted it to wake me, so it did. Once or twice, careful not to wake Juno, I snuck downstairs to join them. They were pleased to see me, in an absent-minded sort of way. They asked me about school and my friends and my hated dance classes in a way that they never bothered to in our everyday encounters at breakfast and dinner and in front of the TV. It was as though we were all part of some underground community, meeting in the hush of the night, speaking in low voices, the last cigarette of the night going round, casually equal. It was only years later that I realized they were probably stoned out of their heads as they focused intently on my banal answers to their polite questions.

I loved it but I felt so dumb, in both senses, and young, in my stupid little pink going-to-the-bathroom socks which I tried to hide under myself as I sat on the sofa. When I *did* say anything the sentence would just come out so helplessly, hopelessly wrong that I could practically see it stranded in mid-air in front of me, dying in the silence. Eventually I would mumble something that sounded like an explanation or an apology or a straightforward goodnight but which didn't have any actual words in it and wasn't properly any of them, and I would sneak back to the cowardly safety of my room, my awful mumble ringing like a persistent tuning-fork tone in my ear, a blaze of embarrassment consuming me as I climbed the stairs in a rage of self-pity and fury at my youth and immaturity and stupidity, stupidity.

I did it twice, cried myself to sleep both times. But I still liked to hear them below me, murmuring, even after I gave up trying to join them.

As Juno and I accompanied Paul to Connollys then, I found myself almost giddy with excitement. I'd been to Connollys a billion times with Juno but this was different. Look at me, going out on the town with Paul! I felt like singing, so I did.

'I could have danced all night, I could have danced all night . . .'

I didn't know enough words, it was one of my father's favourites and I'd never really listened to it closely.

'You're in flying form,' said Paul.

'Mm, yup.'

39

And I was. All my melancholy had vanished, *ping!* as the front door closed behind us. I did a giddy little dance and nearly tripped on the cracked pavement. I felt quite drunk and we hadn't even arrived at the pub yet.

Paul pushed Connollys door open and waved us in. It was like putting your head in a kettle. The heat and steam would have overwhelmed me if the noise hadn't got there first. Every exile on earth seemed to have arranged to meet here, just inside the door, tonight, and most of them would appear to have arrived in the previous sixty seconds. The air juddered with back-slaps, roared greetings, howls of recognition and delight. Seamus! Jaysus! How'r ya! Moira! Feckit! Odysseus! C'mere t'me! Is it Napoleon is it! Shake, man! Cain, begod! How's the brother?

All the Christmas returnees met up and exchanged histories in Connollys at Christmas and now to my shock I found I was a returnee. People greeted me, greeted Juno, greeted Paul, shook hands, offered drinks, refused money, piled coats, pushed over, and in a dizzy minute I was sitting at a table with a bunch of semi-strangers, a glass of Harp in front of me and another on the way. My protestation that I didn't like Harp, or glasses, had been as benignly overlooked as my proffered ten pound note and my request for a pint of Guinness. Paul leaned over to calm me as steam leaked from my ears to aid the general smog. 'They mean well,' he said softly. 'They're idiots but they mean well. They probably don't even remember beating the shit out of myself and William in the Christian Brothers. If I can forgive them that, you can forgive them buying you Harp. I'll get you a Guinness later. Sit back and enjoy the comedy. It's Christmas.'

So I sat back and calmed down and even drank some of one of my Harps before the flailing elbow of a new arrival swept them both into Paul's lap.

'Oh Jesus Paul, I'm sorry, buy you another, what was it?'

'Harp, but don't worry.'

'Shit no, I'm not buying you that piss, Guinness is it, and what're your sisters having?'

'Hello Aengus, I'm grand.'

'Hello Aengus, they were both mine and I'd have paid you to get rid of them, don't worry about it.'

Aengus settled in among us and the night began.

'God you're looking lovely, are you old enough for Guinness, grand, three then, I'm shagging loaded don't touch that, oh fuck it's murder at that bar let me get a breather first, is it English Paul tells me you're learning, well that'll come in handy if you ever visit me in London, not that any fucker speaks it there anymore, did you hear the streets are paved with gold there, shagging right they are, but it's like lead, sure it causes terrible deformities, the people there have hearts the size of gooseberries and fierce short arms, every bastard in Soho must owe me a pint.' Having had his breather he leaped up and squeezed through the scrum towards the bar.

'He's a dote,' said Juno.

'He's a sexy dote,' said I.

'Jesus, hands off Aengus, he's a friend,' said Paul, alarmed. 'And if I hear he's laid a hand on you, I'll kill him.'

'OK, no hands,' I said

'Jesus,' said Paul mopping his brow. 'You *are* joking, aren't you? Don't answer.'

The night grew increasingly ribald, energetic, and drunken. Paul and Aengus vied to ply Juno and myself with pints. Juno found herself at the eye of a hurricane of male attention and as I grew increasingly relaxed and less inclined to scowl at rubbernecked passers-by, so did I. I almost began to enjoy the attention, a *very* rare feeling for me. When James Power fondled my upper arm and playfully tousled my hair in his familiar creepy way I told him to 'piss off' rather than 'fuck off' and didn't even stop smiling. Of course he took that as a come-on and did it again, brushing his forearm 'accidentally' against my breast as he did so, and then I had to say 'Fuck *right* off James, I mean it' and tread very hard on his instep to make absolutely sure he understood I meant it, but all in all it was a lovely, relaxed evening. By closing time I was pissed as a coot and up for divilment.

III. *Divilment*

We swayed the very short walk from Connollys Bar to Connollys Disco, out the pub door and in a door six yards away, paid our money, found a table on the edge of the dancefloor, and the night roared on. I leaned against Aengus.

'Tell me more about advertising,' I said.

'I'm boring you,' he said

'No, tell me more. I love your voice ... it's all mixed up, all London and Tipperary.' Either Aengus went red or the disco lights did, I wasn't sure and didn't care.

'Ah, they love me Irish accent over there,' he said. 'It's worth an extra ten K to me no bother. They think I have a fiery Celtic creative soul. They *know* I can't be as thick as I sound so they mistake their estimations in the other direction.'

He said 'thick' as 'tick'. And 'mistake' as 'mishtayk'.

'What's kay?' I said. He had to think back.

'K. A thousand. Thousand pounds. Forty K. Ninety K. It's a stupid way of talking about money, real casual. Came from the City. I don't even know where the fuck I got it. I don't even know if it's fashionable anymore. It just slipped out cause I was drunk.'

Thrunk. I wuz thrunk. I thought of saying something and thought better of it. 'Let's dance,' I said.

He hesitated for a moment, not sure if I wanted to dance or if I was merely identifying the tune. 'Let's Dance' by David Bowie throbbed from the speakers. Someone should have slapped a preservation order on the DJ box as a Site Of Special Historic Interest. Someone probably had. Was this DJ stored in one of the hotel freezers and only thawed out at Christmas, carefully shielded from the shock of learning the year, or indeed century? Certainly the preservation process seemed to have had an alarming effect on his shirt-collar. 'Let's Dance' segued jarringly into 'New Year's Day' by U2. Mother of God, it was like going on the piss in a time-capsule. It was a fucking museum with a mirror-ball. We danced. I was having a great time.

Suddenly I felt a hand on my knee. On my *knee*? As I was *dancing*? I looked down to see one of the Gleeson twins grinning up at me, fag in mouth, head shaved to stubble, denim shirt, jacket and jeans. They hadn't changed since they were ten. Chain-smoking their way through primary school, secondary school, reform school and prison (rumour had it they lied about their age to get in) they had perfectly preserved their youthful figures, yellowed fingers and, unfortunately, heights. Frankly, the two of them hadn't a height between them. It had been a very long time since they'd been able to headbutt anyone their own age in the face without the assistance of a stepladder, but they were still tiny objects of fear in the town, on the rare occasions they weren't in prison.

'Jimmy?' I said 'Johnny?'

'Johnny,' said Johnny Gleeson. 'Jimmy's gone for a slash. They let us out for Christmas.' He leered up my skirt.

Juno and I had always had a soft spot for the Gleeson twins, partly because they were twins of roughly our own age and therefore somehow kindred spirits, and partly because they would steal things and give them to us when we were of an age to find that rather romantic. At ten they were giving us Toblerone, at fifteen they were giving us earrings and on one memorable occasion they gave us a video recorder which we made them promise to give back. They got caught giving it back and were given another go in reform school. We felt terribly guilty. They were one year older than us and neither had a half an ounce of sense.

'Oh it's lovely to see you, Johnny,' I said. I could never tell them apart, they were always wearing each other's clothes and they had identical prison tattoos on their knuckles.

'Where's Juno?' said Johnny.

'Over there, at the table by the pillar,' I said. 'Johnny, do you know Aengus Cleary . . .' but Johnny had already vanished among the dancing knees.

Aengus looked at me, faintly appalled. 'You know Johnny Gleeson?' he said.

'Oh, Johnny and Jimmy are lovely,' I replied.

'They're fucking *psychopaths*,' Aengus said.

I stopped dancing and began assembling furious words towards a reply.

'We'll agree to differ,' he added in haste, hands raised in surrender.

I restarted dancing but at a much slower pace than before, and wearing a pout that could knock out a pack-mule. It took him 'til half-way through the Bryan Adams set to disarm the facial expression and bring me back up to speed. Then we realized what we were dancing to and returned to our seats.

'Oh Joolz,' said Juno, 'You'll never guess.' She was holding what could only be a Christmas present from the Gleeson twins.

'The Gleeson twins have given us a Christmas present,' I guessed.

'Well, yes,' said Juno 'They said we should open it together.' She frowned. 'In fact they said we shouldn't open it here . . . they wouldn't tell me why.'

'Because it's stolen,' said Aengus and I simultaneously.

I gave Aengus a startled look before realizing that he didn't actually know anything about our relationship with the Gleesons, he just knew a lot about the Gleesons.

'No,' said Paul. 'That's what Juno thought.'

'Jimmy swore it wasn't stolen. Although I suppose buying it with their money is only one step away from theft, really . . .'

'Oh hell, we ate the Toblerone,' I said gaily, to the puzzlement of Paul and Aengus. 'Open it.'

Juno hesitated. The small, flat, extraordinarily badly wrapped present lay on the palm of her right hand. Juno lofted it slightly a few times as though weighing it. The wrinkled wrapping paper, striped with bands of crumpled sellotape, much of it (by the fluff on it) sticky-side out, sat enigmatic on the palm, its white ribbon, oily with thumbprints, tied in no knot known to Scout, Cub, Guide or Brownie.

Jimmy, or Johnny, whizzed by, seeming to my startled eye to pass beneath our table without stooping as he did so. I blinked.

'Hope you like your present,' he Cagney'd from a mouth-corner as he orbited me. 'Don't open it here.'

And he was gone. They had always been shy.

IV. *In which our Heroines Giggle like Schoolgirls*

Giggling like schoolgirls, Juno and I raced across the dance-floor to the toilets to open our present. Giggling like a schoolgirl is never more *satisfying* than in the year after you've left school. The knowledge that no nun will ever again have the right to say 'Stop that sniggering, girls' seems to triple the pleasure somehow. Actually that's probably just true for me, rather than a universal rule of iron, but for months after my Leaving Cert I couldn't pass a nun without giggling vengefully.

Anyway, still giggling, we entered the toilets. Every cubicle occupied, every mirror besieged. The air was beige with foundation as girls I half-recognised tried frantically to deal with the sweat-damage sustained during 'Summer of '69' in time to get back out for 'Everything I Do (I Do It For You)'. We were greeted distractedly by a couple of old classmates, one re-applying lipstick, one standing on one leg with a hairpin in her mouth.

'Mmm, m'no, mmm m'l't.' She risked a smile at Juno and the hairpin fell to the filthy floor. She glared at us. Obviously hadn't been a close friend.

The other girl gave a theatrical wave from about a yard away,

45

and greeted us warmly without bothering to stop touching up her lipstick. 'Juno! Just a ... there ... ? ... yes ... and Juliet, how *are* you?'

Juno told her. I couldn't be arsed, she'd never liked me anyway and I'd always found her as brittle as our grandmother's hip and as artificial as its replacement. She was one of the ones who'd acted in a school play and never bothered getting out of character. My memory refused to supply me with the part or the play. Julie Bleeding Andrews in The Sound Of Bleeding Music no doubt. I bared my teeth as she passed me and she chose to treat it as a smile. Sensible of her. I had a mad desire to snap at her like a dog and bark lustily to see how she'd react but I fought the urge down. It was a bit too like our old school toilets in here for my liking. Connollys doormen wouldn't ask for ID if the entire cast of The Great Escape turned up with the contents of a kindergarten stuffed under their greatcoats, so a good half of the girls, unsteadily swigging from their smuggled naggins of Smirnoff while they waited for a free sink to spew in, were still attending our old school, and thus unpleasantly familiar to me. I felt nausea rather than nostalgia. It was a bit too recent for me to have romanticised it. Spots and braces. Homework. Dress codes. Ye gods. An unfortunate called Pam whose mother was an alcoholic and who'd had to repeat fifth year, came out of one of the cubicles. She'd always liked me, God knows why.

'Hello Juliet,' she said shyly. Her braces shone in the fluorescent light.

'Hello Pam,' I said, and it was absolutely too much for me, I hauled Juno into the vacated cubicle and slammed the door on Pam's startled orthodentistry.

'Open the present, I'm going mad.' I said.

Juno opened the Gordian bow and pulled off the paper. We stared.

'It's a *stamp* album' I said. 'It's a ... flipping stamp album. I think I'd have preferred Toblerone. And to think we made them give back that video recorder.'

Juno giggled and said, 'Well it's the thought I suppose ... and they *are* a bit dim ...' which was a charmingly uncharitable remark from her and made me think all the higher of her.

She flicked the tiny stamp album open and I said, 'Well at least they've stuck in some stamps.'

'Oh dear ...' said Juno, with the observational advantage of being slightly less drunk than me. 'I don't think these are stamps ... I think they're ...'

V. *Trips*

'... trips.'

It is a tribute to the sheltered nature of my upbringing and to the sheer breadth of my ignorance that I did not know what my sister was talking about.

'Trips?' I said, vague images of foreign travel in my head.

'Trips, tabs, acid, LSD,' said Juno impatiently, sounding like an unusually specialised drug dealer with a Thesaurus, offering her wares. '*Drugs*, you idiot.'

Now, I had *read* a lot about drugs and I'd seen Drugstore Cowboy three times (for Matt Dillon) and My Own Private Idaho six times (three times for River Phoenix and another three times for Keanu Reeves, and I *still* couldn't decide ... hey, I was young) and countless TV programmes and news reports, but Tipperary and Galway were not exactly the drug capitals of Europe and I'd never actually seen a Class A drug for real. I had the vague impression that 'drugs' came in whacking great kilo bags of white powder with 'DRUGS' written on them.

'They're not *drugs*' I said. 'They're *stamps*.'

I peered at the stamp album again in the bad light of the toilet cubicle. It consisted of a number of small plastic pages, each with a number of small plastic pockets for stamps. In each pocket was a small paper square. I peered even closer. They were a bit small for stamps and all the same size. And they didn't have proper perforated edges. The first row of three were white with a blue globe on them. The next row of three were white with an Arabic squiggle on them. The next row of three were white with a cartoon explosion on them. I turned the page.

'Jeeeesus,' I said.

'It's a selection box,' said Juno. 'They must be microdots,' and she pointed at three pockets each containing what looked like a tiny ball of, well, snot.

I looked at Juno suspiciously. 'How come you know so much about it?'

'Because I didn't skip religion when Sister Imelda showed us that video on drugs.'

'Oh yeah.' I shrugged. I was still glad I'd missed it. Someone hammered on the cubicle door. 'Fuck off,' I said absently. I fished a square with a heart on it from its pocket and examined it. 'Acid,' I said. '*Aciiiiiiiiieeeeeed . . .*'

Now you will mock me for my innocence in what follows but I blame it firmly on National Drug Prevention Day, the Press, the Guards, the Government and Society. I had been bored to tears for years with the message that drugs, from hash and grass through acid and ecstasy to heroin and crack, were intrinsically evil and exceedingly dangerous. My experience had shown me that half the people I knew smoked marijuana in its various forms and that the message simply wasn't true. I'd smoked Satan's cigarettes a couple of times but couldn't inhale without coughing with embarrassing vigour for an impressive duration, so the full health-and-life-destroying joys of Reefer Madness had been denied to me. I'd drunk mushroom soup once at a party, too. It was meant to be magic-mushroom soup but after two hours of sitting around watching MTV we reluctantly decided that our morning on the golf-course had been wasted. So I didn't really, deep down, *believe* in 'drugs'.

Also I was a little drunk.

So I popped it on my tongue, sucked it like a sweet, and swallowed.

'Oh Juliet!' wailed Juno.

'What?' I said, a little belligerently. I was already starting to get the horrible feeling that I'd done something very silly. Juno had covered her face with her hands and was peeking at me through her fingers.

'You *absolute* idiot,' she said in a muffled voice. 'Oh God, *what* am I going to tell Paul?'

'I licked a stamp,' I said, facetiously. 'When will it start to work?'

I was rather disappointed the world hadn't been transformed immediately, as though a switch had been thrown. I felt exactly the same. Boo.

'Shouldn't notice anything for half an hour. Forty-five minutes. Something like that. And it lasts for *hours*, what are we going to do with you? Is it too late to get sick?'

'I'm *not* getting sick,' I said firmly. I'd done that often enough here as an under-age drinker. Reading the fine print of the Armitage Shanks logo at the back of the porcelain bowl. (Head down, clutching the seat. Did the Queen *really* use one of these by appointment? Bet she didn't use it for what I was using it for. Whoops, here we go. God, I promise, never again . . .) Indeed one of the reasons I'd cut my hair so short back in transition year was to keep my fringe out of Connollys toilets on Friday nights when I'd get sick. Not the main reason, but it had helped tilt the balance at the time. Juno, you will be unsurprised to learn, avoided throwing up on her fringe by avoiding throwing up. Hey, different strokes for different folks.

I snapped back the bolt. 'C'mon, let's get ready to rumble. We gotta fight for our right to party. I'm kool and the gang, don't worry be happy.'

She sighed but she joined in the game. 'Oh lord, please don't let me be misunderstood. Let's stick together, and every little thing's gonna be alright. Idiot.'

'Idiot's not a song,' I objected.

I swung open the cubicle door and we walked past a cross-legged, bug-eyed girl with carrots in her fringe. I banged open the swing-door with a nonchalant hip and we were back in the noise and the heat on the dance-floor's edge. I gave a little whoop of giddy joy and we plunged into the wash of hormones, deodorant and dancers. The air was volatile with cheap perfume and the kind of aftershave that comes free with petrol. The same kind of aftershave that could be added to petrol to make it burn better, and smell worse. As we emerged on the other side to rejoin Paul and Aengus it briefly occurred to me that of all places and times to sharpen the senses and throw open the doors of perception, perhaps Connollys the night before Christmas Eve was not entirely the ideal choice, but I immediately put aside the unworthy thought. Why, Connollys was the best Tipperary had to offer, by God, and only the best was good enough for me tonight. I felt fabulously drunk, and the constant checking of my senses for signs of lysergic impact had the effect of making me feel super-alert, super-alive.

Juno was telling them what I'd just done. Paul was horrified, Aengus was amused but pretending to be horrified, I didn't give a damn.

'If you're not in, you can't win,' I said.

Paul was really annoyed with me and began to say so. I stood up, walked onto the dance-floor, and lost myself.

The night had begun.

VI. *The Martian Dance-floor Experience*

Juno and Aengus calmed Paul down, but I didn't care about that either. I danced with absent-minded fury in the heart of the crowd to half-forgotten songs half-remembered from my brother's ancient record collections.

I'd spent most of my life in Tipperary, locked in my own head, feeling like a visitor to a place where everybody else belonged. It was in Galway that I felt at home, and felt it was safe to relax, that no one would come smashing vindictively into my life if I pulled back the bolts and let in a little light and air. It had been so *lonely* in Tipperary, feeling like an observer, living in my mind, feeding it books that showed me a world that felt so much more real than my own. I looked around me at the town I'd been born in and it seemed so thin, so poor a version of the world. It made me sad in the way that the cheap imitations of good toys almost made me cry when I saw them piled high in the Connollys Super-Store toy department coming up to Christmas every year. I know this sounds pathetic and stupid, but the thought that kids who wanted Sindy, or Lego, or World Wrestling Federation figures, or Power Rangers, or whatever was popular that year, were going to wake up on Christmas morning and run down to open their presents and find sad, cheap, bad imitations of the present they'd dreamed of for months, that their parents had bought because they couldn't afford the real thing, or because they didn't know the difference, its enormous, heart-breaking *importance*, the absolute perfection of what you truly wanted and the desolation of unwrapping a fake, that didn't move right, didn't look right, that was nothing, worse than nothing ... the thought of these other kids with their wrong presents as useless as the stuff they came wrapped in, hiding their huge, gulping disappointment, or letting it show and tearing at their parents' hearts ... to be honest I *did* cry, every year.

It began to prey on my mind coming up to Christmas each year of my childhood, those great piles of cheap imitations, bad copies, with their deliberately misleading names. I would cry at night, I even cried in the aisles of the toy department itself a couple of times, feeling like a perfect fool, wiping my eyes on my coat-sleeve and trying to pretend I had a cold. But I think, now, that what I was crying for (and this is just amateur psychology at its worst, I have no way of proving this, it just feels to me to be true) wasn't

51

really the toys and the other kids. It was my life, and me. My life was somehow tangled up in those toys, lived in the huge shadow of the special-offer stacks. I'd been given the wrong life, in the wrong town, and there was nothing I could do about it, and every single day of my life I had to hide my disappointment, because it wasn't my parents' fault, they thought I was happy here, they came from here, it was home wasn't it. But to me my home felt cheap and wrong and my life felt like an imitation of a real life and every Christmas I'd dream about my father healthy and strong and my brothers happy and myself and Juno happy in an England I'd never known, that didn't exist, that I could never know, because it didn't exist.

And I would wake up just torn apart, in a thin, poor town that I hated. Cattle roaring from the abattoir. Connollys owning the town. A town without a river through it. Oh Christmas, I hated you.

And as I danced, furiously alone, in Connollys on the night before Christmas Eve I was back in my head, locked in, sobbing silently about nothing, with no reason for it and no outward sign (because Christ you don't let them see that you're wounded). Galway had almost ceased to exist, even as a memory. I felt like I had been here forever and I'd be here forever and I'd die here if I ever died. I felt as if I'd dreamed the rest of the world. All that existed was this moment in this town. Oh, this fucking town. I was in absolute, frozen despair inside as I danced and danced and danced. Juno came over and danced with me for a while and asked if I was OK and eventually went away again. The songs were taking forever to turn into other songs. I had no idea how long I'd been dancing. I looked at my watch. The song went on forever. Eventually I looked at my watch again. Less than a minute had passed. The chorus came around again and I felt a shivery feeling that I'd heard it too often, that it had come around too often, that it should be over, but I'd heard it a million times before, when I was younger, and it had always ended, so it would be OK this time too. But I always heard it again, didn't I? I'd heard it a million times when I was young and I was hearing it now and it hadn't ended, it wouldn't end.

My mind was exploding with speed, my mind felt shivery, I was thinking too much, it was fine. I looked at my watch again. Oh God, no time was passing. No, the second hand was moving, I could see it moving, but Christ it was slow, how could I ever get *out* of here if time moved so *slowly*, how could this night ever *end*, time had always moved faster than this hadn't it, I'd never noticed time pass so slowly, could it be slower now? It *felt* slower so it *was* slower, I had to trust what I felt what else have you, you have nothing, what you feel is real or nothing is but if you are mad what you feel isn't real but how can you know because you can't get outside yourself to see if what you feel is really real oh this is a new song oh thank Christ that song is over oh thank Christ I won't look at my watch but if I don't look at my watch how can I know if time is moving fast enough to ever, ever let me out of here but looking at my watch won't *help* oh God this must be the acid it has to be I don't normally feel like this do I no oh Jesus I want to go home.

VII. *Caution, Children Crossing*

I began to try to walk back to the table. Light like liquid flooded heavily amongst the dancers so that several times I had to stop, unsure whether I could walk through the thick, viscous beams of red and orange. When a strobe came on I had to stop again and wait for it to end. The world looked like the inside of a madman's head. Arms and faces froze and disappeared and reappeared elsewhere, still frozen, but in new positions, with new expressions. Very very fast things were happening very very slowly and I felt a drowning sense that I had quite, quite lost my hold on time, that time had abandoned me and I could never be fixed now, that I had made a mistake that could never be fixed or made right. A big tear slowly crawled down my cheek and touched the corner of my lip and disappeared across my mouth in a burst of salt.

The tear-trail left a cool line down my cheek as it evaporated.

The strobe stopped and I walked on.

Eventually I reached the table.

'I want to go home,' I said numbly to Juno.

VIII. *The Connollys Illegal Chip-Van Experience*

Outside, in the car-park, Paul decided he wanted chips. He'd left with us to look after us on the walk home, and he'd helped me into my coat when I'd had difficulty finding the armholes, but he was still pissed off with me and he was damned if I'd rob him of the pleasures of the chip-queue. I didn't mind waiting, once I was away from the heat and noise and light. Out here it was cool, quiet, dark. A pleasant, fine drizzle prickled on my face. I'd retreated so far into myself by now that I didn't really feel connected to what I saw and heard at all. I'd been so overloaded in the chaos of trying to leave the building, by the impossible intricacies of answering the questions of Aengus and Juno and Paul, of stripping their voices out of the noise and taking the words out of their voices and squeezing the meaning out of their words and making some sense of the meaning of the words in the voices from the noise ... and then trying to reply ... that I had now shut down completely. I just heard and saw, without any attempt at comprehension.

Which was rather a pity, because the camera of my mind was running on quite an interesting scene. If you were an anthropologist. Or a zoo-keeper. Or a prison governor with some spare beds.

It was by now coming up to chucking-out time, you could tell because people were coming out to chuck up. My distress had cut our evening short, but not by much. Connollys Illegal

Chip-Van was already busy serving the first wave of drunken clubbers, the smart ones who'd left early to beat the queue. They were all standing round in the rain feeling smug, in a huge queue. Actually, to pick nits for a moment (and you could pick nits all night in the Connollys Chip-Van queue) it wasn't really a queue at all. It was a kind of seething, low-key riot designed to deliver the minimum number of people to the van counter with the maximum discomfort, inefficiency and violence. 'Queuing' was considered an activity fit only for Brits and homosexuals. And Kilkenny hurlers. And Dubliners in general. (These categories were not rigorously exclusive. All Brits were homosexuals. Most Dubliners were Brits. Kilkenny hurlers weren't Brits but they might as well be, shaggin' homos. That was never a goal. We was robbed.)

In a peculiar kind of way, standing in the rain in the dark of the car-park staring at the queue with my brain in mush was oddly soothing. I'd done this so often before. This was a familiar, reassuring childhood scene of just the sort to calm my acid-drenched mind. There was little Benny Reynolds leaning over casually to puke on the feet of the person beside him, his cousin Jacinta, who was too drunk to notice. Rumour had it that Benny was the father of Jacinta's child, but then rumour had it that I was a lesbian and that Juno had gone to England for an abortion when she was fifteen (she'd gone to the Gaeltacht for a fortnight to learn Irish from nuns, along with half her class, but why spoil a good story).

There was a Toohy picking a fight with a Sheehy over a sachet of tomato sauce. The Sheehy wouldn't give him any of his, or had squirted too much on, one or the other. The Toohy had knocked the Sheehy's chips flying anyhow, and now some older Toohys and Sheehys were intervening with confused shouts.

'We don't want any fucking trouble, now,' said Billy Sheehy, smacking Sean Toohy in the face.

'Hold me back, lads, hold me back, I'll feckin' kill him,' shrieked the offended Toohy, throwing himself backwards into the arms of a couple of his brothers. It was a ritual as old as time, and as soothing as a cool hand on my brow. It *was* a cool hand on my brow. Juno, checking I hadn't overheated while dancing. I had the peculiar sensation of her hand melting into my head but Juno didn't seem to notice anything strange and took her hand away satisfied.

'Are you OK?'

I laboriously deciphered her question and risked a nod in reply. The drizzle was falling sideways, which was worrying me a little, but I had a vague idea which I was trying to pin down that this was somehow due to the triumph of wind rather than the failure of gravity and that I had no need for concern. Then people started to fall sideways and I moaned in horror before I made the back-connections necessary to interpret what I'd seen, which was a lot of people being knocked over by a small fight sprawling into them.

I closed my eyes again, and got way, way lost in the electric impacts of a billion specks of drizzle on the tight skin of my face.

IX. *In which the Stars go out*

The tap on my arm woke me back into my body. I had been someplace very, very far away, almost without ego, spread thin across a great dark space. The *violence* of sight when I opened my eyes frightened me. Colour and movement and noise (I was mixing them all up by now, the light seemed to me to be causing the noises that I'd ceased to notice when I'd closed my eyes).

If this doesn't make sense to you I can only shrug helplessly. Words cannot bring you to the place I was.

'C'mon, we're moving,' said . . . I deciphered the mass of features which sat without perspective in front of me, moving under light till sound came out . . . Paul. My brother.

We moved.

Information was arriving very late.

My mind was lagging half a footstep behind what was happening, perceptions were coming in, felt early but recognised late and now cause and effect began to cross over. I felt the pavement suck at and reject my feet, again and again. We got to the start of the main street and in a peculiarly distanced, numb despair I stopped to try to count the strands of coloured bulbs that crossed it. If I could only get the right answer, the answer that I knew to be right, it would give me a finger-tip ledge to cling to, a tiny proof of the existence of an objective world outside of my collapsing mind, and the knowledge that there was still an objective world out there would mean I had a fragile, impossible hope of returning to it somehow, somewhen. So it became very important to me.

And I couldn't do it. I couldn't add. Nothing would connect and stay connected. My thoughts were a babble to myself. Word and number were blurred, chopped into fragments so small they failed to form units of meaning, so charged they repulsed other fragments or snapped tight to them with no regard for meaning or truth, or with no regard for regard or regard for with or or. Thoughts spiralled out and broke apart or spiralled in tighter and tighter and vanished. The pitch of my terror grew as I tried to count the strands of light but I'd lost the words for the numbers and the words for the words and the lights were finally and forever uncountable and above me forever and I couldn't find that tiny ledge to hold me and I fell up into the light forever.

Johnny Gleeson said, 'Is she alright?'

I am to some extent now depending on what Juno told me later, because though I remember every detail of the night very clearly, I remember much of it through the crystal filter of powerful acid, as sound and symbol rather than word and deed.

I stood staring up at the Christmas lights, blurred with the acid and hard, salty tears, as Juno told Johnny that no, I wasn't alright. Johnny asked her what I'd taken, brushing off Paul and Aengus who both seemed in a mood to do him injury on my behalf. Jimmy materialised to back up his brother.

Even in Juno's recollection Jimmy seems to have shimmered into existence rather than walked up to her. The drizzle made everything inconstant and tentative. Juno described the picture on the tab I had taken.

'The red one or the other one?'

The red one.

'Oh, that sheet, I don't know what they did. Half of it did nothing, we had a lot of complaints. It's not even, d'you see, not at all, at all. Very unreliable, we don't deal with them fellows at all any more. Mad London bastards. It's all Dutch we stock now. The lads in the 'Dam have the quality control.'

Johnny talked on as Jimmy reached up to grab my chin and pull my head down to his level. His eyes seemed to have a pulse in them, and the pupils seemed to shudder, to snap small and then expand slowly and I couldn't tell if that was an effect of the drug I was on or an effect of the drug he was on.

'Oh Juliet, are you hurting?' he crooned.

'The lights,' I sobbed. 'Make the lights go away.' And I pulled my head back up to look at the hurting lights that barred me from the sweet oblivion of the dark and the silence that lay beyond them. They burned me through my tears, as uncountable as stars.

Jimmy followed my gaze and as he put his hand on my hand I felt *understood* somehow. No less ruined, but comforted by the sure and certain knowledge that Jimmy could see what I saw.

And then he was gone again, grabbing Johnny by the shoulder, shouting 'I'll fix it' as they disappeared into the drizzle.

And then they reappeared after a million years of tears and Aengus and Paul and Juno looked up from their discussion of what the fuck to do with me because I wouldn't bring my eyes down from the lights and I wouldn't stop crying.

Nobody recognised them right away. They were driving an ESB maintenance lorry.

It roared with clashing gears out of Barrack Street and swerved to a halt at the top of O'Connell Street, twenty-three uncountable strands of light away. The engine bellowed again and then calmed to a mutter. Slowly the inspection platform rose above the cab like a great metal cobra's head, on its enormous hydraulic arm. The joint straightened till the platform towered above the street and the lights and the world. I saw it disappear above the foreshortened sheet of lines of light and I prayed from the heart of my terror for something I couldn't name.

The engine rose to the pitch of my terror and suddenly lurched with a howl towards me and entered the realm of light. And the great metal arm bent the first strand of light into a tight, astonished V that snapped with a noise that felt to me, as the line of light vanished, like a crisp explosion of pure silence in the heart of the great roar of light that still poured on me from the uncountable stars of light that made up the uncountable strands. And the next strand bent to a faster V and was gone, and the next. And the roar of the engine grew closer and greater as it extinguished the roar of the light until the lorry tore through the powerlines that crossed the street fifty yards from us and in a great explosion of light and sound the Gleeson twins ripped every star from the sky. The town went black and the streetlights went out. The last of the strands were torn down in darkness. Tiny sparks flared in the gutter from the severed powerlines, and then even they died.

Sirens began to go off and emergency lights flickered on in a few windows. But the huge sky above me was black and stripped of its great strands of torturing stars.

The ESB lorry braked hard in the darkness behind us. Jimmy and Johnny jumped down from the cab and ran back to join us.

'I fixed it,' said Jimmy to all of us, but only I understood what he meant. 'You'll be alright now,' he said to me, and touched my hand again.

Then they were gone, and I was left staring up into the night as slowly the true, tiny stars emerged here and there in the gaps in the low clouds that moved low and fast over the dark town. The drizzle swirled and cleared and for a moment I could see the moon racing across a gap in the clouds.

I could go home now. I felt everything ease and soften. I would be alright. Twenty-three, I thought. Twenty-three strands. Jimmy had cut through the knot of my problem. I would never have to count them now. Never have to count them again. Things could be changed. I wasn't doomed to repeat and repeat and repeat till I died.

I was happy as we began to walk home then in the strange, siren-filled dark. My new tears, as I walked with Juno holding my hand and with Paul's arm in mine, weren't for me at all, or not directly. They were for the knowledge that I had gained as I had looked up into the blackness after the veil of light had been torn from the face of the night.

Jo Baker

'A SMALL CUT'

His face was fat and red and angry and his eyes were all puckered up and piggy. There were hairs crawling out of the open collar of his shirt. The whole place fell silent when he suddenly scraped back his chair and yelped

— Fuck!

Which was fair enough; I was pouring hot coffee all over his crotch.

— I'm sorry. I made to dab at the coffee with my tea towel.

— Fucking hell!

I shrugged. I didn't want to discuss it any further. I turned and went to fetch them their bill. At the counter, Eamonn said,

— Take your wages too. And don't bother turning up for work tomorrow.

— But, Eamonn, he's an arsehole. Did you hear what he said to me?

— You can't go scalding people's dicks just because they're arseholes.

— You have such a way with words.

— You're sacked.

— What about my tips?

*   *   *

I'd never really liked waitressing anyway. Never liked serving, as such. Like, it's fine when the people are polite, you know, treat you like a person. But you get the dickheads in who think they're better than you because they've got more money than you. And I hate that. Getting your arse felt isn't really the worst of it. It's the stuff they say that really turns me over. It isn't just the blokes either.

I untied my apron and left it behind the counter. As I made for the door, I got a few hostile glances from the other waitresses. Understandable. Didn't envy them a Friday night playing with only ten men. Eamonn was leaning over the fat red guy and murmuring something consoling. Unnoticed, I walked past his table and out through the heavy wood-and-glass doors, into the air.

Outside the evening was cool and soft, the sun low, catching the clouds, picking out the edges of each brick in the pavement, bathing the BBC building with peachy light. I stood there in my black-and-whites, sniffing the air, blinking with pleasure.

The Crown is where Cathy and Emer go on a Friday evening, when its snaky innards are seething with Suities, letting their metaphorical hair down. Cathy's got a soft spot for these guys, and they seem to reciprocate. She seems to be getting quite sleek on a diet of accountants and systems analysts. Emer's Cathy's friend. I met her back in September, the start of the year. I've known Cathy like forever. She's a year ahead of me, now, though we used to be in the same class at school.

When it's light outside, The Crown's like the bar in StarWars. You come in out of the bright Alderaan sunlight into this murky dark room and for a moment you can't see a thing. Even in Belfast, the contrast of the bright evening light outside and the dim crowded bar can leave you blinded for a moment. You have to stop, wait, let your pupils readjust, while everyone else gets a good look at you. I hate that. I always blunder on, bumping into people, just to avoid that embarrassing pause at the door. Tonight, Cathy saw me first:

— Una!

I turned blindly towards the call and found them, at the corner of the bar, leaning on the marble top.

Cathy is, always has been, sexy. Sexy in a kind of understated way. Just talking to her you find yourself considering the contour of her breast, the curve of her buttocks. Wondering what's going on in her pants. She's beautiful; she's got light, clear, wet eyes, and smooth straight dark hair, and her skin's always perfect; but she's not sexy because she's beautiful. She just seems so altogether ripe. She has a small, ripe, round body. It fits her. In a way my bony breastless whiteness will never fit me.

She was leaning on the bar, blowing smoke up into the thickly smoky air.

— What are youse drinking? I asked as I leaned across the counter, looking to catch the barman's eye.

— Vodka and white.

I ordered us the drinks. As I fumbled with my wage packet, dragging out one of the three twenty quid notes it contained, Emer pointed out that I usually worked on a Friday night. I agreed, taking a step backwards and gesturing to my clothes.

— I don't wear this stuff by choice.

— I've always liked those trousers on you, Cathy commented.

I paid for the drinks and stuffed the change into a pocket. She has this way of left-footing me.

— Thanks.

— So why aren't you working? Cathy asked, leaning towards me, her hair falling down around her face.

— Got myself sacked.

— Ach, Una. Cathy sounded annoyed and worried.

— Well, I said.

— Well? She sounded motherly. Like, someone else's mum.

— Well. It was this fat fucker kept saying stuff.

— What did he say? Emer asked.

— Well, the last straw was when he asked 'do you take Visa?' and I said yes, and then he asked, really straight faced, 'and do you take it up the bum?' And all his mates thought it was really hilarious and were laughing their tits off.

— You must've been scundered, Emer suggested, but Cathy made a snorting noise. Her 'wee buns' noise.

— Not really. I poured coffee all over his crotch, I said defensively.

Cathy had one of those silent giggle-fits she specialises in, shaking noiselessly, helplessly. I love watching her laugh like that. Her whole face creases up and she just throbs with laughter. Sometimes, when she gets the giggles really bad, and completely loses control, she'll let out a fart. Which of course makes her giggle all the more.

The girls didn't want to sit in a snug. There's not much scoping can be done from inside of one of them, so we stood at the bar with our drinks and I watched their half-focused conversation and felt their eyes shift from me or each other to the middle distance as they checked people out.

— So what are you going to do? Emer asked, looking over my shoulder.

— Fuck knows. I rummaged in the change in my pocket, thoughtfully. I've got just over fifty quid left from my wages and nearly a grand's worth of overdraft. Rent's due next week.

— Can you not ask your parents?

— No. Cathy answered for me. Like I said, I've known Cathy for years.

— So what are you going to do? Emer asked again.

I realised then that I'd been a bit of a dick. Scalding that bloke's knackers had seemed like a really good idea at the time, but now it was me who was fucked. I was getting that creepy nervy feeling in my stomach. The kind of feeling that oozes up your throat and before you know it you're retching with fear. It's something I hadn't felt for a while now. Not since I'd left home. Cathy must've seen me go green or something; she reached out a hand and held mine, cupping it. The cool dry softness of her palm made me notice how cramped up and hot my hand was. Emer, tactful, or in need of a piss, headed for the bogs.

— You're a wee eejit, so you are, Cathy said gently.

I suppose I thought Cathy would make it better. She always had. I suppose that's why I'd come straight there, without stopping to think. Cathy would make it better before I had to deal with it. She began to make conversation, to cheer me up. Her choice of subject wasn't the greatest.

— I'm meeting someone later.

— Oh.

— At The Europa. D'you want to come along?

— I'm hardly dressed for it.

— Ah, you look class. Those trousers are great on you. And you'll like this fella.

— Who is he? I asked, doing my best to summon up some interest, because she meant well.

— His name's Sean. Mid thirties. Well-off. Generous.

— That's the best type. I was swallowing down my nausea with gulps of vodka-and-white and beginning to feel a little better. There was a distinct pause before Cathy spoke again, and I glanced down at her. Her little face was thoughtful, and she twisted a slippery lock of hair around a finger. With her other hand, she gripped mine tighter for a moment, and then let go. Her lips formed the words precisely and she leaned in towards me, speaking softly.

— Listen. She paused, seemed to give what she had to say some thought, smiled, and then began again.

— You're taking the Women's Studies modules, aren't you?

— Yes, I replied, puzzled.

— Well, don't you think it's about time you gave some thought to rejecting patriarchal bourgeois morality and taking control of your life and your own sexuality?

— Uh?

She realised she wasn't getting through to me and leant in closer still. I could smell her. She breathed the words to me. I could feel them graze my skin.

— Listen, Una. You can make a fortune. Well, you can get your overdraft paid off. And I can help you out. Sean's not the only guy. You can be back in black in no time flat. I can help you out. Set you up.

She leant back, opening her cigarette packet and selecting one thoughtfully. As she lit up, she was squinting up at me.

— For a small cut, she added.

Cathy's always been enterprising. Like, when we were at school together, she faked a whole pregnancy-miscarriage drama to get more lenient marking on her 'A' levels. The nuns wrote to the exam board and everything. She got the marks she needed and I got another year at home, doing my resits at the Tech. Which was just lovely. She almost had even me convinced, even though I knew she was a virgin, at the time.

Nonetheless, this came as a bit of a shock. That year of me at home in the sticks, her up here in the big smoke, had made more of a difference than I'd realised, but I was mainly surprised that she'd kept it hidden from me. That she'd managed to keep it hidden from me. That I'd not noticed. I know she's got a big raised brown mole on her left buttock, the size of a Jaffa Cake. You'd think if you knew that kind of thing about someone, you'd know everything there was to know. But then I suppose that mole's pretty common knowledge nowadays.

Apparently, she'd been seeing this guy, not Sean, but this other guy, back at the start of her first year. A good bit older. Very good looking. A lot of cash to throw around. Generous with his dope too. As she described him I recognised him as someone I'd seen her out with once or twice. One of the few beautiful men in Belfast. So she'd been fucking him.

Anyway he'd introduced her to some people, some other young women, who were all working already. And they were all young and fun to be with, and were making good money too. And spending it. And of course, Cathy's grant ran out. Grants always do. And like me, Cathy's not got the kind of parents you can just ring up and ask them to lend you a few quid.

— So, he said he could set me up with a guy. And it wasn't like great sex, but you soon get used to it. And you get used to the money. And he makes sure you're safe. Like, you're not going to get some weirdo. Not going to get beaten up.

— I thought this stuff was all run by the 'RA, I said.

Cathy shrugged.

She was watching me thinking, her sheeny eyes studying me through the veil of smoke. I managed a smile for her, and said:

— And this is what they teach you in Women's Studies.

— Fuck, no. She was laughing up at me, that irrepressible, infectious shake beginning in her belly. No. I made that stuff up.

Emer rejoined us, and Cathy bought another round, and we drank. Maybe I was quieter than usual. Maybe I was less of a dick than usual. I was fairly detached from what was going on around me. When Emer picked up her jacket from the floor and Cathy slid off her barstool, I was surprised at how quickly the time had gone. Out the front of the pub, in the orange glow of the street lamps, Emer climbed into a black cab, and waited for us to get in. Cathy said:

— Una and me'll walk.

Emer nodded, probably thinking that Cathy was going to give me some sound advice and moral support on our trek back.

We stood on the pavement while the taxi moved off, the noise of the bar dim behind closed doors, then flaring loud as customers pushed in and out. The air was cool and I shivered, remembering the jacket left hanging on the hat stand at work. I promised myself a new one. A soft tobacco-coloured suede one, like Cathy's. That thought brought back the lurching nausea in my gut, but it also amounted to a decision.

— Well? Cathy asked. In the orange half-light of the street, her eyes were intensely bright, the skin around them dark and bruised-looking.

— Well. I assented.

I waited in the corridor. The carpet was blue with a tiny flecked pattern, like a feather or a lily, repeated again and again all the way up the corridor. Past all the closed blue doors. Cathy had left the door ajar and I could hear her voice, speaking calmly, persuasively, but I wasn't making out any of the words. I felt someone come to the door and look out at me. A long moment's appraisal, then he went back into the room and they began to talk again. After a little while, Cathy came out, closing the door behind her, giving me a smile.

— It's sorted. You can go on in. I'll wait for you in the bar.

I'd never felt so nervous. Not even exams. Not even at home. My stomach had kind of melted, and I really needed the toilet. I could feel my hands were sweaty but my face felt cold and kind of hollow. My teeth ached.

I turned the doorhandle and walked in.

The fella, Sean, he was sitting on the edge of the bed, with his back to me, speaking into the phone. He had a southern accent.

— Yeah. Just now. Thought you'd be interested.

He half turned, saw me and then finished:

— Listen, I'll talk to you again. Bye.

And put down the phone.

— You must be Una. He smiled at me. It wasn't a bad smile. It was quite a nice smile. He heaved himself up from the bed and came round it towards me. He was wearing a slightly crumpled suit and shirt, his tie was off, his collar loose. He said, Cathy tells me you're new to this.

I swallowed, nodded.

— She knows what I like.

— You just have to tell me what you want, I said.

He laughed. A real, genuine guffaw. I suppose I did sound ridiculous, standing there sweating and trembling, trying to talk like a Hollywood whore.

— Cathy's done well. I think we're going to get on fine.

* * *

70

I didn't relax. I couldn't. As he undid the buttons of my shirt I just froze, my skin tingling with apprehension. He undressed me, even untied my boots and dragged them off me, so I was soon standing there pale and skinny in my old BHS knickers and bra. I was fiercely embarrassed that I was wearing such untarty underwear. I was fiercely embarrassed that I couldn't make a better attempt at a come on to him, and wondered vaguely if he'd still pay.

He didn't seem put off. He dragged off his clothes, and turned to me. His erection was terrifying, enormous. And I was scared and cold and dry and knew that it would hurt. He came up close to me, put his arms around me, and undid my bra, slid it off me. He hooked my pants down with a finger and I stepped out of them. He cupped my right breast with one hand, bent down and sucked briefly on the nipple, then smiled up at me. He pulled me over towards the bed, and I sat down then lay stiffly upon it. He rummaged in a bedside drawer, picked out a condom, tore off the wrapping and put the condom on. He climbed on top of me, and I opened my legs for him and he pushed his dick into me. It hurt. I didn't relax. He didn't want me to. I lay there, cold and dry and shaking as he fucked me, and then he came. Then he pulled himself out of me, and went to the bathroom, to clean himself. I lay there a moment, my legs cramped and sore. Then I stood up, found my clothes and hurried them on. I felt sick and sore and still in need of a shit but somehow I also felt relieved. I heard the toilet flush as I was just stepping into my black trousers. He came back into the room, still naked, and laughed again to see me losing my balance as I dragged the trousers on.

— Thanks very much, he said. I couldn't think of anything to say. He continued, That was really nice. He passed me, went round to the bedside drawer he'd got the condom out of, and lifted out a neat, leather wallet. He opened it, peeled out several notes and handed them to me. I realised I'd no idea how much I was worth.

* * *

Cathy wasn't in the bar. It was a small place, it wasn't crowded. Compared to the other people there, I felt a mess, but more together, more sober. Strangely clear. And sore. I found myself a barstool and ordered a drink. She was a long time turning up. I was getting some hassle from a couple of English fellas in suits, who wanted to buy me drinks. I noticed someone standing close, to my left, too big to be Cathy. I glanced up at him. He was tall, beautiful, elegant. Cathy's guy.

— You must be Una, he said. Cathy's waiting outside.

Strangely, I wasn't scared. I followed him out of the bar without a question, even in my own mind. I felt clear and calm and even a little confident. Cathy wasn't waiting at the front of the hotel. He put an arm around me, across my back and down so his hand rested in the dip of my waist. He led me down the street a little way, then round a corner and we were out onto the dark wastelands of car parks. Ahead of us there was a car, sitting in the murk. It was a big car, an expensive one. A BM perhaps. He felt warm and comforting against my side as he walked me up to it. He opened the back door and gestured me in. I slid in, he closed the door, then got in the front seat.

As the front door opened, the light came on. I saw a crumpled form beside me on the back seat, face pressed into the leather upholstery, hair spread out in tattered knots. She was almost crying, choking back her sobs. She raised herself to sitting position, slowly, painfully, leaning on one hand. Her eyes were bruised with running make-up, her nose swollen and dripping. She had a hand cupped against her cheek, pressing a cotton handkerchief to it. It was soaked with blood.

The light flicked off.

— Give me the money, he said.

I fumbled in my trouser pocket, drew out a handful of crumpled notes and handed them to him through the gap between the seats. He took them from me, and I could hear him straightening the notes out one by one. He shifted round in the seat and handed me back a single note. And a small white card.

— That's my business card, he said. In future you go through me.

For a moment, I sat and looked at the little bit of white paper glowing bright in the darkness of the car park.

— Well, off you go then, he said.

Emer Martin

'THE POOKA AT FIVE HAPPINESS'

I was on my way to Five Happiness when I saw three veiled women standing on the steps of the Wellington Monument in the Phoenix Park. I stopped the car to look. They were completely shrouded, small slits for their eyes. Their children might have played at the back of the monument, and their husbands could have been there too, but all I saw were the three ghostly figures, like black crows on the slanted steps. The dark cloths billowing and their imagined eyes gazing.

My parents own two Chinese restaurants in Ireland. One in Dublin and one in County Meath. Both are called Five Happiness, which might add up to ten happiness but not for me. My family came from China proper to Hong Kong when my brother was six. He didn't want to leave China so he hid by the river. When my grandmother and aunt found him they tied him to a stick and carried him on that same stick to the bus. My brother thinks they only tell that story to be cruel. He is fourteen years older than I am. I was born here.

My mother was wary of foreign doctors so I was born over the restaurant in Trim town, Co Meath. When I was three, my mother went back to Beijing for many years because my father's mother was difficult. The woman who minded me was from Galway. Her family had been moved from the west of Ireland by the government and given land in Meath. They were Irish speakers and the government thought that they could spread the language through settlements of native speakers. The locals didn't like them much; they called them Gaeltachts. Because of this woman I spoke better Irish than English when I was little.

I loved the woman who minded me. She believed in fairies. She and I often had picnics in a field behind Friar's park on a fairy ring. The fairy ring had greener shorter grass than the rest of the field. She laid the cloth on the flattened circle of grass and we drank diluted orange from plastic cups and ate cheese sandwiches, and she would tell me stories. I loved her more than my real family. My father was busy setting up the Dublin restaurant and avoiding my grandmother. My family spoke to me in broken English and I didn't speak Chinese. The woman who minded me died five years ago when I was fourteen years old. I found her in her chair by the fire. Her mouth hung open. I tried to shut her jaw before I called my grandmother but it sprang back open with a popping noise as I reached the door. The funeral was at her family's place in Rathcarn. As we buried her, the sun shone, and her family spoke softly in Irish. They made a few disparaging remarks about my family but I felt embarrassed to let them know I understood.

I forgot the Irish I learnt from her and forgot the Chinese I had when I was a baby. If other things happen I might forget the English I think in now. The castle ruins I played in, as a kid, were solid even as ruins, but words are just shapes of thoughts, moving as shadows from our heads and hands. I know more than most the faithlessness of words.

It is impossible to find parking in Dublin these days as everyone has a car and a cellular phone and a swanky new job. I finally found a spot on Fade Street and walked to the Five Happiness on George Street. I was wearing my bright red fake fur coat but it did not seem cold for the beginning of winter.

'Late,' my mother said to me as I walked in the back door. She was making a tray of dumplings in the kitchen of the restaurant.

'Hungry?' she then said. I shook my head. I don't like Chinese food. 'Never eat,' she said and I shrugged.

'Too thin,' my aunt said.

My father came from the front and shouted his order. He saw me and instinctively adjusted his black bow tie; shaking his head like I was already dying just because I went to NCAD, The National College of Art and Design and did not study medicine or law. My older brother put my paintings up in the Meath restaurant he now managed. But here in Dublin the walls are decorated with calligraphy. Bold unintelligible strokes; the same strokes I paint with, and I don't know what my paintings mean either. These days they just want you to be abstract.

'Halloween,' my father whispered to me in dread. I peeked through the door to the restaurant floor and saw a witch and two men in cow suits with plastic udders. They were eating noodles. Halloween was always trouble. In Dublin the kids set fire to horses and dogs, and tied frying pans to cats' tails. In Meath they used to come to the door and say 'Penny for the Pooka'. My Grandmother would wrap cold pork dumplings in paper for them. I watched from the window, as the kids pelted the glass with her dumplings. The woman who minded me would give me sweets to give to them instead. I would fire them from the window and try to take their eyes out with my Milky Way missiles.

I took off my coat and my father clipped a dicky bow to my collar. He liked doing this. He squeezed my arm affectionately. He was in a good mood these days. My grandmother was dead and my mother was back from Beijing with her sister.

My aunt and mother cooked without chefs' hats. They had an old Chinese man doing the dishes. He hunkered down on the speckled linoleum floor and ate a bowl of noodles. No westerner of his age would have the agility to eat like that.

'He learn English classes now,' my mother said to me, nodding in his direction.

'You should too,' I told her.

'No use,' my mother shrugged. 'So many Chinese here now.'

'You could talk to me,' I said.

One of the old man's jobs was to put the dressing on the salads. We had One Thousand Island dressing, Blue Cheese dressing, and French dressing. Known to him as Thousand Island, Cheesy Island and French Island.

'Which Island?' he said to me as I marched up to him with my orders.

'Cheesy Island' I said back, amused that he confused the brand name with the word for dressing. I could have corrected him but I liked his mistake. Besides, I got fed up with him always wanting me to teach him English.

'Give me kishy!' he demanded, puckering his lips. 'You come to Hong Kong I buy you jacket!'

'Sexual harassment,' I said. 'That's today's new word, asshole.'

'Ashhoe?'

My mother and aunt laughed. At least they understood.

It was nine o'clock and I had served an assortment of freaks. Hippies, punks, sluts, vampires, aliens had all partaken of my family's Pu Pu platters and Moo Shoo pork. Three black men walked through the door and my father let me take their table. He was fussing over a Chinese Mafia wanker who was over from London. He told my mother in the kitchen that there were three black men at one table.

'Before never this,' my mother said, as she handed me a plate of General Tao's chicken and chips. 'Before only us.'

My aunt nodded. 'Only Chinese and no trouble.'

'Too many come now,' my mother said. 'Soon the Pakis and Indians.'

'And after that the cowboys and where will we be then?' I said, in mock horror.

'Which Island?' asked the old man.

'Frenchy Island.'

He administered the dressing and I grabbed my salad and left them to it, swinging through the doors. My father was laughing loudly at the Mafioso's joke.

I had three tables: the black men, a group of NCAD students I recognized from a senior year, and the last table had to be the strangest. They were a group of ten blond German speakers. They ranged in ages from twenty to sixty, and all wore purple sweatshirts and loose black trousers. Both the women and the men had yellow hair cropped closely to their heads. 'What are you guys dressed up as?' I asked them. 'The Branch Davidian?' They looked blankly at me, but were scrupulously polite. I floated between these three tables and in and out of the kitchen.

'Are you going to the rave tonight' One of the students had recognized me from college.

'I hadn't heard about it.'

'This one has been a big secret cause of where it's at. Here's some flyers.' She handed me a bunch.

I read it. POOKA PARTY TONIGHT IN THE RUINS. There was a map. 'I know this place. I'm from Trim. My brother manages the restaurant down there.'

'Great. Come along.'

'Sure. I could sleep over with him.'

'I'm not sure how much sleeping you'll get done.'

'Oh yeah? You got any E?'

'Nope, but there'll be plenty there. And they say the DJ is just fucking brilliant. He's from Ballymun.'

'She shagged him at a rave up the mountains. That's why.'

'Fuck off he *is* brilliant.'

'A brilliant shag?' I asked. 'Or a brilliant DJ?'

'Both.' She handed me an empty rice bowl. 'Honestly though, you have to come. It'll be good craic. And these might be the last of the raves. You never know, the Guards are cracking down.'

'Come early though. They'll bust us at some point for this one. It's a historical sight or something but we thought we'd go all out since it's the last Halloween of the century.'

'Aye, I will so,' I said and took their plates.

'Last one we threw was deadly.'

'Who were you there with?' her friend asked her.

'About forty of my closest friends.'

We all laughed. She smiled guiltily, 'I guess that's a real E thing to say.'

'What's with the Aryan nation, or whatever they're dressed up as? Do you know them?'

'No. Haven't seen them in before. They seem harmless. Everything's a little edgy these days. They could be just a volleyball team or something.' I went over to clear the group's table. They all ordered the same dessert, banana fritters and ice cream.

'We were looking for somewhere special tonight. A place where people gather outdoors,' one of the older ones asked me.

'This is Ireland, people don't gather outdoors.' But I gave them a flyer.

Back in the kitchen the old man was making origami out of the napkins. He showed me one. I assumed it was a Chinese dragon. His eyes lit up and he pulled the tail of the little paper creature to make the head move. Its wings fluttered.

'What word in English?'

'Napkin. I need a salad. Thousand Island.'

'No. Not napkin.' He was pissed off.

'Dragon. I think that's a dragon,' I relented.

'Dlagon. Dlagon.'

'Dragon. That's right.'

The party girls were gone and had left a good tip. They had put the rave flyers on some of the tables. Two of the black men were American, but one of them had an Irish accent that was identical to the accent of the woman who minded me.

'I don't wanna go to no rave. I came to this country for some old world culture,' one of the Americans said.

'OK, this is business for me,' the Irish one said. 'I can get my own ride. I'll call Maura, she's probably already heard about this.'

'I'm driving there after work,' I said on impulse.

'Deadly! Can I catch a ride?'

'Indeed you can.'

'Hey, young lady,' the large American one said. 'Tell us what's there to see this country.'

'What are you looking for?'

'Do you have video games here?' the skinny American said.

'You come here to play those damn games?' The large one threw his eyes to heaven. 'Look Miss, this is our first time out of the U.S. Tell us what to do.'

'No problem. It's easy. Dublin is New York, Galway is San Francisco and Limerick is Detroit,' I told them and the guy wrote it down. They were smiling. 'Where's Mexico then?'

'Cavan.' I didn't miss a beat.

'And Cootehill is Tijuana.' The Irish one laughed. 'Hey, great dumplings you have here.'

'I don't like dumplings,' I said. 'They remind me of drowned flesh.'

I had said good-bye to my family, changed my clothes, married the ketchup, and wrapped the cutlery in napkins. I was leaving out the rubbish when I saw the old man stand by the skip staring at the sea gulls perched on the side. He turned to look at me and pointed to the birds.

'Dragon. Dragon.' He seemed to be beseeching me, but I turned away silently and went back to lock up. I had given him the wrong word. Forever he would call birds 'dragons' and people would think him mad. The Pooka party man was waiting out front.

'What's your name,' he asked.

'Daisy. What's yours?'

'I am the Pooka.'

'Figures. You're from Galway, aren't you?'

'How did you know?'

'Your accent.'

'You're spot on. I was raised in an orphanage in Clifton.'

'Who were your friends back there?'

'I met them in North Carolina. They're all right. I was in the States for a bit but I didn't like it. All my friends are here, like. Those two were lads I worked with on the boats. I think they got a fright when they came here and realized that I was the only black guy in the country.'

We walked to Fade street to my car. When I started to drive he asked me to swing by and pick up a friend of his. John Paul was a traveller and lived with his family on a caravan site by the side of the road in Blanchardstown. I got out of the car and walked with the Pooka through the site. John Paul was short and had red hair and huge freckles. He wore a tracksuit and pocketed his red laser pointer when we told him it was a rave. I fascinated his sisters and brothers. They all knew the Pooka. He introduced me to them.

'This is Sigourney, this is Brad, this is Winona, this is Keanu.'

Sigourney, Brad, Winona and Keanu grinned back. 'Are you from China?' Brad asked. Some of the children had cheap plastic horror masks on.

'No, are you?' My stock response.

'Do you speak English?' Keanu asked.

'You fucking eejit. Sure isn't she speaking it now?' John Paul shooed them away and walked out with us.

'Your mother must watch a lot of films.'

'Fuck yeah. We were in Tallaght for ages beside the multiplex at the Square. Sure when she heard of the new one opening here in Blanchardstown state of the art and all – there was no stopping her.'

'You were born in 1979 weren't you?' I asked him as we passed a pile of burning rubbish. Children danced about and threw more sticks on the pyre.

'How could you guess?'

'This one knows everything,' the Pooka said.

'Pope's visit.' I shrugged.

'Can I come with ye?' A little fellah was already sitting in the open car dressed in a Zorro outfit. 'No you can't River. Wait a few years and then we'll take you.'

'Go on to fuck.' John Paul turfed him from the back seat. 'He's soft in the head so he is.'

'Arra, sure he's only a wee one.' the Pooka said.

Magically the Pooka produced a bag of of E. We all took one. Twenty minutes later they had the nerve to ridicule my music collection.

'Beck, Garbage, Chemical Brothers, Prodigy, Chumbawumba, Jaysus this one is into all the celebrities. Kronos Quartet, who the fuck are they when they're at home?'

'Fuck names man,' John Paul shouted. 'Raves are about the crowd not the fucking idiot rock star. We're into the music not the worship. We want our music to be anonymous.'

'Like it was made by machines,' the Pooka agreed.

I grabbed a tape and slammed in *'Fuck the Millennium — We want it now.'* They shut up and started grooving. The Pooka turned in the front and poked John Paul in the back seat. 'Hey John Paul, I've a new joke for you.'

'What?'

'There were these three fellahs sitting outside the hospital in Dublin. A black man, an Irish man and a knacker . . .'

'Traveller,' John Paul said sharply. 'Knacker is a bad word. How'd you like me to call you nigger.'

'It's just for the joke. The nuns always called yiz the tinkers, then it was the itinerants, now it's the travellers. Would ye make your mind up? What'll it be next, inter-galactic Pad-dies?'

'What's the fucking joke, Negro!'

'I'm African Irish,' the Pooka corrected him. 'Ok, three guys outside the hospital, real nervous. The nurse runs out all happy and says 'Great news altogether, you've each had a son. Only one problem, in all the excitement they got mixed up. Yiz'll have to come in and decide which is which. So the Irish man jumps up, runs in, grabs the black baby and starts to cradle him and kiss him and coo over him and the black man says 'what the fuck! Isn't it obvious that one's mine' and the Irish man holds on tightly to the baby and says 'No way, I'm keeping this wee fellah — one of them two is a knacker.' '

John Paul laughed. 'We'd enough trouble between us Irish without you lot showing up.'

'Today I saw three Muslim women in the Phoenix Park in full veil,' I said. 'On the steps of the Wellington Monument.'

'Lord Nelson's spies.' John Paul said.

'Iranians. I bet.' The Pooka said. 'The embassy crowd are very strict.'

'Fuck's sake!' John Paul said. 'We just got rid of the Catholic Church and before ye know it we'll be Islamic.'

'The women who minded me told me about all the Irish invasions. First there were the Nemedians who actually came from the Caspian Sea in Iran, and they fought with the Fomorians who were already here, then came the Firbolg. The Firbolg were defeated by the Tuatha De Danann and the Tuatha De Danann were conquered by the Celts.'

'So?'

'So we're not the first foreign settlers on the soil.'

'That's fine by me,' John Paul said. 'At least you'se lot come in peace to feed us sweet and sour after the pub closes.'

Crowds were gathering in the ruins and music was pumping. Everyone was drinking water and people seemed to know the Pooka and know he had E. He was dosing everybody. John Paul and I, we were dancing by a tomb. The tomb had a life-size carving of a man and a woman in medieval clothes. The Pooka came over and started picking up rusty safety pins that were scattered on the figures.

'Don't.' I slapped his hand. 'People leave them there to cure warts.'

'Genital warts?' He dropped them and wiped his hand on his jacket. I thought he looked so handsome all of a sudden. The ruins were bathed in yellow and purple and green lights. Mardi Gras colours. He was tall and his face angular. I hoisted myself up onto the tomb. As I wrapped my legs around his torso, he kissed me. I licked his brown neck and felt him shiver. 'Jaysus, the mere mention of genital warts and the two of ye get all fucking randy.' John Paul ran off, leaping over the stones and shouting, 'Fuck the Millennium, it's come and gone.' 'And how was it?' some girl shouted at him. 'It was mighty,' John Paul declared.

I was wearing a short black suede mini skirt and thigh-high leather boots. The Pooka was sliding his hands up my skirt. drum 'n' bass music sucked us into the belly of the night, and churned us around in there, digesting us. People were dancing on the graves and snogging in the empty stone arched windows.

'You grew up here?'

'Yes. Then I went to boarding school in Navan. My brother lives here now. He was carried on a stick from China to Hong Kong. Now he has a new Chinese wife from London.'

'What's his name?'

'Tony. He was given that name in an English school in Hong Kong. I don't know his Chinese name.'

'What's your Chinese name?'

'I was born in Meath, remember?' I dislodged his hands, which were edging under the elastic of my knickers. I lay down on the tomb on top of the woman and kissed her lips. Someone came up and bought four E's.

'Are you jealous?' I asked, stroking the life-size effigy's stone chest.

'Are you tripping yet?'

'I am.'

'How did these two die? Do you know?' He pointed to the carvings on the tomb.

'They're the jealous man and woman. The woman who minded me said he killed her and then himself. I asked her what jealousy was, and she told me if I saw a friend with a lovely red ribbon, and wanted it, and hated her because she had it, then that was jealousy.'

'So he killed her for a stupid red ribbon.'

'Who cares? They'd have been dead by now anyway.'

He took my hand and led me away. We blended into the throng of sweating happy people. They were dancing so seriously and trance-like. Everyone was moving to the same repetitive rhythm.

It was as if we were breaking through to somewhere else. So much was possible. I swear I felt so happy that night. The Pooka was a great dancer. I saw the three girls from NCAD that had given me the flyer. They were feeling each other up and swapping cigarette smoke from one mouth to the other.

'Let's go off somewhere,' he suggested.

'I can't go to my brother. He'll tell my parents. I need that job.'

'What's over there?'

We walked out of the graveyard toward the Tower of Leprosy. As we crossed the bridge there were a bunch of local lads. 'Have you got legal papers?' they shouted at us. 'You need a visa to come to here from Dublin, you know?' The Pooka shouted back. 'Go dance in the graveyard, it's free and you're welcome.'

I put my hand on his arm to silence him. 'They're just local guerriers. They don't like Dublin people coming here and throwing parties on their territory.'

'Bunch of culchie skinheads,' he said.

'Who's being prejudiced now? Remember I'm not only Chinese Irish, I'm culchie Chinese Irish.'

We climbed quickly over the wall and I pulled him to the middle of a ruined church. We lay on the ground and I took a condom out of my pocket. 'Let's fuck,' I said, and he laughed. We could hear the music from across the way as we kissed. His tongue was slightly bitter tasting, and I could slip my tongue underneath his and feel every bump on the floor of his mouth. My skirt was pushed up to my waist but I still had my boots on. We were really screwing hard and wonderful when we heard noises.

'It's them.' He said. 'The bastards have come to get us. Let's go.'

The Tower of Leprosy was a tall, hollow medieval building that was once a hospital run by monks. As we passed by I noticed the iron door had been prised open.

'I used to spend my life in all these old places when I was a kid. It's a wonder I never fell and broke my neck. Then they came and put up iron gates here and at the castle so I couldn't climb up anymore.'

'Were you always alone?'

'I had a woman who minded me but other than that I was a solitary creature as a child. You should know all about that, they say the Pooka is a misshapen animal spirit deformed by solitude.'

'Not me. I was a local celebrity. The nuns doted on me. How come the gate is open now? Can we go up?'

We walked inside and climbed the stone spiral staircase. There was a ledge where the roof must have been and it was possible to walk around comfortably. 'I always felt I was on top of the world here. You can see the town and the Boyne river and the castle and the graveyard. There's the echo gate over there. Can you see it? If you stand at that gate you can shout across the river to the ruins and the ruins shout back.'

'Those local guys must have joined in the party. There's no sign of them.'

We sat and smoked a joint and watched the rave from our privileged position. Tiny bodies moving in and out of the lights; a synchronized throng of people woven inside the throbbing music. His fingers sneaked under my sweater and grazed my belly and spidered up to my breasts. I could feel the tip of one of his fingers circle my nipple. 'In Belgium in the Middle Ages,' I said, 'there was a phenomena of dancing groups who moved through the countryside. They would dance into a town and like it was a contagion the people would drop their work and dance off with them. It caused quite a disturbance to the whole economy and everything.'

'Are you always this full of information?' He stood up.

'Fuck you,' I pushed him. He almost lost his footing and a stone was dislodged and crashed over the side.

'Hey, don't push me up here.' He looked over the edge and down the sheer side of the stone walls. It was a long drop to the ground. 'Certain fucking death. Let's get out of here.'

As we climbed down there were a group of people standing

in front. One had a crowbar. The Pooka almost bolted on the spot, but I realized who they were. 'It's the Germans from the restaurant.' They were all wearing purple robes. One of them saw the Pooka look in terror at his crow bar. 'This was just to open the gate,' he said gently. 'Peace, brother and sister.'

'Whatever.' The Pooka shrugged and we climbed the outer wall giggling and ran back over the bridge. The rest of the group were unloading crates from a van. 'Fucking nutters.' He shook his head. Back at the party we danced to the wildest noise. We were so high we could dance to machines, to a refuse of sounds. There were no words. The track the DJ was playing was one I had never heard before. Jazz and techno was cut up and mangled by urban nightmares – and if we could dance to car alarms then we would be prepared for the beginning of the next thousand years. 'I love you,' the Pooka told me. The first words breaking into my world of pure sound. And I thought I could take those words and for once have something of my own. I loved him too. Then, all of a sudden, we found ourselves dancing to police sirens.

'COPS!'

'I was wondering what was taking them so long.' The Pooka slipped away. I tried to go after him but the crowd was panicking as a bunch of Guards were roughly pushing through to find the source of the music. More police came with loud speakers telling us all to sit down and not move. But some people kept dancing, and the Guards were grabbing them and trying to drag them off. When the music stopped abruptly, I scoured the crowd for the Pooka, but saw no sign of him. Over at the Tower of Leprosy a firework shot into the air. My fellow dancers and I stood and cheered as firework after firework reverberated like battle sounds through the ancient walls and stones. The sky was a cathedral of moving light. Then little robed figures, casual shapes, began diving off the tower's high walls.

'They're killing themselves,' I grabbed a Guard who was spinning around in the confusion, and I pointed to the Tower of Leprosy.

'Holy fucking Mother of God!' He shouted and all the Guards left us and ran in their direction. The DJ started the music up again and everyone was applauding. Why go on if you don't have to? What's the tragedy in wanting nothing? Where's the shame in surrender? The whine, hiss, and bang of the fireworks exploded into sparkling reds and greens and blues and yellows over the dark October night, leaving the sky bristling with bright falling sparks. As one by one the men and women jumped, wisps of ghostly smoke trails hovered high above and marked the black air. I stood on a grave with my hands covering my mouth, and saw John Paul stumble towards me. He was in bad shape. His nose was smashed and bleeding, and blood was flowing from a gash across his forehead.

'John Paul!' I grabbed him and hugged him. He bled over my face, and down my neck. 'Poor John Paul. What happened? Did you fall? Was it the skinheads that got you, or the Guards?'

His eyes were closed, and he held onto my wrists with both his bloody hands. His legs were jiggling and I realized that he was trying to dance. Our fingers interlocked. 'Have you seen your friend the Pooka?' I asked him. 'Where did he go?'

'You mean Seamus? That slippery bollix?' he murmered. 'I saw him jump into a car and fuck off.'

'He's gone?'

'He'd done his business. Too much gear on him to stick around.'

'Whose car, was it?'

'His girlfriend Maura. She'd been looking for him all night.'

'Oh.'

John Paul was out of breath, and leaned heavily against me. And so we danced as dawn approached, under the shower of light, among siren screams, and in front of newly arrived press photographers. The drum 'n' bass echoed over the Boyne river, and on out through the farms and small towns, and on toward the cities and the sea that lay beyond the cities – out into a shifting world that sent its eerie echo back.

I danced with the fierce longing to tell the woman who minded me my own story; the three spooky women on the steps, the dragons the old china man pointed to at the rubbish bins, the travelling children with movie star names. She had told me about all those who once came here looking for a home – the Nemedians, the Firbolgs, the Tuatha De Danann, and the wild Celts. And I would tell her of those that chose this place to die. And then I would have to tell her about the Pooka; his galloping gunpowder hooves in the sky, and the terrible journey he took us on, holding onto his horns, and how he left us all in the gray morning, with blood on our hands, in the jealous ruins.

Colin Carberry

'DIGGING A HOLE'

There are three ladies in the house (four if you count six-month-old Francesca snoozing in an upstairs cot).

Sally Brannigan perches forward in an armchair in the living room, her cigarette resting on the rim of the ashtray lying by her foot. She is scribbling down each lottery number on the top of the day before's newspaper as the balls come to rest on the thin plastic shoot. In between glances at her Lucky Dip ticket, she mutters 'fucksake' and wishes that Scrappy, the household cat, was still alive so she would have something to kick.

Yvonne Staunton is in the kitchen, lifting plates from the cupboard, preparing to dish out the Chinese meal, delivered only moments before by a man who bore an unsettling resemblance to Billy Wright. She has no interest in the Lottery. She has never bought a ticket, fearing that, as the course of her twenty-four years on the planet has hitherto been all snakes and no ladders, the fates would, inevitably, conspire to rob her of any winnings in an imaginatively horrific tabloid manner. She loves the smell of hot sweet and sour sauce. She opens the little plastic container, brings it up to her nose and sniffs greedily. If she didn't smoke, she thinks, there would be more of a kick.

Her sister, Anne-Marie, is coming down the stairs in her socks. She has peeked in on Francesca, sighing with relief that Wee

Gurny Bastard is resting her lungs and tear ducts. Anne-Marie is hungry, her hang-over has finally began to ebb and now she craves some beef noodles. Beef noodles, with chips, stuffed between two pieces of thinly buttered brown bread, eased down the throat with a cool mouthful of vodka and coke.

The house is being lightly pelted with spittles of rain. The front lawn, spongy after the day-long mizzle, glows yellow — the lights of the living room falling softly, through the closed blinds, onto its lap. The street is empty. It is quiet except for the echoes of TV programmes, radio stations and conversations that creep through single-glazed or half-opened windows and mix with the crackle of the power lines above.

A car slips quietly along the road, rolling to a halt directly outside Anne-Marie's house. The five men inside have been listening to a Brian Kennedy song on the final stage of their journey. The occupant of the passenger seat had brought his wife to see the singer play at a concert at the Waterfront Hall and enjoyed every minute. He had especially liked it when Brian untied his pony-tail, freeing his long dark hair to the escaping squeals of a hall full of women.

— Silly auld bitches, he had said to his wife, as he looked all around, shaking his head.

— Fucksake, says the man by the back left window. — Missed the fuckin Lottery draw, listening to that fuckin fruit.

His words sink to the floor and no-one responds. He thinks of the duo sitting beside him, they are almost ten years younger than him but they show little respect. When they are not ignoring him, they make disparaging remarks. They may be bigger, he thinks, but one day they will push him too far.

The pair by his side are twins. They are both thinking of the two sisters they met at the club last Friday. They are thinking of their short, firm thighs, their tight breasts, their high-pitched sighs. They regret not having gone back last night. They determine, at the same time, to return next week to try to talk them into a swap.

'Digging a Hole'

The driver gazes at Anne-Marie's house. He has spent the last twenty minutes attempting to shift his posture, unable to sit comfortably in this seat. His back will ache in the morning. He unbuckles his seat-belt, leans forward slightly and rolls his head in a slow semi-circle from one shoulder to the other. Then, switching off the radio, he turns to the others.

Sally can hear the rain begin to spray against the window. She reaches over to feel the radiator and, after it chills the palm of her hand, she shouts for Yvonne to turn on the central heating.

Anne-Marie walks into the kitchen and opens a cupboard, taking out a glass. Yvonne asks her what Sally was shouting about. Anne-Marie doesn't answer, just walks to the wall and switches on the heater. She then tugs at the fridge door, taking out an almost full two litre bottle of Coke.

A drenched tree drops water onto the side-mirror of the car parked beneath the edge of its branches. Inside the vehicle all but the driver are pulling on balaclavas. As four step outside, three can be seen carrying baseball bats, the other is holding a handgun. They walk a few half-paces and then jog up the drive-way of Anne-Marie's house, like schoolkids chasing after a bus.

The driver of the car watches. His eyes, between glances at his rear-view mirror, fix on the rectangle of light spread across the front garden. He twitches when the orange glow begins to shake. Like something had fallen over.

Anto Quinn had ripped the corners from every beer-mat he could lay his hands on. His table was littered with so many tiny flakes of card it looked as if it had contracted leprosy. He had started to sniff a lot — a nervous, shallow sniff that made its presence felt at thirty second intervals: a legacy, Anto was convinced, of the speed he had vacuumed since the afternoon before, which he now felt prickling his eyeballs, clogging up his throat and stabbing his sinuses. One of his knees was jumping uncontrollably, almost

97

hitting the table and disturbing the pint of Cold Flow Guinness that stood amongst the ripped-up paper. Anto took a long drink and wished that he could fall asleep.

Anto had a problem. A five foot ten problem with access to guns.

It was the first time Anto had been in that bar in almost ten years and, when he had stammered through the door, the transformation was blinding. What had previously been a cider-smelling den of under-aged drinkers and refugees from disintegrating marriages, ringing to the sounds of breaking glass and one-armed bandits, had grown to resemble a mid-Atlantic submarine. What walls there were carried huge black and white pictures of baseball players, American footballers and basketball stars. In every corner, eight feet high, flashed honeycombs of television monitors.

The place shone with brightness and youth. You would almost feel ashamed being sick in the toilets of a place like this, Anto thought. Which was ironic considering that, back in the Stone Age, he had stuck his face down one of the piss-rimmed bowls of the bar and spluttered up the first six pints of cider-and-black ever to pass down his fourteen-year-old neck. The location had seen a number of firsts in Anto's life: it was the first place he ever saw someone being glassed; it was the first place he ever saw the RA pick someone up for a knee-capping; and, in the bushes of the car park, with a red-headed chain-smoker called Donna, it was the first place he'd ever put his hand between a girl's legs.

Fucking dump, he thought. An ugly, fucking dump.

All those years ago, he had looked around at the clientele and staff with a haughty, withering contempt. He would stare at the middle-aged, greying men (they were always, always men) failing to hold the attention of the disinterested barstaff and know that, no matter what, he would never end up as pathetic as that.

That made him laugh. His knee shook a little faster.

Two attractive young women glanced worryingly towards him

from a nearby table. He thought he would probably be thrown out soon. Once the place began to fill and the space around his table could be occupied more profitably by free-spending, well-dressed gangs, the bouncers would have him out on his ear. Which, Anto concluded, had a certain poetic appeal.

When he was younger, that bar represented everything he was never going to allow himself to become. For Anto to finish that night, to finish that horrific fucking week, face down in the puddles of its car-park had a charming sense of closure.

Anto's problem was commonly banal. Anto's problem was money.

When Tom had originally told him the idea Anto had thought it was one of the worst suggestions he had ever heard.

— You need your fuckin head examined if you think that's gonna work.

But Tom remained committed. He had it worked out. Or so he thought.

He knew the owner of a local scrap-metal yard, somewhere that had recently done a deal with a second-hand car sales-room to buy up the rusty dregs nominally offered in part-exchange deals. These cars were strictly bottom of the food chain – vehicles living out the last, skinny days of a terminal illness.

— He'll give us a few dirt cheap. I'm talking fuckin chip shop money here 'Anto, he said, his eyes wide with conspiracy. — We clean them up a bit, just enough to keep them going for an hour or two, and we get kids to pay us to drive them. Y'know, kids with no licences, too young to drive or haven't the money.

Anto shook his head.

— Up at the auld quarry there's a huge big square of waste ground. No-one ever goes near it and there's a big whack of fields all around it. We bring them up and just let them rake about for an hour. You know what the fuckin kids round here are like with cars. The wee cunts'll love it.

Anto had had a response to that very point tickling the very

99

tip of his tongue. — But Tom, he was going to say. — The kids round here do not need us to provide the cars necessary to quench their road-lust. No, the resourceful little tykes are more than capable of commandeering their own vehicles — vehicles, I must add, of a demonstrably higher standard than the Eastern Block rejects we have at our disposal. But he had remained silent.

Why?

Well, the Anto twitching and sniffing in the submarine bar, with the full benefit of autoposycal hindsight, came up with a theory. As he had listened to Tom's scheme, Anto had been fully aware of the total unlikelihood of it being a success. There was no way it was ever going to work. But Anto had become sick of the torpor that had descended upon every facet of his life. He was sick of unemployment, sick of having no friends he liked or trusted, sick of being twenty-seven and still living at home, sick of never being worth a girl's second thought.

It felt like digging a hole in the fine sand on a beach. No matter how careful you were, the sides would collapse and the space would be filled. You could never make an impact.

At least Tom gave him the chance to do something.

But maybe that was shite. Or self-pity. Anto took another mouthful of Guinness. Maybe, he thought, he had actually allowed himself to be persuaded by Tom. He had been, after all, very drunk and smacked-out after a party at Gerry Cush's house. Tom was a confident sort. The type who could carry you away a little.

— Leave it to me, he had grinned. — No problemo.

— Do what you want, Anto had sighed, still feeling hungry. This is where the money comes in.

Tom said he needed two grand.

— That's some fuckin chip shop money, said Anto.

— We need at least two motors starting off and we need plenty of equipment — tools and shit. For doing them up.

— What kind of tools?

— Mechanic's tools. Gabriel Donaghy's closing his garage down. He said he'll flog us some of his auld stuff on the cheap. Our Harry'll come over and give us a hand till we find our feet.

Neither Tom nor Anto had any experience when it came to fixing cars. Anto couldn't even drive one.

— We'll only have to get them up and running, Anto, not fuckin Grand Prix racing, Tom had laughed. — How hard can it be?

Given the uncomplicated illegality of the scheme, and the uninsured risk to public health that it posed, the usual financial avenues open to small businesses remained shut to the pair. They were subsequently forced to consider all manner of possiblities in regard to raising the necessary funds. However, the options were strictly limited. Medical experiments having been ruled out, the stark choice fell between theft and loan.

For two grand it would be necessary to rob a warehouse or a store-room, with all the planning that would entail, and, besides, Tom was only ever a half-hearted opportunist when it came to burglary – he was not a play maker. Anto decided to leave the decision up to Tom, he didn't want to think too much about it. It scared him.

— If we borrow two grand, we'll end up paying back two thousand five hundred. We'll make that in the first three months and still have a profit. No fuckin problem Anto.

Anto gazed at the wall of television screens that flashed across the room. The door of the pub opened and a couple walked in, hand-in-hand, making their way straight towards the bar where they were greeted by a smiling barmaid.

He had realised that Tom was full of shit. He had known that there was no way on Earth he could persuade groups of hoods to pay twenty-five quid to drive around a dirt track in a glorified dodgem car. But he had barely raised a single objection once the plan began to unfold. He had nodded his head and snorted with affirmation every time Tom made another ludicrous suggestion.

Anto looked at the grinning barmaid again, not exactly beautiful, but pretty with energetic eyes. He could not remember the last time a girl had aimed a smile like that in his direction.

It had not been long before Anto realised that he was not a full partner in Tom's enterprise. A day after revealing their need for two thousand pounds, Tom called to his house.

— I've got the money.

— What? Anto yawned as he ushered Tom upstairs, out of the rain.

— Frank Wallace said he'd give us the dough.

Anto felt something dissolve with a fizz in his stomach.

— You haven't, he moaned, collapsing backwards on his bed, pulling the pillow over his face.

Tom spoke on, his back to Anto, trying to convince himself.

— It's no problem. He's sound about it, said he liked to help out young entrepreneurs.

Tom's voice was unsure. He would clear his throat with weak little half-coughs. Anto wasn't listening. The moment he had heard Wallace's name he had felt like wetting the duvet. He did not want to owe that man money.

— We should've ram-raided Dixons.

They sat in silence for a while, the rain falling like marbles on the window.

— So, asked Anto eventually. — When do we get the dough.

Tom turned and smiled. — Tomorrow.

— I didn't know you liked them, said Tom, pointing at the U2 poster on Anto's wall.

— Used to, replied Anto, rooting through the old socks and pornography below his bed to snatch two tins of beer. — They're the biggest load of auld bollocks now.

Both had a drink. They didn't speak much, just looked through the window at the water falling on the roofs of the street outside. But, as they drained the last of the warm beer from their cans, they had looked at one another and began laughing, like heads in a guillotine's basket.

— There you go lads, said Frank Wallace as he handed them a stuffed, white envelope. — Don't go spending it all at once, he added blankly.

He had been on his own. He had walked into the club carrying two grand and he was on his own. That frightened Anto, the fact that there was no effort made to intimidate. That there was no need to.

That night Anto and Tom had gone into the city centre to celebrate. They had toasted their entry into medium-scale debt with pills and cocktails. As always, Anto was the first to fade. The night developed into a fuzzy show-reel of whiskey and strobe-lights. At one point Tom put his arm around Anto's shoulders and yelled in his hazy friend's ear.

— You know this is all a load of auld bollocks.

Anto had spluttered a giggle into his drink.

They laughed as the music thumped.

Tom brought a girl over to the table where Anto was slumped. She said something that Anto couldn't hear and then laughed. Anto laughed as well and gave the thumbs-up sign. Anto thought she was beautiful. He thought that Tom went off with her. He couldn't remember if Tom ever came back.

He woke up the next morning on a park-bench, the sleeve of his jacket smeared with the vomit that lay on the pathway below. With much effort he scrambled to his feet and set off for home.

He slept for a day.

Then he spent twenty-four hours indoors, mostly in bed, with the television on.

When Tom didn't call, he remembered the girl and assumed that he had better things to do.

When, by the evening of the fourth day, Tom still hadn't been in touch, Anto decided to go round to his house.

— Tom's away love, his mum had said on the door-step. — Took off with some girl he met.

She had never liked Anto, it was obvious that she had enjoyed the sheer look of shock peeling across his face.

— Away where?

— God knows love. All I know is he's packed his stuff. He had to get a lend of two cases from our Andy. You know what our Tom's like — his feet aren't the part of his body that moves him about.

Anto was frozen with disbelief.

— Were youse meant to play snooker?

Anto turned and walked away.

That had been exactly a week before. Anto had been left with nothing but an eighty pound giro and one hundred quid, swiped from Wallace's envelope. He had bought bottles of gin and wrap after wrap of speed. On Monday he had watched the News, seen the story of the Staunton sisters being *knee-capped*, not beaten but knee-capped. The kid upstairs had slept through it all. It was said to be drugs related.

Everybody knew that it was Frank Wallace.

One afternoon Anto had started sobbing in the back seat of a bus. The other passengers looked around and shook their heads, some wanted to ask the driver to throw him off.

He needed another drink. He made to get up but felt his thighs begin to buckle and decided to stay seated for a moment more.

— Here you go big lad. Looks like you could do with it.

An old man placed a pint in front of Anto and sat facing him across the table.

Anto looked at him and nodded his head.

— Cheers.

— No problem big lad. He took two cigarettes from his packet, gave one to a grateful Anto and, as he slowly scanned from one end of the bar to other, lit up his own. — Fuck me, this place has changed.

— Tell me about it, mumbled Anto.

The man began squinting at the baseball pictures on the wall with an expression of complete puzzlement. He took out a pair of glasses and put them on but this did not seem to lift his confusion. He stood up and walked directly towards the plaster, pushing his nose to within two inches of a picture showing a black batter, posed on the mound, ready for action. Shaking his head, he took off his glasses and walked back to his seat.

— There's this fella at the club I drink in, he began, bending forward towards Anto. — I'll not tell you his name in case you know him. Anyway, his wife, God love her, she's not the full shilling. She has that auld Alzheimer's. And they've only one child, a son, I think he'd be in his early thirties. Quiet big fella, never any bother out of him. But he's terrible ugly. You'd actually notice him if you saw him on the street, y'know go – 'Jesus, he's fuckin ugly'.

Anto began laughing, but the old man continued speaking without even a shadow of a smile flushing across his lips.

— Anyway, apparently in the last couple of weeks the auld ma's head's really gone up the blow and she's started torturing the son. The husband was telling me that the language coming out of her's shocking every time the fella walks in – 'Take yourself off you ugly effing B'. It's got that last week she went round the house taking down every photo of the son they had up. She ended up cutting photos from the newspapers and sticking them on walls instead. Doesn't know who half of them is, he finished, lifting his pint for a drink. — She'll stick up anyone as long as it isn't her son.

— By the way, started the man, after a pause for refuelling, holding out a chunky hand. — The name's Jack.

— I'm Geordie, lied Anto as they shook.

Jack smiled at him. It seemed to Anto that the old man

suspected he wasn't being entirely honest. But no, he told himself. It was the speed. Good old-fashioned paranoia.

— So, are you a regular here Geordie?

Anto was tired. He liked the company but he had no desire to encourage a conversation.

— No, he replied, in a rather sharper tone than he intended.

If Jack picked up on the harsh inflection in Anto's voice he didn't let on. He leant back regally on his stool and, once again, cast his gaze around the quickly-crowding bar.

— Honest to God Geordie, he sighed, leaning forward again. — I can't believe the change in this place. I used to come in here when Sean Ferris had the licence. You'd still see sawdust on the floor in them days. Now look at it. Thousands spent on it, music, lights, crowds, noise. All young ones in the best of gear.

He paused, trying unsuccessfully to suppress a burp. As he made to continue, Anto expected the start of an All-Our-Yesterdays rant. Instead, Jack broke into a warm grin and his voice began to bubble.

— It's great son. Do you not think?

He didn't look for Anto's reply. — This used to be a terrible grotty auld hole, like all the bars around here. At least there's a bit of life to the place now. Like look at that.

He pointed to a girl who had just walked in wearing a silver mini-skirt. A beautiful girl who caught gazes from everyone she passed.

— Like, I don't want you thinking I'm a dirty old man, but that's great, isn't it?

Anto didn't want to look at her because he knew that she would never look at him. He stared into the bottom of his glass as it tilted towards his mouth.

— I tell you what, continued Jack. — You don't get that down the Theobald.

He laughed the kind of manly laugh that made Anto feel like

a passive smoker. Anto was glad when he had changed the tack of the conversation.

— Do you know the Theo, Geordie?

Anto did. It was one of those dark bars that looked like the inside of someone's liver. Its customers, he had always thought, reminded him of balding, fat snooker referees.

— No.

— Drinking there for years, so I have.

— Yeah?

— Aye. Went down the night there. Lot of auld fuckin gypsies knocking about. Up for a funeral. One of their wee kids was knocked down, God rest his soul. So, they've come from all over. Very good people for all that kind of stuff, any time there's a wedding or a funeral, they all come together. Anyway, you've to watch when they go out on the drink. It's not that they give any hassle to ordinary punters, but they're terrible fuckin wild for fighting among themselves. Friggen hatchets and everything. Terrible bad for holding grudges, so they are. Terrible friggen bad.

Jack finished off his pint and noticed Anto's glass was empty.

— Fancy another wee swall then?

Anto put his hand in his pocket and took out a ten-pound note.

— I'll get them.

— Sure you sit there and I'll go up.

Jack took the money from Anto's fingers. As he made to turn, he looked at Anto and shook his white head.

— They say the gypsies bury money with anyone who's died. It was a powerful big funeral for the wee lad. He must be sitting on a fortune. God bless him . . . Same again is it?

Jack walked away, scratching his back.

Anto swept the pieces of paper strewn around the table onto the floor. He sat back and thought about the young gypsy child. He couldn't help but wonder if the money was thrown on top of the naked coffin with the first roses and fistfuls of soil, or if it was placed beside the body, in the fingers – twisted amongst the rosary beads.

Maybe they spread it over the shroud, or put it in the pockets. Providing, of course, the garment had pockets. Which would be absurd because it was unlikely that the pockets would be of much use. But, then the money would hardly be of great benefit either. Anto imagined a little angel being stopped by a doorman at Heaven and refused admission because he didn't have the entrance fee.

It actually began to annoy Anto. Why couldn't they have given the kid the money while he was still alive. What joy was it ever going to bring moulding away with him in a muddy Belfast cemetery.

For some reason he thought of Tom. Thought of him lying on a beach with his girl.

Try as he might, Anto had been unable to genuinely resent him. Tom had seen the chance and gone for it. The scheme had been blindingly unworkable. That Tom had realised this and decided that the cash would be put to better use with a girl in the tropics was completely understandable. It would have been nice if he had told Anto. It would have been even nicer if he had not left him to face the wrath of Frank Wallace. But Anto had taken his chance when it was offered. He, as always, had his eyes closed and wasn't even looking. It was his own fault.

When Jack returned with the drinks Anto attacked his with black intentions. As the night progressed, the words passing over the table fell in regularity as both men swallowed the hours away.

. . . Staring directly at Anto, his eyes like tomato juice, his chin almost touching the wet table, Jack reached over and touched his companion's arm.

— Listen, let me tell you, he whispered loudly, — I fuckin envy you.

The muscles in Anto's face had been so disorientated by the alcohol he couldn't laugh.

— I'm telling you. See being young now, it must be a fuckin ball. No auld priests to worry about, no worrying about the Orangemen getting your jobs, no worrying about getting shot or the like. I watch the TV. I read the papers. I know the girls are all free with themselves these days.

His grip tightened on Anto. His whiskey breath was hot on his face.

— I'm telling you son, go out and enjoy yourself. Don't let nothing hold you back.

Anto counted the last of his money as he leant on the bar. He had, he thought, six pounds and eighty five pence, but he was finding it difficult to focus. Every time he counted, he came up with a different amount.

The girl with the silver mini-skirt was standing beside him. She seemed to Anto to be even more beautiful than when she first entered the bar. He decided that he had to tell her. Life was too short. It was important that she knew. It was important that he made some sort of impression.

She could tell Anto was staring at her and turned her shoulder away from him. Anto was finding it difficult enough to stand straight, when she moved he tried to re-balance himself, shifting his weight onto one foot. He reached out his hand, looking at the pale, white flesh of her arm.

— Excuse me, I think you're ...

Anto tipped forward, crashing straight into the girl's back. She tumbled into a group of men, spilling drinks, drenching shirts.

Anto felt a quick dig. He was far too drunk for it to hurt.

He woke up in a puddle outside the bar.

The first thing to catch his eye was a spade, leaning nonchalently against a drainpipe.

His nose ached. His lip had begun to swell.

... He didn't blame Tom. How could he blame Tom? The

only person Anto could blame was himself. For all his miserable life he had allowed himself to float like a crisp packet on the breeze, swaying half-heartedly from the wishes of one person to the wishes of another,

— Do you fancy a Chinese or a Pizza, Anto?

— I don't care, whatever you're having?

— So, United or Liverpool for the League then Anto?

— Not sure, who do you reckon?

— Ramraiding or money-lending?

— Not fussed.

. . . He stumbled along the street, the spade dragging behind him on the shiny pavement.

. . . He would have bought the kid a BMX with the money. Kids love bikes. Anto had had a blue Raleigh Burner, speeding every day around the park during the summer he had got it.

. . . A hole in the beach. The sides falling in every time the sand was disturbed.

. . . Something had to change. Couldn't just lie down like a badger in a trap, waiting for Frank Wallace.

. . . Anto had drunk in graveyards when he was younger. They never bothered him. The kid didn't want the money. He would know that Anto was thinking about him, that Anto cared about him. But all he needed was a start, a few quid to send him on his way without a backwards glance. All Anto needed was a mark, a dint, something to impress upon the planet.

. . . Anto was under the stars and a white moon. He knew what he had to do. For the first time he realised how much easier life was with the comfort of a single, cold idea. He zipped his coat up to the neck and determined to walk quickly. He knew his destination, it was where his grandmother was buried. It wouldn't take long to get there. He set off briskly, still sniffing, finding it difficult to focus. But he was resolved. He gripped the shovel with both hands and leant it across his shoulders. The drivers of the odd car that, now and again, would pass him on his route would wonder why he looked so relaxed. Anto had a hole to dig.

Helena Mulkerns

'SURABAYA JOHNNY'

This winter past, in the Connemara rain with the heavens drowned doves, and the only solace being the scent of burning turf and the pavonine-crystal night sky like no city dweller could ever imagine, I would remember her standing against a palm tree in Senegal, naked and completely calm, looking at me with roan eyes, curious.

She was warm and light, laughed a lot, and mostly I remembered her like this. But her vagabond pedigree pulsed, at times contrary, capricious, even cruel. She could drive you to distraction at treble the velocity of any national speed limit and then turn around and ask sweetly, *what's wrong?* Then sometimes she could love you so hard that you could forget everything and everyone else on the planet.

The weather didn't bother me too much, as I had set up a rudimentary darkroom in the bathroom, and was trying to get through my portraits project. Mostly I surfed, when I felt the need of a little escapism. I looked up '*africa.com*' and got myself a cool Senegal screen saver, then replaced it two days later with an Arctic dawn, wondering why she was on my mind.

Then three weeks ago, almost summer, I knew. She stood there for real on my stony pathway, early morning, rented car and no wedding ring. But all the love in the world for me, apparently. As if I couldn't do with a little right now.

'*I hev crossed oceans of time to zee you,*' she hissed.

'No, really, Siobhán. It took me two years to find where you were!'

She pronounced it 'shiv-onn', misinterpreting the fada, like she used to. 'Shiv-awn,' I corrected, beginning to smile as she did that flirty 'ah, gowan' thing, pinching my nipple and slipping her arm round my waist.

I was dazzled, as always, at the sight of her. Heads would have turned at the airport and in the car rental office, even though she was relatively dressed-down for Lani (white suit and Lolita shades strangely replaced by black pants and tracksuit top, her hair cropped, now lion-blonde). But she always had that campy sense of drama: arriving unannounced, unexpected, contrasting stark and sultry against the whitewashed walls of my small parlour.

There I was, earnestly toying with the notion of playing it cool, when she waltzed me towards the bedroom and slid up into me against the wall, pinning my arms over my head, kissing me, mumbling in that bourbon voice how much she missed me. She smelled of sandalwood and hair conditioner and, as she licked down my neck, I was rapidly forgetting all my good intentions. I pushed her over onto the bed. Kissed her eyes, kissed her tummy, zipping open her top, her nipples like coffee-bean rosebuds. She was laughing. I asked her once – and only once – what she was doing here and she goes:

'Holding you to your promise to show me a Rossaveel sunset.'

John Hinde eat your heart out. Her suitcase went under my bed, her socks went into my laundry, and after a few days I didn't care anymore.

Tonight she is wearing turquoise and it reflects a little sky into the grubby mirror in the ladies toilet where someone has puked in the wastepaper basket and there is no paper in the stalls. Somehow, she has come by this high-quality batch of mini-moons and we have been indulging ourselves a little. Leaning back on the sink, she laughs at the bubbles in her whiskey-and-red as they zoom up from the depths of the glass, hitting the ice cubes gently before making it up to the surface. 'Irish whiskey-and-red,' she says. 'It's a trip.'

She has taken to speaking English with as much of an Irish accent as possible, just for the laugh, I suppose. It amuses her to have people ask her where she's from and to answer, *Tullamore. Black Irish, that's me.* She has covered her shoulders with some kind of glittering stuff that glistens and emphasises the *café au lait* of her skin.

We finish our drinks, and when we go back inside the club, the place is beginning to shimmer like her shoulder-glitter. This stuff is all we need to set the night off. We dance to Hazy and to Foaming Lash and when it's time to take a walk, I bring her down to the Spanish Arch.

She wanted to come to Galway. Always said this, but I couldn't imagine her here. But then, you never know with Lani. After Singapore via Jordan, Berlin and Paris, what the hell would she do in Spiddal? Well, for a start she wants to know how to say 'suck my dick' in Irish, but I only know '*póg mo thóin*'[1] and she falls around laughing. She looks like a far eastern Fairy Princess from a Victorian storybook – all innocence, eyes dark pools, slim and fine, her London convent school deportment lessons evincing not one uncouth bone in her body. Then she opens that husky, irreverent throat and mouths off like a sailor. I used to call her Surabaya Johnny.

Also because we met in a submarine in a lake in the Bois de Boulogne. No, really. It was an actual club submerged in an old sub in an actual lake right in the middle of the Bois. Very late night, alternative, and I never heard of it since. Outside the Brazilian trannies stalked the side roads, their long, nude limbs smothered in Tiger Balm to keep from freezing. Truck drivers stopped, wives unsuspecting.

Inside the sub, another less-convincing and unfortunately chubby pretend-girl was on the dance floor all alone, freaking out to Juice Me Down. I was amused by this until Lani materialised in front of me asking for a dance, like an Asian *aisling*, the most beautiful human

[1] 'Kiss my ass'

I'd ever seen, dressed in those Gaultier boys clothes, hair slicked back smooth and wearing a sideways striped mariner tee-shirt like an extra from *Querelle*.

Lani's Indonesian great grandmother was sold as a slave in the market in Jakarta, to a Portuguese colonial family. She was so irresistible to the patrão's son, however, that they married and he took her away to Singapore. Their son married the daughter of an Indian businessman and by the next generation Lani's father was Malay aristocracy, and she was the extraordinary outcome of Javanese, Portuguese, Indian, Malay and some Dutch blood. Aged seventeen, she duly married a wealthy landowner, who kept her locked in his mansion, despite her beauty, her British education and her ceaseless rebellion. Through a cousin, she arranged a divorce, and through contacts, managed to get it passed through the Kuala Lumpur court system before he knew any of it. The day she was leaving, the husband came in and threw thirty thousand American dollars in cash down on her bed, *This is to stay*. She didn't.

In my Paris bed that first night – with Lani's satin sepia thighs so soft, her hairs like pert moss underwater – I lay buried in her scent, intoxicated. She loved me better than anyone, ever. Before Lani, I had never known the loss – complete loss of this world, transcending loud and breathless into some far realm of ecstasy, a force more potent than any drug. The swirl of her dark mane down my pale breasts and the thrashing zebra of our legs, echoing our sticky, fragrant zebra-fingers, interlaced, beautiful. Only these, and our spellbound eyes, brown and blue, mattered in these sheets. Earth and sky in the dawn gloom, only she was sky. And I wondered if I'd ever really touch her.

After, she'd leaned back on the pillow, claiming she'd seduced me with her *pussy perfume*. 'You slip in your finger and then up behind your ears and round your breasts – old girlie trick. I charmed you with it while we were dancing and you didn't even know. Ha Ha.'

She likes the swans down by the Spanish Arch. They are surprised to see us at midnight, snippering up the curried chips we got down the road at the late night with their dainty beaks.

Lani loves this: Irish potatoes covered in Indian curry purchased from a Chinese take-away. It's the *New Ireland*, I tell her. Very international. The Celtic Tiger just loves curried chips, baby. The swans crowd around, aviatory super-models, their long, fine necks gleaming and their eyes bright as the broken beer bottle fragments glinting under the streetlights. Long ago, according to legend, a Celtic chieftain's children were turned into swans and lived for nine hundred years. Now they putter around the dockside rubbish eating curried chips.

We go to Kane's for the midnight Cabaret. Miss Conduct is delivering a mimed version of Piaf's *C'ést à Hambourg*. She has Debbie Reynolds shoes and a tatty dress, covered in mauve sequins (many missing), with the hem down at the back. Her make-up is pretty good, but in a booth nearby my friend Terry is wearing make-up, not for show, but to conceal the patching that daubs his delicate skin. His face bears up reasonably well, all told, the dagger cheekbones almost passing for fashionable thinness. But he slumps weakly, and there is a walking cane beside the table, there being no truly effective concealer for impending death. I tell Lani how beautiful he once was, and she is not surprised.

We move into the booth, she talks to Terry and makes him laugh. He is charmed. They speak French and she tells him the clubs in Paris where she will take him, and of the trashy boys who go there. She makes him laugh more. I don't know who she is, really, this one whose compassion can blitz out every nasty, bitter, sorrowful vibe in the entire room, and yet part of me is still bleeding from her insouciance. She leaves the club with kisses and flowers from all round the table.

'What's your name?' they ask.

'Johnny!' she says.

Lani introduced me to Georges, her French husband, a few weeks after we first met. He took us to Senegal, five star rooms, happy-hours at the bar with diplomats and mercenaries, and tumbling, fun sex (although I preferred Lani alone). My friends

119

didn't get it. *She's no good for you*, they said. That was probably some of the most useless advice I ever got. I mean, when have I ever liked what was good for me? *You deserve better* . . . But how could that be, when Lani was the world's most beautiful girl, the most charming, funniest, wildest, and she loved me. The best was, *Why don't you get yourself a nice man?* I had a nice man. Georges was very nice. Always. I loved him too, in my way.

We managed for about year, Lani and me, Lani and Georges, Lani, Me and Georges, Me, Georges and Lani – etc, etc, etc. An unholy triptych pursuing a dubious passion, the ephemeral, risky edge of which made it even better, most of the time. Despite everything, despite fights, Georges leaving for months, her capricious tangents, she was so in love with me and I with her it was like some fucked up Swedish movie. But reality is not the movies. Somebody always ends up running out to the kitchen in tears.

I ran as far as Galway, nursing my wounds solo, moving into my grandmother's old cottage way out on the westward road. It was far enough from the crowds, but near enough to the city for sanity, just about. A phoneline, but only a modem connected to it, deliberately. Just me and my negatives and, of course, the laptop. I called him Baby Hal. My sweetie, modem-packed, earth-linked, sky-aspiring, addictive little bundle of chips and interfaces, the joy of my life. With my rusting Fiat Uno, an Arts Council Grant, and a little government assistance, I was *ar dhroim na muice*.[1] That is, until my real-world visitor.

Apart from attacking me in my bed, or in the kitchen, or garden, or bath or wherever it took her fancy, Lani seemed to devise endless amusement from Hal. She logged on to a password-coded e-mail account the day after her arrival. One night, pissed as newts, we hooked up an instant link with some surfer called *chemicalwiz* – and we had a blast. Fucksake. Here we are in a tiny coastal village on the arse end of Europe, zapping one-liners with some freak on

[1]On the pig's back

the other side of the planet, telling us the weather conditions in Karachi. Right.

After Kane's, we head off to a party near Barna. It turns out to be a mixed crowd, a thundering, anarchic cornucopia of this fabulous seaside city – trad musicians, rock stars, a smackhead model or two, students, stray tourists, returned emigrants, advertising scum, a few glorious queens, journos, acktorrs, Arts Fest/Film Fleadh people, last-call drunks, and everything in between. I discover, by complete chance, that if a human – any human – lies down under a table – any table – it is immediately forced to explode into paroxysms of uncontrollable laughter. It's a brilliant discovery. We move through the crowd, hauling in volunteers to test the theory. A girl in a crochet dress complies. She laughs her ass off. It works every time.

Later, Lani is sitting on the bony lap of an old fisherman with a face like a junkie and three teeth. He looks like it must be Christmas, yappering on about Chicago, where he had a young one once, dark as this one, only African, mind you. 'More of an arse on her.' He tells Lani to go to Dún Aengus, more ancient than anything else in Europe, he says, and fuck EEC regulations.

The following weekend, Lani insists on going to the island to see Dún Aengus. 'Three weeks to wait is long enough,' she says. Already she knows everybody in Spiddal, we've done every Galway bar and club, she's educated the stuffy barmen in the *Skeffington Arms* in all the new European cocktails, and she even knows how to say *suck my dick* in Irish. Only of course, now she won't tell me what it is.

She packs a rucksack and potters around the bedroom, zapping off her hotmail every now and then as I do the laundry. I'm in the garden, hanging out the bed linen, an action somehow atavistic really. The swathes of blinding white cotton fluttering against the blue seem to echo not just centuries of wet washing, but the flutter of each generation's new hope. Sheets being the fabric between which we make love, bear children, and eventually die.

Yeah, well here I am contemplating the meaning of sheets, when all of a sudden, we realise what time it is, and she belts over, grabbing me.

'Let's go, let's go. I'll finish this – get your stuff!'

As we board the last powerboat to Aranmór at Rosaveel, the singular smell of open salt air, and a seaweed-heavy, full-moon tide swirls our senses. She is subdued, strangely, as the boat moves out over Cashla Bay. Could she be affected by the brutal beauty of the marine processing plant, stark against the sky? Or is it the celestial layers of salmon and gold, cerise and indigo, colours that cannot be argued with. 'Here is your sunset,' I said. She just smiles.

Lani is out on deck, as we pull into Kilronan, talking to an old dear about Mary Robinson. I am more concerned with getting a trap up to Kilmurvey. Except that, silly me, ha ha. No more traps. The full moon shines only on Hiace vans, not many, of course, being as this is not the high season, nor the peak-time ferry. Seán O'Flaherty drives us over the island, stone walls and ancient monastic ruins contrasting with new bungalows, the old dwellings sometimes still visibly disintegrating round the back. We talk in Irish, about second cousins in America, and for once, Lani shuts the fuck up, enthralled. She's only ever heard me speak French or English, and this strange, singing tongue is a wonder to her.

We've booked into the hotel that rests just below the climb up to the cliffs, where Dún Aengus reigns tough over the Atlantic Ocean, majestic, eternal. The oldest, most mysterious outpost of pre-Christian European peoples, standing strong despite the ravaging storms of centuries, plunderers, and the threat of the Interpretative Centre freaks. We are also just up the hill from the old pier, which I have promised to show her tomorrow.

It's dark as we head off along the path. Lani is barefoot – an unlikely Pilgrim on the long trek upwards. She carries stuff in that rucksack, I don't know what, as we ascend. Since my childhood, this has been designated a 'National Park'. There actually is a man-made path now, which we follow for a while. Its tended borders are so disappointingly fucking civilised, I'm beginning to regret coming. But it peters out into untameable, fissured rock, arbitrary clumps of bright grass and flowers, all visible under the full moon. You can't tame the islands.

'Nowhere in the world is this wild,' I tell Lani. 'The *Fir Bolg* built it, a pre-Celtic race, around 1000 B.C. They were thriving at the same time as the Egyptians were sealing up Tutankhamun in his burial pyramid. The same time that King David brought the Ark of the Covenant back to Jerusalem.'

She is quiet as I tell her this, staring up at the stone bastion. We ascend into the second circle, there being three in total. There, with the waves crashing far below us, their force muffled by the cliff face and the light wind, we witness the stunning army of slim vertical stones, shooting up from the ground, thousands of them, surrounding the back approach to the citadel all round the second circle like warriors, fringed by thousands of dramatic shadows on the grass behind them.

'What are they?'

'Sentinels.'

She squeezes my hand, and we move into the interior circle, massive and sobering in its stony blue, the open sea glittering out as far as our view extends. She seems unusually perturbed.

'I'm not sure where I belong,' she says. 'But it might be here ...'

At the cliff's edge, her eyes shine with the prospect of flight. Three hundred feet down, what could such a drop be like?

'I used to feel like flying, too,' I tell her. 'Now I just look out to sea, and wonder what they were protecting themselves from.' She doesn't seem to be listening.

'I have a friend who wants to sail around the Solomon Islands,' she whispers. 'Maybe you could come ...'

The moon has moved stage right as we make our way back down, after I have persuaded Lani to put her shoes back on her bleeding Cinderella feet. It takes about an hour to get back, and we sneak into our room quietly, snuggling into the bed and our bodies' warmth, whispering, melting into zebra.

I awake towards eleven, remembering that Seán O'Flaherty is

probably downstairs, waiting to drive us over towards *Poll na bPéist* ... But when I reach over in the bed for Lani, there is no Lani. When I go to pee, to my confusion, nothing of Lani is present. The usual underwear curled into ball on the bathroom floor is missing, no toothbrush. Rucksack not there. Abducted by aliens, obviously. I look for her downstairs, outside, the *Bean An Tí* has not seen her. I pay and pack up, and make Seán drive me around the island instead.

She's not in any of the bars, or the tourist centre, and she's not on the first boat back to the mainland either. My heart is sinking. Lots of sea, lots of stone — stone everywhere, all turning dark, sad grey as a soft mist begins to creep over the island, turning to rain as the afternoon progresses. On the way down to the boat at Kilronan, finally, Seán is rattling on about some yacht that came in last night in the early hours at the old Kilmurvey pier and set off again before dawn. Seán loves tall tales, and this sounds like one of them.

'*Ag ithe na muisiriúní, arís, a Sheáin?*'

'*Ní ag magadh atáim, Siobhán, ní bhfaca mé a leithéid ríamh. Beadh tú i ndán seoladh timpeall an domhain intí ...*'[1]

She's gone, I thought. That's all. Left me lying alone in that blank hotel room while she pulled one last prima donna caper. Fuck her.

By the time I get home, it's last-light evening time. I pull around into my cosy bay to the bizarre spectacle of all the lights on in my cottage, illuminating a cop car, a flashy new black Range Rover and a battered maroon escort (drugs squad, obviously). Cathal McDonagh, local baby Gárda extraordinaire, who once bit my elbow in third class, is apparently standing guard at my gateway, his russet skin tones sweaty and flustered.

'*Cad a tá ar súil anseo?*'[2] I ask him, incredulous.

---

[1] 'Eating the mushrooms again, Sean?'

'I'm not kidding, I never saw the like. You'd be able to sail 'round the world in it.'

[2] 'What's going on here?'

He answers in Irish, rushing his words and slipping into English as two suits get within audible distance, bearing officially down towards us.

'That one! Your friend. What possessed you to have her in the house, Siobhán? She's a fuckan nightmare – they've been following her round Europe for the past two months.'

'John Hazleton, London Special Task Force. Could we have a word with you, Mrs Dineen?'

'Ms.'

'Excuse me?'

'Ms Dineen.'

'They have a search warrant, Siobhán . . .' Cathal seemed very upset altogether.

I am waking up from this full-moon dream now fairly fast. I'd still been a little out of it all the way home, but with one cop sounding like Mr fuckan Steed and the other like Klaus Kinski, I know this isn't just about my television licence.

'We'd like to ask you a few questions about Ms Rochet, whom you've been harbouring here . . .'

'Harbouring?'

An array of local kids are hanging goggle-eyed over my stone wall and I can see Mrs Flanagan and her sister standing at the bend of the road, arms folded in fascination. I can't resist it.

'Better than *Ballykissangel*, girls!' I shout. The police escort me inside.

I sit in my kitchen while they ask me about Chalandra Kumari Raj Rochet. French National, Malaysian of origin.

'Never heard of her.'

The two foreign plain-clothes boys have matching ties. I want to ask them if they're cloned like *Dolly* or actually choose to dress in that naff style, but I'm distracted, as I glimpse, sideways through the bedroom door, the vacant spot under my bed, where Lani's suitcase once parked its arse. The place has been well-worked over, cupboards opened, drawers pulled out, the usual prime-time police-show carry-on. Except for old Chief Gárda Seamus Mullen, who is carefully going through the contents of my bathroom cabinet on the kitchen table.

'That's really excellent lube. You should try it,' I tell him.

'Ms Dineen,' says Steed. 'Your friend has been under the observation of Interpol for some months, due to her activities in a large international drug cartel operating out of Pakistan. Just over a month ago, she slipped our net after a money-laundering transaction in Zurich — which my colleague Mr Holtz can tell you more about.'

I look on the mantelpiece, her jewellery and her mini digital multi-time zone alarm clock are gone. Worse still, Baby Hal is gone. Interestingly, the modem wire and the mains plug and converter are also missing. Lani has cleared every last trace of herself out of my life.

Now I am beginning to strengthen, not weaken. My anger seethes up my neck, invisible, like a current. It's funny. My anger usually fucks things up for me. I lose friends, family, lovers, and even jobs as a result of its uncontrollable power to rant and wound and rage. But it also, sometimes, has a strange capacity to silence me, to render me smart-ass, insolent, fuck you. To render me a stone.

'That operation also involved laundering for a Croatian fascist splinter group in the former Yugoslavia, among other things,' continued Klaus. 'These people are not playing games, you see.'

'She slipped out of your hands?'

'This young woman is a dangerous customer, Ms Dineen. But we do know she was here. We finally located her to this outpost through your telephone line.

'I don't have a telephone.'

'But you are *westgirl@siar.net*, is that not correct?'

'I don't have a computer.'

'We've been trying to trace certain communications over the last three weeks on Siar Net, and we patched into you yesterday afternoon.'

'Do you see a computer around here?'

'Ms Rochet's partner is an Irishman named Peter Connelly,

also wanted in Europe on drug trafficking charges. The third party is one Kareem Abdulayam, who is a manufacturer of methylenedioxymethamphetamine, or MDMA, known to you perhaps as *ecstasy*. Pakistan is one of the few remaining countries where the manufacture of this chemical is still unregulated. However, once it leaves that country, it's a different matter.'

'Have you found any? You've messed up my house enough.'

'No, we haven't. Now we are more interested in the whereabouts of Ms Rochet.'

'But you can't locate my 'computer' to prove this ridiculous theory.'

'We can summons you, and you can be charged with conspiring to traffic drugs.'

'I don't do drugs.'

Gárda Mullen interrupted, with sudden viciousness. 'We have members of the *Connaught Parents Against Drugs* committee who can testify to the contrary. And they're not without clout in the courts, as you know. Not to mention *outside* the courts.'

This sounds so much like a serious threat that for the first time I shiver. The Euro-badges are one thing, but Mullen and his savage CPAD thugs are not to be fucked with.

'*A dhaoine Uasaile,*' I counter to himself and Cathal, '*Ní bhfuir sibh aon rud ar bith amhrasach i mo theach, agus tá sé ag eirigh déanach.*[1] Mr Hazleton, Mr Holtz, I'll let Cathal know my lawyer's number in the morning when I've got in touch with her.'

The boys left, en masse, stony faced. Fuck. Now what. Normally, in such a desolate, deluge of panic, I would have hit the keyboard and logged on, letting Hal ease me into my nice, soft, surfing oblivion. Click: another time and place, yada yada yada. But she's taken Hal. Bitch.

Okay, now what. Don't panic. A patter of rain hits the window, and my mammy-instinct goes on auto-pilot as I rush out to the washing

---

[1]'You've found nothing of a suspicious nature in my house, and it's getting late.'

line to take in the damned sheets. The sky is distinctly angry as I argue with the clothes pegs, plucking down the dry bed linen and racing back inside the cottage to beat the storm, breaking furious and full now, thundering all round my tiny house. I throw the sheets down onto the bed. Odd. The main bottom sheet has been stapled at the edges, and appears to have stuff inside. Now what.

Ripping it open, I realise that I was wrong in thinking that Lani's last, campy high-drama stunt was her disappearance. It's pitch dark now, the wind howling like a Banshee. But I daren't turn on the bedroom lamp, just trying to count these bundles of notes by the porch light and the lightening flashes. Now what. Thirty thousand American dollars. Cash. Very funny. But enough for a new Hal. Or a flash Land Rover. Enough to finish my portraits project. But enough too – I hardly dare entertain the idea – to finance me at least as far as the Solomon Islands.

I move into the front room, still in the dark, peering out my cottage window at the open Atlantic, now broiling and crashing like some demented god. The force of the towering waves' impact, and the lofty spray alone soaring off the outer rocks of the bay, is enough to freeze your blood. Like generations of women before me, I find myself standing lonely vigil at the window, remembering Seán's tale of the yacht down at the old pier, wondering if it will make it through the battle of surf and swell and wits and rock that is a western storm.

Caspar Walsh

'N52'

9:16:00 pm

Dark blue rain lashes down on the car.

Everywhere; top, sides even underneath. So much water on such an old car makes Kate feel insecure.

The oncoming lights hurt her eyes, each passing car or truck forces a blinding glare into the mist-covered windscreen. She tries to shield them, gives up and puts her shades on.

All this; the rain, the lights, the dark, force her to drive slower than usual. Too much time in a car is a waste. Driving this slow wastes precious time, which there's never enough of. Jack always says this but Jack's a musician. He makes time for himself. Lots of it, which seriously winds her up.

Jack's eyes focus on the tiny circle of light pointed at the map. Both hands holding taut while the orange torch juts out of his mouth, overstretching the muscles of his face. Kate thinks it looks at once painful and stupid. She finds herself torn between sympathy and laughter.

'Ahm fuhct f I no whe we ar'

'I've no idea what you're on about. Take the torch out of your mouth for Christ's sake.'

He lets go his grip. It drops into the centre of the map, ripping an uneven hole and falling through. The light spirals to the floor, haphazardly waking up the insides of the car. The glare hits Kate's eyes twice, she blinks heavily behind her shades, before the torch lands in the footwell.

'Shit. Sorry. Said I'm fucked if I know where we are. Chris said he'd marked the map but I can't find it anywhere. Want me to drive babe? Maybe I'll be able to get us there on instinct.'

'If you can't work it out from the map, forget about driving sweetheart. We'll get a signpost soon. We need some sounds, sort a tape out. It's gonna be too late if we don't suss out how to get there soon.'

Jack contorts his skinny body into the rear of the car rummaging around in the shadows of the back seat.

'Yes!' He slumps into his seat. 'Made this one for us. Some of the coolest tunes recorded. From me, about me, us, to you. Called it "Neon Skies".'

'Why?'

'Sounds good.'

'Are *they* on it?'

'Who?'

'The ones responsible for this journey into the middle of a piss awful Irish night.'

'Course they are. First track.' Jack clicks the tape into the deck. The heads screech, looking for a comfortable roll.

'Let me guess, "Roads"?' Kate's eyes fix hard on the white lines in the road.

'Nope.'

'Glory Box?'

'Nada.'

'Biscuit!' Jack beams into the darkness. 'Should've guessed.' The velvet Portishead tune fills the car, hushing the couple into smiling silence. Jack lets his gaze slide through the closed passenger window, into the darkness beyond the orange haze of Dublin.

9:34:00 pm.

The car slips away from Malahide, onto Swords and another sub urban clone; no different from any other Irish town or road. Jack rests his cheek against the cold, wet glass. He blows a plume of condensation into its centre.

'How many times have we heard this?' Jack muses, covers the window in his own mist.

'Lost count. With you at least a hundred. Never tire of it babe. It's like Miles Davis "Kind of Blue". Never wears out. First time we had sex and it was sliding around in the background. You stopped bang in the middle of my moment to start it up again, breaking my Buzz Lightyear in the process.

'Because your room's always strewn with party fall out.'

'Probably. Why is it that it spins that kind of feeling in one group and not another? You know, to play it in whatever mood we're in.'

'It's blue.'

'What?'

'"Dummy", "Kind Of Blue", both blues albums. "Dummy"'s whole look is based around the colour. Even the video, moody Noir and all that . . . Different periods both hitting the same point; gets into the saddest part of you and turns you on, so long as it reminds you of some kind of sadness, something everyone can lock into, it's going to catch you every time.'

'It's more than that. The blues thing is obvious. It's more subtle, sneaks underneath all your *NME* boyz theory. Something basic. Don't think I've met anyone who didn't get turned on by Portishead or Miles Davis at some time, even when they're up.'

'*Shit!*' Kate fixes her stare on the stop start white lines in the centre of the road, trying to judge where she's driving and not get blinded

133

Caspar Walsh

by the oncoming car.

'Bastards should have automatic dippers. Someone's going to get killed.' She slams her hand on the horn too late.

'Biscuit' finishes and Soul II Soul's, 'Keep On Movin' mixes gently in.

'Not bad babe, so far, so far.'

'All yours. I worked the tunes out over the last couple of weeks.' He hands her the cassette box. She looks between it and the road, long enough to make out the dedication:

'Big boys tunes from the big bad city.'

She looks up, smiles at him, puts the car into fifth and rests her hand on his leg.

'Thank you. And maybe later . . . if you're good.'

'Pleasure. Any idea where we are yet?'

'We're coming to Balrothery. What's it called again?'

'Termonfeckin.'

'We're lost aren't we Dougal?'

'No Ted'

'We are, aren't we Dougal.'

'Yes Ted we are,' Kate chuckles, kicking yet more speed.

'Can't believe there's a feckin' place called Termonfeckin. What are they doing playin' in the middle of nowhere?'

'Usual true to form obscurity. Wherever it is, Chris said it was ten minutes from the sea. I'm in the water the minute we get there.'

'If.'

'It's cool, we've got hours, and each other.' Jack croons a cheesy grin and lurches forward, lips puckered.

'Spare me.' He slumps back in his seat pretending to sulk. 'Keep On Movin' fades out and Beck lurks in with 'Devils Haircut'. Kate scrunches her nose, like she just got a whiff of something burning, somewhere else.

'You reckon the venue'll be big enough? Can't stand that body to body shit.' He lights a cigarette, hands it to her, lights another, settles back into his seat smoking quietly. Kate indicates left, turns down a road.

134

'Well?'

'What?' Jack blows more smoke and condensation against the window, watching closely as it disappears.

'Are you listening?'

'Course I am. Don't you love this tune.'

'. . . *Got a devils haircut . . . in my miiin . . .*' Slick lyrics. Kate shakes her head, her shades slip. She pushes them back up her nose. The speed of the car increases.

9:58:00 pm

She thinks Beck is too loud. Too many guitars. Way too much scratching. Normally she hates scratching but reckons Portishead gets it right. Beck's lyrics sound like pseudo intellectual bollocks. Whatever a devil's haircut looks like in anyone's mind she'll never know. Too loud and about as subtle as a punch in the gob.

The road narrows and with it the bends begin to sharpen. She loves driving through the country at night. She can hammer around the corners, knowing just how safe it is by the amount of artificial light she can or can't see ahead in the dark.

Jack starts to roll a joint but is quickly beaten into submission by the increasing trickiness of the twisting, fuscia-walled road.

'Easy Kate. Man's trying to get something together over here.' Jack scrambles around in the footwell, trying to rescue some of the tiny buds from the ancient carpet.

'You smoke too much. Think of it as a favour.'

'Forever indebted, or at least until I find my weed.' Although tongue in cheek, Jack knows Kate just slung a dig. He gets the feeling a row may be brewing. He hopes they can have a peaceful night. Just enjoy Portishead. He listens and relaxes to the last few bars of 'Devils Haircut' tapping his index finger on his knee. He'd like to get up and shake himself, let the tune wash all over, but

a) he's in a car and b) it just finished. He finishes rolling the salvaged joint.

Van Morrison's 'Moondance' rolls into the protective warmth of the car. Kate gets that sinking feeling. For her, Van has this habit of reaching a saturation point. She found one day, after months of easy listening, she suddenly broke the this-is-bollocks barrier. She couldn't listen to one more Celtic whinge from a fat moody old man who looks more like a builder on eight pints than the rock genius Jack keeps telling her he is. She doesn't want to listen to it and doesn't have the heart to tell him his tape is taking a down slide. She knows how much he loves music. She does too and most of his stuff she's into, but she also knows how over-sensitive he is to any criticism of what he considers classic tunes. He always takes it so bloody personally. She sinks deeper, trying to bring her concentration to the high lined hedges looking down on her. Deep pink, fuscia rockets of light reflecting and bounce back through the wet windscreen. They ease her a little.

She decides to bite the bullet, sighs and sinks into her seat.

10:03:00 pm

'What?' Jack shifts about.

'Van the Man.'

'Yes?'

'I'm not really into him. You know I'm not.'

'You've always liked him. We play him all the time.'

'*You* playing him all the time doesn't necessarily mean *I* like him. "Brown eyed Girl" was OK until Julia Roberts fucked it up in that awful movie . . . what was it?'

'Why didn't you say anything?'

'You never asked.' Kate feels her blood start to boil. 'You just bang it on in the morning and start prancing around the flat singing along to "Tupelo — bloody — Honey" or whatever you're into that day.'

'Shit.'

'What!'

'I'm gonna have to remix this whole side again.'

'You don't have to do that.' Now she feels bad. She tries to placate him. 'The first two tunes were great. I'm sure the rest will be cool. I know you've got good taste in music, we just diverge a little at times that's all.'

'Christ that's patronising. I suppose you hate Beck too!'

'Ja . . .'

'You know what it's like. One duff tune on a tape and you'll always think twice about playing it.'

'Jack.'

'I'm serious.'

'You're too sensitive, it's not that important.'

'No! That's my point, it *is* that important. Have you got any idea how long it takes to make a tape like this. A tape like this, it's part of you. You make a statement about who you are and the connection you make with the person you give it to. If you get it wrong, just one track and you've missed the signals of what that person's into. It's about observation. If you don't observe, you're not paying attention and that person notices. "Well he obviously hasn't got a clue." Looks like your whole angle on the relationship is fucked up.' He starts muttering into the window, drawing a small but imperfect circle in the condensation, then rubs it out. The window is the only sign of how cold it is outside as the night slips past. He blows across the tips of his fingers.

'What angle? Oh for Chrissakes.'

Kate feels bad and angry. Confused. She wants to stand her ground but doesn't want to get into another pointless row. This bullshit is trying her limits. She doesn't feel she could take another row about nothing. She looks over to Jack who looks pissed off.

Without looking back at her his mumble fades back into to some kind of coherence.

'It's a part of me. If you don't like that part of me, the music, I doubt you could take the rest of me, Till death 'n' all that, know what I mean.' He starts to roll another joint.

Kate approaches another big bend making no attempt to slow down.

The tobacco and weed take another dive.

'Fucksake Kate!' He lurches forward, ducking into the footwell again. As his head slips into the darkness he hears Kate gasp. A backward scream stuck somewhere in her throat. Something's happening.

10:07:00 pm.

The brakes of the car scream.

Jack reels back, whacking his head on the underside of the glove compartment.

'FUCKIT, shit!' He falls back into his seat holding his forehead, covering his eyes. He feels the car jerk to the right then slide sideways as the brakes lock. He thinks it's Kate's side. He keeps his eyes covered for what seems like a minute but in reality is only a fraction of the single second it takes for him to realise the car is crashing. He can hear metal crunch and twist. Shouting at the object it's found.

10:07:01 pm.

Van Morrison exit stage left, Massive Attack enter stage right. Kate definitely likes this, I knows she does. They had sex on top of her dad's car to this tune.

The front of the car continues to fold into whatever the object is. Jack can't for the life of him figure out why everything is taking so long to happen. Like someone just hit the slow mo on the video. He's wondering who shot the front of the car.

No change in speed. Everything still full ahead slow. Even the music:

'I was looking back to see if you were looking back at me . . .
to see me looking back at you.'

Jack remembers the video. Shara Nelson walking coolly down a Soho street in London. Singing along to the timeless base line of Massive Attack's 'Safe From Harm'. In all this slow deliberate movement he can stop and think. Get his head round why he made such a horse's arse of Kate's tape. It may only be a tape but it's what it represents. A soul laid out nice and clear on a brown magnetic strip. Spoken, sung and base lined far better than he could ever express himself. If music be the food of love, mine's a large one.

Nice. Plenty of time; like sitting on the edge of a cliff at dusk. When everyone's gone home for safe keeping and you just sit there, huddled against the wind. Nothing to do except think. Everything's slow except his thoughts, which are sharper now than they've ever been.

10:07:03 pm

Kate feels detached. She knows she's in trouble. She can't remember if Jack has his seat belt on? She can't see him, only her immediate area. The front of the car is caving in. Metal folding toward her like a thick wool blanket. Rolling up and moving slow. A cracking, crunching sound that runs an ice strip of fear down her back. She feels sick. The hairs on her neck spring up to see what's happening, followed by every other follicle on her shaking body. Does Jack have his seat belt on? She hopes so.

139

The small gold block of Benson & Hedges jolts off the front dash and makes it's way through the gap between her and Jack, to the back of the car, in the anti gravity kind of way Neil Armstrong made his way up there, back then.

'One small step for man . . .

. . . One giant leap for twenty B&H'

She watches them closely as they make their way toward the back. She lifts her hand, which moves as slow as the packet. She touches the gold block and it spirals off toward Jack's side. She's smiling but she knows she's in trouble. She can see Jack now all right, staring ahead, a childlike terror written across his grey face. He does have his seat belt on. Good. Jack always was a sensible boy.

Another tune, no, this one's been on a while now. Massive Attack:

'. . . looking back to see if you were looking back at me . . .' Maybe Jack's present isn't so bad after all. She loves this tune. And despite all the bullshit she loves Jack too. It's playing slower than usual, which fits in well with her new slowed down view on things, gives her time to think. She hasn't had much time to think for a while. Which is why she drives too fast, so she never really has a chance to think. The car, this car, which she doesn't reckon will be doing much more line eating for a while. She also reckons they won't be seeing Portishead. Not this time round. She loves that tune. The one with the weird title, that Jack put as the first tune to his slice of himself compilation. 'Neon,' whatever it is. Great lyrics. Great to make love to.

Jack looks at the packet of cigarettes making their way thoughtfully toward him. No gravity. Which reminds him of Sting. Of the moon.

That would have been a good tune for the tape. Kate loves the Police. She doesn't have to tell him that. He knows by the way she moves when Sting sings. When she closes her eyes and twists her body all over the shop, clasping her hands round the back of her head smiling, smiling. He could watch her do that forever. Just lie back, listen and watch. That would be Jack's first idea of heaven: Kate and this tape on an infinite loop.

The front of the car seems to have arrived at the windscreen, the front grille anyway. The glass begins to crack. Over on the right hand side, about level with Kate's eyes, a hairline crack branching like the roots of a tree looking for water, more space.

To Kate it sounds like lemonade poured over ice, splintering and dividing. To Jack, a good sample for Goldie or Roni Size.

10:07:04 pm

For the first time in the last few seconds, however long it's been, Jack can feel something in his body, his toes to be exact. A prickly, tingling sensation, like too much heat got into them and is bubbling over. This is one of two things, or both.

1) His feet are looking for the brakes. Blood rushing to stop what is already happening; because Cack, as Kate sometimes calls him, reckons he's a bit tasty behind the wheel. Better than Kate. But then he would.

2) The old fear is trying to get him the fuck out of this life-threatening situation, to run away, which is pretty hopeless because it's happening, and it's nearly over.

10:07:06 pm

Kate remembers drowning when she was six. Well not completely, almost. In Greece, while her mum and dad were still into each other enough to be at it in the villa, least that's what she reckons now. She remembers falling off the end of a pier and slipping down a ledge into deep water. She couldn't swim, knew she couldn't and knew she was in trouble. Like now. Although she was too young to really understand death. She got the feeling she'd been in that situation before. It felt very grown up to think like that. But it didn't help the fact that she thought she was about to die. She remembers looking up into the orange football sun, hoping it would reach down and wrap her up. It didn't, it just stared down at her and blazed. Then she remembered seeing the faces of her mum, her dad and all her friends flashing through the centre of it, getting faster and faster until finally, they turned into a citric blur.

She remembered thinking, Help! Then, as if she'd said her prayers and got into bed, a big leathery, hairy Greek fisherman with a dirty hat, dipped a fishing pole into the water. She grabbed it.

Her dad came sprinting down the beach a minute later, whilst she was throwing up the contents of her stomach. He was late as usual.

Kate remembers this now because she can see more faces scattered in and out of the spider web cracks in the windscreen. More faces, places, events and sounds.

Steam rises from the engine briefly before evaporating into the night sky.

The crushing sound of metal continues to fill Kate's ears along with the reverberation of Massive Attack. If she could pick a track, a single track to take away with her and play without getting bored, it would have to be this one. This one always makes her feel safe, even if it were the last tune she listened to. Her very own desert island bassline.

'You can free the world,
You can free my mind,
Just as long as my baby's safe from harm.'

10:07:06pm

Jack remembers falling off a building near George's dock when he was ten. Chasing his best mate Tom across the roofs of a warehouse. He's wondering what he's doing now, all these years later, if he's still alive. They definitely shouldn't have been there, on the roof. This gave them both a double shot of adrenaline. That's what they did as kids; see how high they could get their adrenaline going before they burst with excitement. Up on this roof was the limit. Thousands of feet in the air, that's what it felt like. A fat, sweaty security guard lumbering after them shouting 'Oi you little baastards ... stop.' In a thick 'Norf Laandun' drawl. They knew he couldn't catch them in a million years but they also knew he had the advantage of knowing the lay out of the roofs. This was their first time up. The first time they'd managed to get past Fat Bastard. Which is what they're shouting after him now. Egging him on to sweat and pant a little more. Tom runs ahead because he's faster. Runs in all the races at school and beats everyone. Jack looks up to him. Tom leaps over a gap between two buildings. Tom's good at leaping, he does long jump. As he lands he turns, panting, sweating and shouting to Jack to 'Come on!' Jack picks up speed and leaps. As he does, Fat Bastard shouts 'Oi!' again, which puts him off. He almost makes it; hits the edge and sees Tom's face drop in horror. He holds on with his elbows for a second and then ...

... slips.

He sees Tom's face disappear as he slides down the wall. He tries to climb, scrabble, claw his way back, like Spider Man. It doesn't work. He carries on sliding then all of a sudden tips back. Now he's looking up into the blue white sky above him. He starts to pick up speed, going down. He can see the silhouetted figures of Tom and Fat Bastard peering over each edge, head and shoulders. He can't see their faces. Tom shouts down to him, 'JACK!' Jack can hear the tears in his throat. He keeps falling and keeps hearing Tom call his name. It sounds slow and strange, bit like Darth Vadar but not as scary. He keeps going down. The further he gets the more the red bricks of the wall in front of him fuzz and blur. The further he gets the safer he feels. Warm and soft, like he's in bed, at home, hiding under his duvet waiting for a parent to come and say goodnight. He feels like he's floating. Then, just as he's getting used to this new feeling, this new kind of adrenaline, more than he's ever had . . .

CRACK!

He lands. Wind knocked clean out of him.

His lungs sting. He's awake, still here.

He looks around to see himself surrounded by a huge pile of empty cardboard boxes. Safe.

10:07:06 pm

Jack's knees are hurting. The glove compartment, where he stashed his hash, is crushing slowly against them. He's starting to wish that things would speed up so this pain, this knee splitting pain, would just reach it's peak and then maybe he could pass out, or die. Whatever it is, he wishes it would hurry the fuck up.

Kate is finding it hard to breathe. Her chest hurts. She takes her eyes off the movie screen cracks in the glass and looks down.

She sees the steering wheel, sliding gently into her. She wishes it would stop.

She hears her tune, 'Safe From Harm'. She hears the part that means the most to her. Jack must have looped it because it means that much to her. He does know what she likes, thinks he doesn't, gets all riled but he's just over reacting. He's always over reacting but it doesn't stop her loving him.

'You can free my mind . . .
Just as long as my baby's safe from harm.'

She wrenches her arm slowly free and grabs Jack's hand. She feels like she's Thelma and he's Loiuse. Louise is better looking but hey. Like they've made a choice to run into the back of this stationary

144

truck in the middle of the fucking road, in the middle of the night, straight after a bend like that. If she wanted to be with anyone at a time like this, it would be Jack. Course it would. She hopes they'll get the same fade to white that Ridley finished with. Freeze frame into heaven.

Jack's knees have stopped hurting. He can hear Portishead's 'Biscuit' again. The tune he knows hits the same spot in him and Kate at the same time, every time. Just gets right in there and melts them.

The folded car is now still. Finally silent. Perched on this empty stretch of the N52, dead centre between the towns of Kells and Ardee.

10:07:38 pm

Everything has stopped.

Silence.

Jack looks over to Kate. She smiles back at him and squeezes his hand.

Not a sound in the world, not even music.

Just as the pain becomes unbearable, everything finds its real time again.

As they look into the breaking silence, Jack and Kate both get the feeling, the sensation, that everything just came together.

10:07:08 pm

Fade to white.

Olaf Tyaransen

'GOLDFISH'

Twenty seconds after swallowing the entire sheet of Goldfish blotter — twenty seconds too late — I suddenly realised that I'd just made a huge mistake. Really huge. No doubt about it, I'd messed up bigtime, blindly jumped out of the psychedelic plane without a parachute. I'd panicked, body and mind all charged up with unwelcome adrenaline; heartbeat going like a drum machine on overdrive, manic thoughts neither ending nor beginning, everything happening in a frantic fast forward. And in all the confusion I guess my instincts just took over. Which doesn't really say much for my instincts.

Bad instincts! Bad! Bad! Bad!

Standing over the blue toilet in our tiny bathroom, anxiously watching the last stray pills of what had been my ecstasy stash bobbing up and down like baby white seals in the bowl before finally disappearing in the last chemical swirl of bubbly foam, it suddenly occurred to me that dropping prime LSD while the police were busily busting my home probably wasn't a very good idea. In fact, come to think of it, it wouldn't have been a particularly good idea even if the shades hadn't been there. There's a time and a place for everything, particularly the ingestion of serious mind altering chemicals. Then and there, both were wrong.

And I'd eaten the whole sheet!

What the hell had I been thinking?

It was a dumb move. Story of my life. I'm the Master of Misjudgement. The Earl of Error. The Count of Cock-ups. The Prince of ... you probably get the message.

Ugh! I could still taste it burning at the back of my throat, tingling away like electric sherbet or something, but I knew it was too late to attempt to do anything to reverse the pharmaceutical process I'd just foolishly embarked upon. I'd crossed the chemical Rubicon. I'd torched the bridge.

I could hear them downstairs. Trashing the gaff.

'Why do I do these things?' I asked my reflection in the tiles. My voice sounded weird.

I just stared back at me. Dumb and dumber.

It wouldn't have been so bad if the tabs had been Strawberries or something. I've taken enough trips over the years to be able to handle a mild buzz like that, but no, this stuff was something different, something new. As yet untested. Little pictures of cartoon goldfish on each tab. Miranda had brought them back from Amsterdam the week before, along with the usual batch.

'A gift from Andreas,' she'd grinned, handing me the page of blotter. 'He says they're really strong so go easy on them. One at a go.'

'Why goldfish?' I'd asked, examining the sheet. It looked like wallpaper for a Barbie house.

'I dunno,' she'd shrugged. 'Andreas didn't either. Maybe they're meant to be zodiac symbols – Pisces or something. Who cares anyway? He says they're mental.'

Andreas was our main supplier – our man in the Dam, if you like – and had consumed so many drugs in his time that the blood in his veins was rumoured to be more chemically polluted than the River Rhine. When he said something was strong, you took it seriously. And when he said something was *really* strong, you knew you were in business. Every now and then he'd pass something special on to me, something too far out to sell. I guess maybe that's why I ate the blotter. It just seemed too good to waste. Or something.

I could hear flat feet pounding heavily up the stairs. Closer. Closer.

I tensed and considered my circumstances.

My circumstances were not exactly ideal.

Not for tripping. Not for getting busted. But particularly not for tripping while getting busted.

There were numerous reasons.

For a start, I wasn't exactly dressed for the occasion. In fact, I wasn't dressed at all. I was naked, completely in the raw (unless my nipple ring counted), with my dick still semi-erect. No way to meet and greet a policeman. It's one thing to be caught with your pants down, but to be caught with them *off* puts you at a serious disadvantage from the word go. But I hadn't had time to get dressed. Miranda and I had been lying in bed enjoying a post-coital spliff when we heard the front door go in. We've been busted a couple of times before so we knew exactly what to do. We have a routine for such occasions, just like they do.

The first – and most important – thing is not to panic.

The first thing we did was we panicked. Well, we were pretty stoned. It was serious skunk – Swiss hydroponic (another gift from Andreas). The moment we heard the bang of the sledgehammer and the crash of shattered glass downstairs, we both jumped out of bed and ran around the room like frightened children for about ten seconds. On the eleventh second we caught hold of ourselves and went to work. The removal business. Drug disposal. Evidence erasure. Luckily, almost everything was in the bedroom.

'Get rid of the scales!' I hissed at her.

'Lose the stash!' she hissed back.

'Get rid of the spliff!'

'The money! The money! Quick!'

'Put some fucking clothes on!'

We had a lot to lose. We lost it all.

Scales, small bag of skunkweed, quarter kilo of Nepalese, the best part of a nine-bar of Moroccan slate – all straight out the bedroom window, from profit to loss in one easy move.

Plop! Plop! Plop! Plop!

The back of our house faces directly onto a canal. Neat, eh? Every drug dealer should have a place like mine.

Miranda grabbed the money from the drawer in the dresser – about £1,500 in old tenners and twenties (rather difficult to explain away when you're officially on the dole) – and sealed it in the weighted waterproof bag we'd bought in a Northside diving shop specifically for occasions such as this. *Plop!* (I'd be out fishing in a couple of days).

'Get rid of the stuff in the bathroom!' she snapped, wriggling snakelike into her jeans. '*Quickly!*'

I ran into the small bathroom off our bedroom. The bag of ecstasy and the Goldfish blotter were in the medicine cabinet over the sink, hidden behind all of Miranda's beauty products and asthma stuff. I'd put them there just an hour beforehand, after we'd finished counting the pills. I should've left them where they were, sitting snugly on the bedside locker. Then they could have exited canalwards, along with the rest of the gear. Looking back, I guess I would've had time to put them out the window. But I didn't. I don't know why I decided to flush them. I guess because I was stoned. And Miranda's stuff took longer than it should have to clear out of the way, panicking me even more. Bottles breaking, pills spilling everywhere – the sink was a real medicinal mess by the time my desperate fingers found the bag.

Anyway, I flushed the lot. Pulled the chain and sent close on a grand's worth of ecstasy straight to a watery rave.

Except for the Goldfish blotter. For reasons I haven't quite figured out yet, I decided to eat that. One second it was in my hand, hovering over the toilet bowl, and a moment later I was chewing it to a ball of evil-tasting pulp and gulping it down.

Down the red lane *en route* to my brain.

I'd dropped them instead of, well, *dropping* them.

Which raised a serious point. Exactly how many trips had there been on the blotter? I had no idea. I'd counted the pills because they're my business, my stock, my stash. The acid was for personal use only, just me and a few select friends, so I hadn't bothered. How many tabs had I dropped? How many goldfish had there been on the page? I remembered Miranda making a joke about 'lifetime supplies'. Had there been fifty? One hundred? Two hundred? A lot, anyway. Maybe more than a lot. Maybe best not to think about it.

Anyway, chemical matters aside, back to the less than ideal circumstances.

Firstly, as I've already mentioned, I was in the buff. Not only was this potentially quite embarrassing, it was also extremely cold. Goose pimples erupted all over my body and a shiver ran down my spine. But maybe that was just fear.

Secondly, there was music blaring. A David Holmes track was still blasting out of the bedroom speakers at full volume (luckily, the cops had smashed the door in during one of his quieter moments). Techno never creates a good impression with the law. Makes them automatically assume that you're a drug user, for some strange reason. If I'd known they were coming I'd have stuck on a Daniel O'Donnell record (not that I have any). Unfortunately, the main stereo was downstairs so I couldn't do anything about the volume.

Thirdly, I still had a plastic moneybag in my hand. It took me a moment to realise this. Less than a minute earlier it had contained approximately ninety-five White Doves. The pills had since been emptied into the toilet but I'd forgotten to throw the bag in after them. I held it up in front of my face. Bad news. The inside of the bag was still liberally smeared with fine white powder, probably more than enough for those forensic fuckers to identify as pure MDMA (well, more likely to be impure actually, knowing Andreas). The cistern would take at least two minutes to refill. *Splish splash.*

Suddenly, the music stopped.

I could hear the bedroom door crashing open. Miranda screaming. I did what I thought I had to. Took the oral option, ate the bag as well, stuffed it into my mouth and tried to swallow. Naturally enough, I gagged on it. It was plastic after all. Two dumb moves in as many minutes. A new record. My personal best.

No air. I fell over.

And that's how they found me. Sprawled naked on the bathroom floor, choking to death on a small plastic moneybag. I could see their feet, their shiny black shoes, their thick woollen socks. I closed my eyes.

I felt myself being hauled up. My mouth being forced open. Someone's fingers down my throat. A taste of nicotine. Lots of swearing.

'Stop biting me you little bastard!' A country accent. Kerry, maybe.

I passed out.

Blackness. Nothing.

Whiteness. Something.

I'm not quite sure how long I was unconscious. A couple of minutes I suppose. Maybe longer. Anyway, when I finally came around I was lying on the bed and there were several people standing in the room. I counted the silhouettes. Five – all male, three in uniforms and two in cheap greasy suits (well, I presume they were cheap and greasy). One of the uniformed cops looked strangely familiar but I couldn't quite place him. I didn't recognise anyone else. My head ached. Must've banged it when I fell over.

Miranda was sitting on the chair, pulling her top on. I hoped they hadn't seen her tits when they'd burst into the room. I'm quite jealous that way – very possessive (despite this, I've never been done for possession).

I looked down and realised I was wearing my boxers – the new pair with a picture of Homer Simpson on them. Miranda had bought them in Duty Free as a joke (she calls me Homer on my particularly lazy days). I wondered who had covered my naked shame. Hopefully her. I wouldn't like to have been responsible for any cheap Gardai thrills.

The familiar looking cop noticed that my eyes were open.

'He's awake.'

'No I'm not.'

I closed my eyes again. A technicolour blaze danced on the inside of my eyelids. Oh yeah, the acid . . . A light slap on my cheek.

'We know you're in there.' A mocking tone. 'Cancel the doctor.'

I blinked. *Oh shit!* It was technicolor on the outside as well. The bedroom walls were glowing, on fire with purple and red and orange, as though we were in the centre of some kind of weird energy field. Or an MTV set. Either way, it was pretty fucking strange.

Keep it together, keep it together . . .

'What's your name?' the cop asked, handing me a glass of water. Ha! As if he didn't already know. I'm fairly fucking famous in police circles. Arrested five times and never once convicted. I'm fairly fucking unpopular as well.

I took the glass and used a line I've wanted to try for ages.

'My name is not important,' I managed to croak, between sips. 'But you can call me Not.'

Miranda seemed to crack up at this. Well, either that or she was crying. I looked over at her to wink but for some reason I couldn't. The glare was too bright, forcing me to squint. And there were goldfish swimming around the room, five or six of them floating around the heads of the cops. I took a deep breath and tried to clear my thoughts, to focus. The goldfish disappeared, I had a feeling they'd be back. Hallucinating already. This was not good. In fact, this was pretty fucking bad.

I dropped the water, soaking the pillow. Closed my eyes again.

The cop slapped me again. Harder this time. A little too hard actually.

'Come on Bishop,' he snapped. 'Wakey, wakey.'

He did know my name. I looked directly at him and suddenly realised that I knew his as well.

'Fucking hell!' I gasped, '*Spud!*'

His meaty face went red with anger. Well, *redder*. It was already pretty red to begin with. Looked like it had been boiled or something.

'That's Officer Murphy to you shithead!' he barked. Or tried to anyway. It's difficult to sound intimidating when you've a voice like Mr Bean.

This was too much. Oliver Murphy. Oliver fucking Murphy! *Officer* Oliver fucking Murphy! I'd gone to school with the prick. Hated him from the moment I first met him. A real nasty piece of work, one of those stupid but sneaky types, the kind of guy who'd get a sly kick in when there was a scrap in the playground and some poor bastard was on the ground, getting hammered.

The last time I'd seen him he'd been working as a Dunnes Store's security guard in the Stephen's Green Shopping Centre. I'd actually stolen a video from the shop (*The Shawshank Redemption*, in case you're interested) just because I saw him there, prancing around in his silly little snot-green uniform trying to look important in front of all the bored housewives and OAPs. And now he was a law enforcer. Figured. I guess he'd always wanted to be a cop. He was certainly the type. Power hungry and desperate for some kind of authority but far too stupid to get any on his own terms. Oh yes, I remembered Oliver Murphy. An insignificant cunt, if ever there was one. An *insignificunt*.

The goldfish came back. More of them now. Ten, twenty, thirty. Swimming around the room. Going with the flow. Flowing with the glow.

'Why goldfish?' I wondered to myself. Then I remembered. Acid. Pisces acid. Maybe.

Keep it together, keep it together . . .

'One, two, three, four, five,' I sang '*once I caught a goldfish alive . . .*'

I started to laugh. And chortle. And guffaw. And snigger.

It wasn't funny. I was hysterical.

Officer Spud looked very aggrieved. He became quite animated. Literally. It was like watching a cartoon. Before my very eyes he turned into Chief Wiggam from *The Simpsons*. Had the voice right and all.

'I'm glad you think it's funny Bishop but we've got you this time, ye little prick.'

I turned my head away from him but he remained in front of my eyes. Tried closing them. Still there. Chief Wiggam wagging his porky little fingers at me. '*Blah, blah, blah . . .*'

Oh shit! This was too much.

'. . . *blah, blah, blah . . .*'

(*How many trips were on the blotter?*)

Miranda turned into Marge Simpson! Miranda was Marge Simpson! Blue hair and all! Miranda Simpson!

(*How many trips were on the blotter?*)

The other four cops all turned into Homers! Homers! Blue trousers, white shirts, three hairs on each head — same as on my boxers. Four Homers, Chief Wiggam, Marge and me! I was in the fucking *Simpsons*!

Me. Who was I?

I looked down. An evil looking python was sneaking out of the slit in my shorts. An animated python. Like the one from *The Jungle Book*. What was the snake's name? Balloo? No, that was the bear.

Keep it together, keep it together . . .

I couldn't keep it together.

'*CALL ANDREAS!!*' I screamed in a high pitched hysterical voice that I'd never in a thousand years have recognised as my own if you recorded it and played it back to me. '*MIR! ASK HIM HOW MANY TRIPS WERE ON THE BLOTTER!!!! FOR FUCK'S SAKE CALL ANDREAS!!! I NEED TO KNOW! HOW MANY GOLDFISH HAVE I TAKEN? ASK HIM!!*'

Or maybe I didn't scream at all. Maybe I just thought I did. Maybe I was still laughing.

This wasn't good. Wasn't good at all. I was starting to really lose it. A goldfish swam into my mouth. It tasted of nothing. The python darted from my shorts and swallowed two of them whole, just picked them out of the air with a snap. Then it belched. Loudly. Pythons don't belch, do they? The fish I'd just swallowed reappeared through my left nostril and swam away across the room.

I tried to focus my mind. Put things in perspective. I knew none of this was really happening. The only thing was, I wasn't quite sure exactly what was really happening. My eyes were lying to me.

Deep breaths. Shallow thoughts.

'*My name is John Bishop. J-O-H-N-B-I-S-H-O-P. I am 29 years old, a human male. I am currently in the bedroom of my home in Dophin's Barn, in Dublin, in Ireland, in Europe, on Earth, in our galaxy. What's it called? Yeah, the Milky Way. Like the chocolate bar. Miranda is here. My beautiful Miranda, I'm lucky to have her. Five policemen are here also. One of them is Spud Murphy whom I once went to school with. This is just a coincidence, not a conspiracy. Don't freak out! The cops are here looking for drugs because they know I am a drug dealer. But there are no drugs here. Everything is in the canal. Everything bar the acid. Which I took — stupidly admittedly but what's done is done. Those goldfish are not real. I am not in an episode of* The Simpsons. *I'm seeing Simpsons because Homer's on my boxer shorts. I'm seeing goldfish because they were on the blotter. That python is not real. I am hallucinating. I have taken LSD. I have taken a lot of LSD. Only Andreas knows how much. Andreas my Dutch supplier. What's his surname? Dunno — doesn't matter. What matters is that I must come back to reality because I have a situation to deal with. My name is John Bishop. J-O-H-N-B-I-S-H-O-P. I am 29 years old. I live in Dublin but I was born in . . .*'

I continued like this for a while. Real thoughts about the real world. Simple sentences with beginning, middles and ends. Deep breaths, deep breaths. I ignored the fish, ignored the glowing walls, ignored everyone and everything. *Keep it together, keep it together*. Deep breaths, deep breaths. It worked.

Reality bit. Eventually.

I was back in the bedroom. Five cops, Miranda and me.

Rhymes with LSD.

The walls had stopped glowing. No *Simpsons* characters. No goldfish.

I looked up. *Peekaboo, I see you . . .*

How long had I been away?

A while from the looks of things.

What had I said? What had I done?

A lot from the looks of things.

The room was very quiet, save for the sobbing. Miranda was crying now, red eyed and scared, staring at me with a horrified expression on her face. The cops just looked like they were feeling sorry for me. I stared down, unable to meet their accusing eyes. The python was gone. Now there was just a purple hard-on poking through my shorts, like a periscope. Same difference. *Peniscope.*

I giggled. *Peniscope!*

Spud cleared his throat.

'Are you on drugs?' he asked with the same evil sneer I remembered him having at school.

Some time passed. I tried to think of something clever to say.

'Congratulations Spud,' I eventually replied. 'You may make detective yet.'

Unfortunately, by the time I said it, I was already in the squad car.

Questions, questions, questions. No answers though. Ying without yang. Balance all wrong. Chemicals, you see. They do that to you. Fuck up your perspective. Confuse your confusion. Christ, I had enough to be confused about!

Where was Miranda? Who had dressed me? Had the police found anything in the gaff? Had I forgotten some secret stash or something? Were they drug squad or just ordinary cops? Had someone tipped them off about Amsterdam or was it just a routine bust? Did the neighbours see me being led to the car? Was I going to be charged with anything? Had I come up fully or was this only the beginning? What had I said in the bedroom? How much time had passed? How many trips were on the blotter? Why goldfish?

Me, Officer Spud and three other cops were sitting snugly in the leathery smelling squad car – Spud and a plainclothes up front, me and the other two uniforms in the back, all not very nice and cosy – taking a magical mystery tour through the Dublin night. Down along the canal to Harold's Cross Bridge, left onto

Clanbrassil Street, right to South Circular Road. Over the pills and far away . . .

'Where are you taking me?'

I tried asking the question several times but whenever I opened my mouth to talk, a stream of goldfish appeared instead of words. They'd shoot out of my gob at high speed, fly straight ahead between the driver and passenger seats and then disappear when they hit the windscreen. *Pop!*

The only thing keeping me sane was the fact that I knew they weren't really there. I was hallucinating.

I had taken acid, a lot of acid.

These things happen when you take acid, a lot of acid.

They're to be expected. They're to be unexpected. That's the whole point.

Shame about the situation though. In less stressful circumstances I'd probably be enjoying the sight of red ribbons of fish streaming from my mouth. Might even have tried blowing goldfish rings. But I was in the back of a police car. Under arrest. With Officer Spud. As far as I could tell anyway.

Where were they taking me? Never-Never Land?

Never-Again Land. If I landed.

Keep it together, keep it together . . .

The cops weren't saying anything. Not even Spud who must have been enjoying himself — it's not every day you get to bust an old school enemy. Maybe they were nervous. I wasn't quite sure what I had said or done back in the house. Maybe I'd freaked out. Maybe they thought I was mad.

A sudden thought hit me: 'Maybe I *have* gone mad!'

It was possible. After all, I'd eaten the whole sheet of blotter! Gorged myself on goldfish.

Mantratime. Quick. Fight the fear.

Deep breaths, shallow thoughts.

'My name is John Bishop. J-O-H-N-B-I-S-H-O-P. I haven't gone mad, at least not permanently. It's Friday night in Dublin — Friday the 17th of October, to be precise — and I've just been arrested. Or maybe not. I can't

remember being charged. I'm in a police car anyway, tripping out of my skull because I've taken an enormous quantity of acid. I'm seeing goldfish, I'm seeing cartoon characters, I'm seeing all sorts of shit. I can't panic because this is all panic's fault. Time to keep it together, whatever happens. If I get through tonight without losing it then this'll be a great story to tell. My name is John Bishop. J-O-H-N . . .'

It wasn't working. My thoughts dripped and disintegrated like Dali clocks, my sanity hung like a loose dribble of snot from a sick junkie's nose. I began to get the fear. A tremendous heat in my head. Sweat down my back.

'My name is . . . my name is . . . my name is John . . . something . . .'

Where was Miranda? I needed her with me!

Losing my grip, losing my grip . . .

A voice, a familiar voice. In my head, not my ears: *JOHN BISHOP – THIS IS IT! YOU'VE CROSSED THE LINE! YOU'VE GONE MAD! IT'S OVER BABY. THIS IS THE LAST DAY OF THE REST OF YOUR LIFE. YOU'RE OURS NOW, YOU SILLY LITTLE BOY . . .'* Miranda's voice!

Panic stations. Nearly screamed. Saved by the car radio.

'ANYBODY FREE IN THE LIBERTIES?' it suddenly squawked. *'THERE'S BEEN AN ARMED ROBBERY AT THE XTRA-VISION. ANYBODY FREE IN THE LIBERTIES?'*

Anybody free in the Liberties? Is there anybody free anywhere? How I laughed.

Spud turned around and glared at me. He opened his mouth to say something and another stream of goldfish drifted out and swam past my ears. I just nodded at him and stopped laughing. I think.

Keep it together, keep it together . . .

The car took off into the air, *BladeRunner* style. I didn't know squad cars could do that.

Up, up and away. Higher, higher, higher. Cartrekking across the universe.

My stomach began to churn. Must have been the G-force. G for goldfish.

What do I know about goldfish? What's the thing about them?
— *Oh yeah, they've got a five second memory.*
What do I know about goldfish? What's the thing about them?
— *Oh yeah, they've got a five second memory.*
What do I know about goldfish? What's the thing about them?
— *Oh yeah, they've got a . . .*

I closed my eyes again. Can you blame me?

Deep breaths, shallow thoughts. The golden rule.

'My name is John Bishop. J-O-H-N-B-I . . . This car is not flying! This car is not flying! This squad car is not flying! I've gotta come down . . . My name is John . . . Why goldfish? What do they . . . John Bishop . . . J-O . . . J-O-H . . . Where's Mir? . . . This car is not flying . . . J-O-H . . . Mir! . . . I need you . . .'

I'd lost it. Didn't even know what 'It' was. Reality had left the building.

Images came, images went. Brightly coloured lights flashed like computer graphics. It was hot, very hot.

Hell?

Fade out. Fade in.

Fade in. Fade out.

Time and space collided. Time and space collapsed. They obviously hadn't been built very well.

Seconds felt like weeks. Weeks felt like months. Months felt like years. Years felt like seconds.

Spin cycle. I felt rather confused.

And goldfish. Always goldfish. Everywhere.

Touchdown. What time was it? *Sometime.* Same night? *Maybe.*

No Spud, no cops, no car, no Miranda. No idea.

I was in a small boxy room with cold grey walls. Alone. Police station? Maybe.

'My name is John Bishop. J-O-H-N-B-I . . .'

The door opened. I didn't see it, I just knew it. A door had opened.

'Mum?'

'John, son, what have you done to yourself?'

'Go away mum! You're dead! You died in a car crash fifteen years ago.'

'Ah, don't be like that son . . .'

'YOU'RE NOT REAL. YOU'RE A GHOST. YOU'RE AN HALLUCINATION!' Screaming.

'That's a terrible thing to be saying to your own mother.'

'MUM – YOU'RE DEAD! DEAD!' Hysterical now.

'But . . . but so are you son.'

Exit mother. I started to sob. Thin rivers of tiny tear-shaped goldfish slipped down my lavalike cheeks in slow motion.

Was I really dead?

Some time passed.

The door opened.

'Andreas? What are you doing here?'

'Sorry John . . . sorry, man. I should've warned you.' Shaking his head. Staring at the floor.

'Warned me about what? The bust? The acid?'

'Sorry man.' Retreating, fading away.

Andreas, Andrea, Andre . . .

'No, come back! Andreas! How many goldfish on the blotter? Andreas?!'

. . . Andr, And, An, A . . .

The door closed.

Where was I?

A goldfish floated by. Stopped dead in front of my nose. Spoke to me, its mouth moving in slow motion. 'John Bishop, you are being formally charged with possession of . . .' — Spud's voice. No, Chief Wiggam's voice — *'. . . blah, blah, blah, blah, blah . . .'*

Floating underwater.

No, swimming underwater. Using my tail. My *tail?*

I am a fish. John Bishop The Fish.

'J-O-H-N-B-I-S-H-O-P-T-H-E-F-I-S-H . . . J-O-H . . .'

I looked upwards. Saw the light. I was in the bowl of the toilet in my bathroom. I'd recognise that light anywhere. Bought it in Camden Market four years ago, back when I was scoring my gear in London. A silhouette, blocking the light's light.

High above me, John Bishop The Drug Dealer, looking somewhat stressed out. Shaking a bag full of White Doves into the bowl. They splashed around me like little meteorites and started to dissove, hissing furiously.

Dive bombed by ecstasy? By my own ecstasy? Oh, the irony of it all.

Bad karma. Shouldn't have sold drugs after all.

Definitely Hell.

High above me John Bishop the Drug Dealer pulled the chain and flushed.

Niagara Falls. Water water everywhere.

Turn off your mind, relax and float downstream . . .

'G-O-L-D-F-I-S-H . . . G-O-L-D-F-I-S-H . . . G-O-L-D-F-I-S-H . . . G-O-L-D-F-I-S-H . . . G-O-L-D-F-I-S-H . . . G-O-L-D-F-I-S-H . . . G-O-L-D-F-I-S-H . . . G-O-L-D-F-I-S-H . . . G-O-L-D-F-I-S-H . . . G-O-L-D-F-I-S-H . . . G-O-L-D-F-I-S-H . . . G-O-L-D-F-I-S-H . . . G-O-L-D-F-I . . .'.

Some time and many spaces later. A voice. A *real* voice. In my ear, not my head.

'John! John! Wake up baby, wake up!'

Someone shaking me. *Miranda* shaking me.

'Whashappenen . . . ?' Groggy. Dazed. Confused. Completely *GDC*.

'You were screaming. Having a nightmare.'

I shook my head and let reality settle for a moment.

I was in bed with Miranda. The sheets were soaking wet.

('I'm in bed with Miranda. The sheets are soaking wet.')

Closed my eyes, opened them.

I was still in bed with Miranda. The sheets were still soaking wet.

'Are you okay?' Feeling my brow. A warm, lightly perfumed hand. A *real* hand.

'Dunno.' My voice sounded strange again – weirdly normal.

'I was getting really freaked out. You kept on spelling your name, over and over. What was all that about?'

'Uh ... dunno.'

'John, sweetheart – were you having a bad dream? You're soaking! Are you sick?'

I didn't know what to say. Miranda shook me again. 'Sweetheart?'

'Em ... can we talk about it later?'

'Sure.' Softly.

She kissed me warmly on the cheek and snuggled in beside me, her lithe little body melding into mine like warm wax. Soon afterwards, she was purring with sleep. We lay like that for what seemed like hours, Mir fast asleep, me just staring wide-eyed at the ceiling. I didn't know how I felt. A bit numb. A little shellshocked. I pinched myself repeatedly. Thoughts trickled snailslow through the corridors of my mind.

(*The bust? The goldfish? The car? What had happened?*)

Had it really just been a dream? This all seemed real enough. Me and Mir – all warm and cosy in the bed. So real it was surreal. I could feel her heartbeat fluttering against my chest. She was definitely there, wasn't going to disintegrate into blurry graphics, wasn't going to drip away the way things had in the ... in the *dream*?

This was all a bit too much like a bad Leaving Cert English essay for me. *And then I woke up?* Nah!

I crept from the bed and padded softly to the bathroom. The Goldfish blotter and the bag of Doves were still in the medicine cabinet, both untouched (two hundred and fifty trips on the blotter!) I checked back in the bedroom – scales, gear, money, all present and accounted for, a place for everything and everything in its place. Nothing had been moved.

A dream?

A fucking dream?

I went downstairs to the phone and dialled a number. The phone rang and rang and rang and rang and rang and *click* and blaring techno in the background and a gruff Northside accent: 'Yeah?'

'Billy, it's John.'

'Johnny! What's up man? It's late . . . nearly fuckin six!'

'Yeah, look, sorry about the time . . .'

'S'alright. We've been buzzin all night. Those are wicked fuckin pills man! Fuckin ace! Got any more?'

'Yeah, eh . . . let's talk about that again, not on the phone.'

'Oh right. Sorry man.'

A moment's silence. I took a deep breath.

'Look, do you remember Oliver Murphy?'

'Who?'

'Oliver Murphy – we went to school with him.'

'Spud!'

'That's him.'

'Used to play on the hurling team?'

'I think so.'

'Complete cunt!'

'Yeah. That's him.'

'What about him anyway?'

'Well, do you know what he's doing now?'

'Why?'

'I just need to know.'

'Jasus, I haven't a fuckin clue man . . . Look, hang on a second, Dean might know.'

Billy left the phone down. I couldn't recognise the track playing in the background. Two minutes later, he came back on the line, laughing.

'Dean says he's in the Joy!'

'What? He's a screw?'

'No, he's doing a stretch.'

'Fuck off!'

'Seriously, man! He's in there for the last six months. He

was working some scam in the Stephen's Green Centre with a few dodgy security guards – ripping off the shops at night or something – got three years for handling stolen goods!'

'You sure?'

'Yeah, Dean reckons he saw him there when he was in visiting his brother last week. Why do you wanna know anyway?'

'No reason.'

'Are you alright man? You sound a bit fuckin wired.'

'No, I'm cool. Talk to you tomorrow.'

I hung the phone up. I wanted to talk to Andreas as well but couldn't call him on that line. Tomorrow. I went back up to Miranda and just lay there, warm and real beside her, turning everything over in what was left of my mind and pondering the significance of it all. I couldn't find any. Spud wasn't a cop. We hadn't been busted. I hadn't dropped any acid. None of it made sense.

Keep it together, keep it together . . .

No need, things are together anyway . . .

Eventually, despite my best efforts, I fell asleep. Dark, dreamless, nothingness. Bliss.

What's the story, morning glory?

Hours later, I woke up to find Miranda going down. Breakfast blowjobs are one of her specialities but, for once, I wasn't really in the mood. I didn't even feel like I was there. Hungover from hallucinations.

'Mir! Stop!' I protested, pushing her head back up. She flashed a sly fuck-me grin and began to kiss my chest, pulling roughly at my nipple ring. 'Feeling better yet?' she whispered huskily.

'Mir! I'm not in the mood!' I laughed. She didn't care. When Mir's in the mood, Mir's in the mood. She brought her hand down between her legs and touched herself. Then she rubbed her wet and salty fingers over my lips. Despite myself, I grew harder. Without saying a word, she turned around in the bed and positioned herself over my mouth. I could feel her bullet-hard nipples grazing against my belly, the warm wetness of her mouth around my cock. I gave in, brought my lips to hers. Her rose petal clitoris grew harder and harder as I slowly stroked it with my tongue. Gradually she pushed herself down even more, completely enveloping my face.

Her clitoris seemed to be growing. And growing.

Fuck! It was growing! And moving!

Suddenly my mouth was completely full of female flesh. I couldn't breath. I tried to push her off but she wouldn't move. *Can't breathe! Choking!* Her clit seemed to have taken on a life of its own, wriggling wildly and slapping hard against my teeth, forcing up the roof of my mouth.

Stop! Stop! Stop!

I panicked. Somehow I pushed her off me, put my hands on her thighs and shoved her so violently that she fell off the bed, falling heavily onto the floor. Her clitoris was still in my mouth, jerking furiously. I turned and spat it out, coughing and gasping for breath.

'What the fuck . . .' I croaked, between heaves.

Miranda's clitoris was lying on the pillow, bright red on snow white, thrashing away like there was an electric current running through it.

'OH JESUS - NO!–'

It was a G-O-L-D-F-I-S-H. Everything began to slip away again . . .

Joe Ambrose

'I HATE YOU AND I HATE YOUR JESUS'

In Tunisia I got a tan. Then I went to London to produce a 12″ for a friend. Christmas coming up, it got too expensive to fly to Berlin, impossible to get a seat to Dublin. So I'm staying on in Clerkenwell the lonely financial zone in a big flat that the Council thinks is still occupied by the Aids victim they gave it to for free five years ago. In reality the Aids guy went home to Australia in '94, is presumably dead. He transmitted his flat, surreptitiously, to a hairdresser who gave it to a dude who gave it to a music journalist who sub-let it to me until her conscience got the better of her and she stopped collecting rent, disappeared from the face of my earth. I got a free London home. I spend about four months a year in London — but I don't live here; nobody does.

I get up in the afternoon, spend two hours drinking black coffee, listening to old CDs. Around six I put the world's smallest turkey into the gas oven and turn the oven on down low. The cosy/Catholic/family/memory smell of turkey floats through the chill tiled hall while I reinvent myself checking out *III Communication* ... Central heating blasts my room full of reassurance — I will never die. Outside my highrise windows the city is almost freezing. While the turkey is cooking, I walk into Soho. Christmas is the loneliest time of the year for the surfer boy and I'm the only surfer boy in town.

The streets are empty, my mind full of vipers. All I feel is the sharp cold. All I can hear is my Berlin-bought Nike trainers slapping the pavement. All I can smell is air. Lack of distraction makes me walk faster — normally I'm a dopey walker — and I'm at Centrepoint on the fringes of Soho in no time.

When I've eaten my turkey dinner I call my mother. Now the soundtrack is Boogie Down Productions, *A Man & His Music*, on vinyl. Mum says a postcard came for me from Alwyn Falklow: 'She says she's living in Dublin now and she gives her phone number if you'd like to call her. The card is horrible, of course, some pop group.'

'Which pop group?'

'They're called Rancid.'

I love my mother.

Alwyn was this linguini-thin kid, limbs delicate as an eyelid, cold as ice cream and just as sweet. She had studs through both nipples and one through her left eyebrow. In 1990, when I was 22 and she was 13, Alwyn was my girlfriend. She had spiked mousy-blonde hair and trusting dark brown eyes. She came from Seattle when all the bands came from there. She wore a t-shirt saying: 'I hate you and I hate your Jesus.'

Alwyn was part of the Seattle Youth Decadence Campaign. The first time I met her she gave me their leaflet Youth of Seattle Demand Sex:

> Much of the neurosis of today's youth is caused by anxiety due to the lack of a decent sex life. Wilhelm Reich recommended that the state provide free hotels for youth to have sex in, to relieve anxiety caused because kids have to have sex in alleys. In addition to Reich's suggestion, The

Youth Decadence Campaign demands that the city provides Seattle's youth with free prostitutes. Youth that are seen as being physically attractive and 'popular' by capitalist society's false value system, hold an unfair monopoly of sex partners. Lack of sex in the early young adult years can lead to an inferiority complex that may never heal, even leading to suicide. Thus, we demand free and decent sex for all youth, regardless of race, gender, class, or physical attractiveness.

I'm Kim. I'm a DJ. I live in Berlin. I'm alone in this world.

New Year's Eve.

Half past midnight I catch a bus into town. It leaves me off near Trafalgar Square. Two lesbians, one looks like Madonna, the other like Bill Clinton, guzzle bottles of fizzy wine. They bump into me aggressively, Bill Clinton nearly knocking me over. I get home around 3 am, listen to Sepultura, ring Alwyn in Dublin.

We talk for the first time in seven years.

2nd January

I close up the flat, head for Heathrow with a bag of records and my tiny black leather travelling bag full of funky t-shirts. I pick up books while I make my way around the world. On the train I'm reading a weird French novel about three lesbians, two white and the third a Moroccan black.

Alwyn is waiting for me at Arrivals. The airport is decorated in Christmas shit. Drunken sentimental peasants wait for planes back to London or New York. She's gone kind of feral. An old sex paperback sticks out of her Nike shoulder bag. She looks kind of stupid, she looks very real. She's a woman now.

5th January

What does she do for money in Dublin? Alwyn's no trust fund babe — Dad's a postman, her mother a teacher. I calculate that she is 21.

She must be a dealer.

She has a totally weird five-storey eighteenth century house on Ardee Street in the Coombe, which is Harlem for white folks. She has the house to herself.

She gives me the second floor, three rooms of my own.

Alwyn has her fortress on the top floor — three rooms just like mine. A small bedroom with a mattress on the floor, alongside the mattress one of those designer telephones made of see-through plastic that lets you see all the wires and components inside. Also in the bedroom she has a rack of grunge clothes. In her sitting room there's a small expensive stereo system and maybe 200 CDs. New wave ska, punk, hardcore, straight edged, grindcore. 'Music for moshing to,' she snaps, when I comment that this is hazardous music. In her third room she keeps snakes and lizards. I like her shiny black tiny swamp snake but the lizards and pythons make me feel creepy. The snake room is hothouse-hot twenty-four hours a day.

'How'd you get this place, Alwyn?' I ask her over a chicken dinner.

'In the late Sixties it got rented out real cheap to a gang of left-field painters, actors, musicians,' she says politely, calmly,

174

like I'm a tedious guest who must be humoured. 'All kinds of allegedly important arty losers lived here one time or another. All total assholes. The place is full of their stuff, going back to the Seventies at least. Take a look around … punks … lesbians … witches … sometimes one or other of them shows up like the Ghost of Christmas Past to collect a packet of rubbers left here in 1973. The rent stayed low. I met this Florida guy — Quique — who was in a band, they had a deal with Interscope, and he lived here. Quique kicked out his Irish girlfriend and I moved in with him, into the top floor where I am today. He lost his deal, went home. I intimidated all the other tenants … an awful painter … a has-been singer-songwriter … an actor who was a total right wing asshole. Over a period of a few months they all kind of fucked off … I had to give the actor £200 to fuck off … so this is where you find me … anyway.'

My floor belonged, before me, to the actor. He cleared everything out except for a blow-up plastic mattress which has a tiny leak somewhere. Every night I blow it up to an erection-like stiffness before crashing. When I wake up in the morning it's at half mast (like me) but still comfortable enough, my ass just about touching the floor.

The house is two hundred years old, it could collapse at any moment. There is a different substantial thing wrong with each and every room, but they're all freezing, somewhat squalid, worn to a thread by history. I tried to open my bedroom window and the whole frame loosened and almost came away in my hands. I keep it in place now with wooden staves I've jammed into the crevices between frame and wall. There are no heaters except for a town gas fire in the ground floor kitchen which is our communal sitting room. Alwyn hangs out there in the evenings with her pals. It got painted dark red about thirty years ago. She likes her time alone. She has lots of pals.

Ground floor hall houses two ancient dusty mahogany presses, full of books, art catalogues, business files, stuffed envelopes, old photographs. Presses and tallboys full of similar archives on every landing.

Most of the stuff — documents, books, furniture — belonged to a young couple living here in the mid-Seventies. A pert Chinese-Irish girl called Anna Chan doing art history at Trinity plus her older boyfriend Niall who ran the Thomas Davis Gallery, then a real cutting edge hotspot for hotshots. Chinese prints. Porcelain Mao Badges. Posters for a Joseph Beuys show at the Thomas Davis called 'I Like Beuys'.

6th January

We're in a subterranean club. The usual arrangement — they built an office block and in the basement they had to choose between having a car park or an unsuccessful nightclub. They went for the club. Alwyn introduces me to this greasy guy called Abdul who could be Turkish or Greek or Moroccan or ... what?

Alwyn gives me her bag and I make for the Men's Room. In the cubicle I open the bag, take out the straw, the baggie, and the CD box. I open up the box but the CD is missing. *Africa's Blood* by Lee Perry. I chop out two small lines on the box and hoover them. I take coke elegantly. I don't snort like a pig. I hate it when people make all that noise snorting coke or speed. It's like sleeping with someone and you find out they snore.

When I step out of the cubicle I stare angrily at my body in the mirror. I look fit and fine. I look lean like a Marine. As the lines hit in I look like a winner. Then in the mirror I notice a queer behind me staring at me intensely. I leave.

12th January

You read about animals, rabbits, deer, who when caught in a trap will amputate themselves, chew off a limb, to escape the trap. I must've chewed off a limb to escape when I quit Ireland. I went around the world a one-legged orphan, no home in this world. All I'm finding in Dublin is the rancid remains of my long lost leg.

Madonna on the radio singing 'I'm Not Your Bitch.'

13th January

She is gone to the Outer Territories. She says she's gone to stay with English hippies she knows in Galway. Tonight I begin my trawl through Ardee Street's presses and shelves and files. I find a box of photographs. Slides, Polaroids, expensive arty signed prints, contact sheets. Photocopies of contact sheets. I make out the story of Chan, a Chinese princess sniffing out sex, funky dyed-blonde hair, small beautiful tits, eyes full of good news and false modesty. In one photograph she is sitting naked on an old couch, the one in Alwyn's kitchen. She is in hot love with her Niall. What does she see in him? Why doesn't she go with a guy her own age? Why do girls who groove like her end up fucking boring guys with good jobs?

In another old box I am marching through the Seventies without paying the price. I'm looking at photocopied 1978 flyers for pro-Palestinian marches starting at Kevin Street, moving down through Grafton Street on the Saturday afternoon, ending an hour later with speeches at the GPO. I'm clutching a voucher for a vegetarian restaurant on Harcourt Street.

I go to bed with a book but I walk down the dangerous path of imagining what kind of girl Chan was.

15th January

Three letters I find in a biscuit tin in my room. Taped to the lid of the tin — the sellotape grown loose and brittle with age — is a small brown envelope with 'Property of Anna Chan. Private.' written in on it.

The first letter written in 1977. Chan was eighteen then. Her dad, a Hong Kong born Professor of Law at UCD, writes to her on old-style UCD notepaper. The stamp on the envelope features a simple calligraphy from Celtic mythology. The UCD phone number is a six digit number.

He writes in his Chinaman's old-world script, he pleads with his daughter. He tells her not to get depressed, that the world is her oyster:

> You are a miraculously beautiful girl, well educated, well reared by your parents, with a wonderful future. I know you feel a need to make your own decisions and to be independent But always remember that your mother and I are here loving you and everything that you do in this life. Above all else remember your religion and be true to it. Save yourself for the man you will eventually marry who will be the father of your children. Those children will give you the same satisfaction that you and your brothers have given to Mammy and me. Ignore the passing temptations of the flesh, place your trust in God. Jesus died for our sins. At least think about what I

am saying. I know I'm old fashioned but I've seen a lot of life.

He just didn't understand. Chan didn't go to church on Sundays, didn't expect to live forever, listened to American punk rock, was a contemporary art scenester.

Letter Number Two is from Niall, dated 1979, written on the back of a Dublin Airport canteen menu where everything seems very cheap. They're breaking up! He's at the airport and he can't stop himself from writing to her. He was a compulsive writer, a compulsive bullshitter, a serial fool.

They're not splitting up because one of them is seeing someone else, because they're bored with each other. Their mutual attraction is still brutally physical and emotional. They fucked like dogs the night before he went to the airport.

Niall loves her too much and she is smothered by his affection. She is trapped — she chews off a limb, the limb is him. In the Seventies women discovered their independence, took their lives into their own hands:

I'm at the airport and Oh God I can't believe I'm really going. Are we really doing this? What kind of fool am I? I can't believe that I am leaving you, that last night was our last night together. I'm sitting in this scummy canteen writing to you — Herb Alpert is playing through the Muzak — on the back of this menu. I'm writing on and on like an idiot and my plane leaves in forty minutes.

He got a job in an Irish bar in New York, worked his way into the art scene, got control of another gallery. Things worked out well for Niall in America.

Photographs of them together, photographs they took of one another. I smell the salty stench of their sex, she is thin and cold, he is stocky and horny. She is nervous and hard-

179

working. I want to reach back into history and rescue her from his earthy mediocrity. I despise his curatorial achievements ... the catalogue for the American Political Posters show ... the touring Fluxus show ... the seminal Bauhaus show acclaimed in *The Irish Times*.

Reading his tearful menu letter I am triumphant. Like I've won. Like the Chinese babe is walking down Grafton Street hand-in-hand with me in the Seventies.

The third letter — also from 1979 — offers her a temporary job as assistant to the art critic of *The Irish Press*.

20th January

She is a dealer, in business with Abdul. He gets her pure moist cocaine direct from the side of a mountain in Colombia. In the kitchen Alwyn uses a pestle and mortar to blend the coke with paracetamol. A quarter coke, three quarters painkiller. She flogs the result in the clubs at the weekends.

Abdul lives five doors away on Ardee Street in a building called Watkin's Distillery. Tonight we're there for dinner. Abdul lives in great style in the middle of the squalor. He has the top floor of the old distillery, full of modern art. The furniture is bulky old Victorian stuff but he only has a few pieces. The floorboards are bare, there are art books and detective novels scattered on the floor. He lectures me on the history of the distillery, one of the headquarters of the IRA in the War of Independence. This is the new Ireland. Even foreigners know more about our history than I do.

25th January

I'm here three weeks — it rains all the time — sleeping all day, playing records all night. I sleep on the left side, sleep on the right side. In the night I hang out at an anarchist/skate coffeeshop/bookshop called Semiotexte about ten minutes walk away, opposite Christchurch Cathedral.

Semiotexte is your typical counterculture emporium. Every town must have a place where phoney hippies meet. Bookshelves full of Chomsky, Hakim Bey, and Luther Blisset. CD music from Aphex Twin, Squarepusher, Plug and Photek comin' atcha from a designer expensive sound system. There are some fine girls there, and pushy Americans of dubious pedigree (a grandnephew of Aleister Crowley, a tall thin geek wearing glasses who says he made a movie with Lydia Lunch, an asshole who claims he went to school with Beck). Semiotexte has good turntables and a good mixer so I spin stuff there when I'm fit.

Tonight I'm playing a CD with a remix of Beck by Aphex Twin when Stan Hatwin walks up to me out of nowhere — I've not seen him for eight years — smiles at me, and says laconically 'Hey, Kim, you must be playing the Aphex Twin remixing Beck. Which means Aphex is losing his touch if I can recognise his work.' Hatwin is a small good looking Romeo from one of the biggest Dublin families. His dad owns an advertising agency and off-Grafton Street property.

Chan's MA thesis is on Picabia, whom I've never heard of. Also an envelope of postcards of his work, the strong punk imagery. The troublemaker. The activist. The man of action. That's what it says in her thesis, painstakingly typed on a Silver Reed electric with a Seventies typeface which is still in Alwyn's kitchen. I plug it in. It works. She writes approvingly of Picabia's

Dada nature. A studious, radical, girl defending an art barricade of some sort.

1st February

I can't sleep.

Alwyn's been gone three nights. She says she's gone to Galway to be with her English hippy friends but she is fucking someone up around Parnell Square. I saw her there one night last week when she was supposed to be on a mission to Galway.

I don't own her. She and me was a long time back. I just fucked her a couple of times — looking over my shoulder to see if the snakes had escaped and were about to attack me — since I got here.

Chan shares the Irish obsession with the written word on paper.

I put an East Berlin DJ mix tape into my Walkman. Then I walk into town.

I go to Semiotexte and stay there 'til four. A prominent Dublin kebab millionaire and his paedophile guru came up with the idea. They stocked the shelves with photocopied Anarchist manifestoes, Beat novels, and rave culture writing. To give it an air of authenticity they handed it over to some kids ... slender European squatters ... American Sonic Youth fans ... generic beautiful kids.

The adolescent rebels, being adolescents, took them seriously, took the millionaire at his word, turned nasty, changed the rules, the locks, and occupied Semiotexte in the name of Anarchism. Right now the millionaire is going through the courts to get the kids evicted. This is a very temporary autonomous zone. Next year it'll be a kebab shop.

Most of the night I'm left alone, reading a detective novel. Stan Hatwin comes in just before I make to leave. Over a joint we decide to form a DJ team. What he looks like now. What he looked like then.

He gives me his mix tape which I check out on my way home. Some ways he's ahead of me, some ways I'm ahead of him. That's the way it always is with good DJs. I think I'm getting pretty good.

3rd February

Invite Stan to dinner. I've cleaned up the kitchen — a forty-eight hour job. Alwyn helped a lot, she says it's something she's been meaning to do since she moved in. We clear away dirt and grime from two decades of bohemian indifference. Then she disappears in the afternoon: 'Don't expect me 'til late.'

The doorbell rings. He's wearing a Paul Smith t-shirt and old combat trousers: 'I've been in a pub gossiping about this hip hop club, Def Row, which is changing venue or has been fired out of Renards. We were talking about the politics of hip hop and how it relates to Def Row ... but I don't know.'

At dawn Stan looks out the window at the sunlight, startled, says: 'Shit, Kim! I got to go home. Phone for a cab.'

Which I do. When he goes I get on the phone to Berlin, tell people I won't be coming back for a few weeks. I tell the guys crashing in my apartment that they can stay a while longer — they're relieved and grateful.

15th February

My mother phones around midnight with some hot gossip. The

183

Joe Ambrose

guy who was my best friend at school when I was five has just come out. 'His poor mother ... he'll not be 'Gay' in Hell!' says Mum.

Mum turned me into a DJ. When I was a kid in Limerick she forced me to take guitar lessons. I hated the guitar, always associated it with bearded idiots sitting round a campfire singing sick-inducing Beatles songs. When my turn came, I wanted two turntables.

There's a file box of business papers to do with the Thomas Davis Gallery. Yellowing proposals for shows by clapped-out conceptualists, printmakers, a Dutch all-women collective. Slides of works. Cassettes of experimental music. Catalogues. Postcards. Our man Niall — man of action — in effect. Countercultural Establishment Can-Do Wonderguy, the Bruce Springsteen of Irish art. Down the bottom of the box are more personal things. Five self-important windy New York letters from him to her. His bullshit ideas and will she join him for Christmas and how much he misses her.

She's a scented oriental Kama Sutra seductress from out of another time. I wish I was living with her back then in Dublin when there was no call for rubbers and she was fresh and fit.

19th February

Stan has a gig at Ratio, which is the size of a football pitch. He asks me to do it with him so now I'm at the decks. We're doing five hours, starting at midnight. We're in a chill out zone called Kulchur. DJing makes me twisted in the head, like making candy floss. You spin it around and around, let it get out of control, then you collect it all up in the middle — vague, pink, moist, and sticky. I take a live album of Lydia Lunch reading her poetry and I mix it with with some Hard Hands techno.

184

I slow and speed up Lunch. Slow, she sounds like a seductress. Fast, she sounds like a witch.

24th February

I'm in the kitchen at the typewriter writing the copy for a flyer. The doorbell rings. I open the door and there she is!

She is fifteen years older than her story in my mind but beautiful still, slim in slick New York clothes. She wears an ankle-length cream silk skirt, an off-white linen blouse, and she protects herself from the cold with an old jet-black overcoat, an expensive man's coat from the Fifties. Her long frizzy hair going grey, she has a slightly petulant air about her but Chan's a game enough character.

'You must be Kim.' She smiles broadly, her accent a nice South Dublin brogue.

'Yep! And you're Anna Chan. I've seen photographs of you around the place.'

She blushes at this comment, knowing I've been through her back pages. I guess I'm looking at her a certain strange way that is borderline sexual. I feel like I'm involved with her but that's not true so I'm careful about what I say, disguising the seedy voyeur inside. I've been sleeping on her couch too long.

'Nice coat,' I say when we're sitting in the kitchen sipping coffee, me relaxed on the ancient sofa where she once posed naked, she casual in an armchair the other side of the gas fire.

'It belonged to my father.'

A silence. I sip my coffee.

'So what are you doing now?'

'I write for a few American magazines, I'm working on two illustrated books for Taschen. One on Frank Stella. One on George Condo.'

At least I've heard of Frank Stella.

Chan is staring at the couch and I'm thinking of the dirty photograph of her.

'Do you mind if I take a look at that couch a moment?' she asks politely.

'No, no, of course not.' I stand up, she comes over and rummages vigorously under the cushions, her long bony arm disappearing into the bowels of the couch where the springs are, like she's fist-fucking it. She doesn't say anything, her brow furrowed, and her attention entirely focused on her search. I get it. She's looking for some drugs.

Eventually the arm emerges from the springs, her thin veiny hand clasping an ancient Seventies cassette tape which she immediately, and without explanation, puts into the pocket of her father's coat.

Everything doesn't have to be obvious and in your face.

25th February

'So what was he like, the guy you moved in here with?' I ask whimsically. We've been doing a moderate amount of coke.

'Quique was a musician, producer. He was a decent boy, he had a nice dick.'

'What's a nice dick?'

'One that is aesthetically pleasing, not necessarily big. I've seen thousands of dicks. I like dick.' She pauses and her serious thoughtful eyes sweep around the room. 'Quique's dick looked real nice, the skin a lot darker than his body skin. Darker at the root. Everything is darker at the root.'

Around midnight she says we should go to Semiotexte. She hates it there so why does she want to go? She says: 'It's like an internet cafe without computers.' Maybe its just that we can get in for free and she wants to escape from Ardee Street.

Abdul is lurking close to the counter so that explains it — we're here to see him. He wants to talk with me, to know what equipment I take when I do international gigs. Do I take amps or heavy equipment? He loses interest when I explain the compact nature of the digital age: 'Man, you need a heavy metal band, that's what you need. They have amps and guitar cases and trunks full of merchandise and lurex trousers. I just use a sampler and a DAT on stage. I lonesome travel with t-shirts and vinyl.'

Abdul files me under 'weirdo' after that but he wants me to explain techno to him and I'm not very good at explaining music. That's why I became a DJ, not a painter or writer.

'Most people get into techno because they've had unhappy childhoods,' I eventually blurt out.

'I never had a childhood.' Alwyn stares at me strangely. 'You had my childhood. You're still having it.'

I'd brought some records with me so eventually I escape behind the decks and disappear into the music.

1st March

It's 3 am and the atmosphere is not good. We flick between CNN and MTV in the kitchen. Then I start playing some promo copies I just got in the post from Berlin.

Earlier we went to an opening at the Thomas Davis. Chan was there with her boyfriend and I small-talked with her a while. We both agreed that the art on display — sculpture — is brain dead, that the Thomas Davis is now the home of bland establishment art in Dublin. The boyfriend is a docile poodle — much younger than her — very tall, thin, black leather trousers, hair dyed Goth-black and cut expensively to a cyber/rockabilly style. A Killiney boy doing an MA in Fine Art. Me and Chan talk happily for fifteen minutes. Mr Killiney says nothing, his eyes drifting towards both boys and girls in the crowd.

Chan says she used to work at the Thomas Davis at one time. I don't react.

Alwyn is staring vacantly at an MTV interview of Marilyn Manson bullshitting.

'So what brought you to Ireland Alwyn?'

'What do you think, motherfucker?'

'Something to do with me?'

'Yeah. Something to do with you. I met this other Irish guy in London . . . you caused me to have an Irish phase . . . I moved here with him.'

'But I'm not very Irish.'

'Maybe you're more Irish than you think.'

Maybe I am. She goes upstairs to her rooms and I make some tea. Lyons the Quality Tea.

10th March

I feel the bass in my face in the crowd. I'm in White Subway, a big club on the quays. The air is wretched with dry ice, hot air, poppers, sweat. This is a big old warehouse with bits of provincial Eighties hippy art everywhere. There's art like this in a big squat gallery in Prenzlau Berg in East Berlin. Most art you see in clubs is reactionary.

White Subway is full of criminals and rich faggots and wretched ageing scenesters from when I used to live here. I think I'm enjoying myself. Wherever there are clubs there are criminals and faggots.

The guy who owns this place used to have a band rehearsal

place in Temple Bar when I lived here. The whole city knows who owns White Subway. His mother used to have a newsagents in Ballyfermot.

12th March

After doing a set with Stan we take a taxi to Killiney with three girls. We stay up all night with them watching videos and coming down. Around 7 am I get a bus into town, and Stan crashes out on the couch.

Two girls, about seventeen, get on my bus in Stillorgan. They've been out at a party all night.

'She's the only girl in the class who hasn't pierced her nose,' one says. 'That's totally weird.'

17th March

She is playing an instrumental track by Sonic Youth from the *Tibetan Freedom* 3 CD.

'Sonic Youth look kind of young for their age,' I tell her, 'and they play pretty well together but they ain't exactly great songwriters or ...'

'Or even good people,' she replies, mimicing my mid-Atlantic Irish accent, accurately anticipating my line of argument. 'But, hey, they seem pretty cool to me.'

She knows I met them when I did a festival with them in Barcelona. She knows I think they're fake punks. She knows I think they're politically full of shit.

'Anyway I think they've got more credibility than Mary J.

Blige,' snipes Alwyn, like I'm always playing her, like I don't know what she was like in the Eighties.

'Oh, I don't know about that ... Mary J. has the kind of voice to make my balls retract in behind my hard-on. To make me cross-eyed when I come.'

20th March

I go with a Welsh girl to the DART, a redhead wearing an Israeli peace camp t-shirt. The weather can't get worse. It's eight in the morning but the sky is black as sin. Heavy rain is falling, storm wind howling, and the wind is Arctic cold.

The Welsh is going home, catching her ferry from Dun Laoghaire. I met her two weeks ago when I was DJing with Stan. I went out with her a few times. At Tara Street DART station I meet Jim Maybury, a clothes designer I knew at art school. He is out of it, spent all night at a 'great party'. Now the party is just over. It's such a horrible cold morning that I don't feel like talking to Jim, still lean as a greyhound and just as paranoid, wearing a totally old-fashioned but very elegant suit. I know nothing about suits, I guess you'd call it a Frank Sinatra sort of suit. Scoobie doobie do.

Outside Blackrock the train travels slowly along the sea wall and through the rain I see six cops huddled on top of the wall, talking with one another, looking down to the rocks below and out to the sea beyond. In Dun Laoghaire I carry the Welsh's bag through to Departures, which is soaked, freezing, and deserted. Dublin yokels in ferry company peaked caps assure us that she can indeed board the ferry, so thankfully she does. I want to be back home in bed. Rain's been falling for three days.

On the return journey just one cop is keeping guard outside Blackrock. Because of the rain and the steamed-up window I can't see anything clearly. I think of getting off the DART to have a look at something too damn nasty but I'm too whacked and it's way too wet and cold.

24th March

I go to Stan's funeral at Donnybrook Church. A desperate occasion where I meet thousands of ghosts from my past. Everyone's in white heat shock because we're burying Stan, a totally bad motherfucker.

His sister the painter and his brother the rock journalist talk with me and Jim Maybury a while before heading off to a waiting limousine. There's drinks and stuff out at the Hatwin home in Blackrock. Jim and me decline an invitation and head for the RTE canteen where we get a cheap dinner while Jim tells me about Stan's last night.

When Jim ran into me on the DART platform the morning I was dumping the Welsh, he'd come from a party he'd been to with Stan — a drug party of course.

Stan was fit and nasty that last night. He'd done coke, acid, crack, and speed. Stan was a waspish rattler when loaded up on chemicals. Jim, wearing the selfsame Frank Sinatra suit in front of me in the canteen, says the music at the party was the best he ever heard. I don't know what to make of this. Jim's taste in music sucks, but Stan knew his stuff. Anyway, Stan — a bottle of vodka in his left hand — danced flirtatiously with a ten year old girl, the kid's mother an old girlfriend of his. A gang of bikers took offence, picked a fight with little Stan, knocked him to the ground, and kicked the shit out of him. He got about ten boot-kicks to the left side of his head. Stan, ironically in the context, was always interested in older women, never interested in girls that way.

Badly concussed and out of it on his drugs, Stan stumbled to his feet. The old girlfriend drove him to the hospital where they decided to keep him in overnight. About seven in the morning — still tripping — he walked out of the hospital, caught the DART to Blackrock, and fell — or threw himself — into the sea. An hour later me and the Welsh passed his poor body, and the fat freezing cops staring at it.

'It's a terrible business,' says Jim, going to the canteen counter to get us two coffees plus two apple tarts and cream.

27th March

Chan phones me and invites me to have a coffee with her in the Design Centre, right across the road from the Thomas Davis. She used to hook up with Niall at the Design Centre for lunch back in the days. All fantasies have been shattered by the reality of knowing her, of bumping into her again and again between Grafton Street and Kildare Street.

She tells me about a show she is curating for the Thomas Davis on the connection between art and club culture. A bit of a so-what idea but I hope it works out for her. I tell her she should start with Warhol and Basquait, Studio 54, work it from there. My big idea seems to be news to her. Maybe she's not as sharp as she seems. They vegetate in Ireland, even the beautiful ones. I tell her that all art in clubs is reactionary.

Much of our talk is to do with Stan. The art scene knew him well — he was a rich kid. If he'd lived he'd eventually have inherited Dad's fortune and become a South Dublin art patron. All art is reactionary.

We agree we'll meet again, she makes small talk about Ardee Street until Mr Killiney, now with his hair spikey and blonde, comes to pick her up. The rest of the afternoon I buy records in Fownes Street.

I cook a pork dinner for five people.

We go to The Pod, Renards, and Republica. Alwyn works, I watch, we have fun talking. We're sitting in a lounge where a fat asshole in a Louis Copeland suit, demi-faggy boys with lime green spiked hair, an Arab girl going to fat, a techno graphic design couple both wearing European glasses, a busty German woman working in the Financial Centre, all want a little cocaine.

'They're a very nice couple,' I overhear a thirtyish woman who looks like she's somebody, an actress or Bjork or something, say about us to her younger boyfriend.

And indeed we are — a nice couple. At least, we're a nice-looking couple.

Alwyn has long curly brown-blonde hair. The spiked stud protruding from beneath her lower lip drags that lip down so that she always has the appearance of pouting. She looks petulant or arrogant or stupid by turn.

29th March

My agent calls from Berlin. They're missing me at the Sniper Bar. I miss them too. Do I want to do a Friday residency in the Sniper for May, June, and July? Yes, I do.

1st April

'You must think I'm a fool, Alwyn, if you think I believe these stories about endless fucking trips to Galway, you're crazy. I've

Joe Ambrose

seen you around Parnell Square and you've been seen in clubs all over town with some band guy called Liam.'

Her face is suddenly beautiful and intelligent.

She laughs at me to my face. She walks away. She has nothing to answer for. Her life is her own.

A black wind blows down Grafton Street. I wrap up tight. I shrug my shoulders.

2nd April

I pick up a girl called Eunice. I give her the poor mouth and the next thing you know we're in a taxi heading for her place.

Eunice has wild red female-poet hair but I don't let that fool me. She pulls out her favourite awful albums and I inspect her shelves — her stuff — her books, her trinkets. She is all kind of left wing, talking to me about a scandal involving the Sandanistas. Eunice works in a editing facility house, where she's doing a project putting the entire Irish national archive of movie shorts onto a website or something. I don't give a fuck, I just nod along like I'm interested. Her apartment in one of the new places up behind Rathmines Rd. I don't fuck her, don't want to, I hope she doesn't want to either. She is relatively silent, has a well decked out spare bedroom which serves as her computer room.

I've lost Stan, lost my friend. Chan is a grey-haired woman, no feline. Alwyn is a a tough American realist, not my friend.

I sleep well. When I wake it's lunchtime and there's a note beside the electric kettle saying Eunice went to work mid-morning, where the food is, that all I have to do is pull the door after me, that if I need to crash there for a few days she'll give me a key. Her number at work.

I turn on the radio to RTE I. The news is on, cheesy Final Countdown-ish synthesizer riffs punctuate snappy American-style

194

news coverage. The big story is a fishing boat in trouble off the Kerry coast. A live on-the-spot report comes in from a reporter in a helicopter which is in the sky directly over the boat.

I'm sitting drinking tea, talking to Eunice on the phone, eating a messy ripe pear. The news says a house burned down in the Coombe last night. Two people killed with others seriously injured. Foul play is suspected — a drug-related incident. Eunice says she must get back to work, she'll see me this evening, goodbye, the news finishes, Liveline surrenders the airwaves to a pervy priest who says he molested twenty-one boys in 1982.

In the name of the Father, the Son, and the Holy Ghost?

'CANAL BANK WALK'

I am standing in an oblong metal box, six feet high and eighteen-inches-by-eighteen-inches wide. There is almost no light at all in here. I can't sit down on the metal seat because my knees hit the wall in front of me. There are about twenty of us boxed up like this, in this modern, efficient armoured van. I have been guessing our route since we left Kilmainham Jail. I think we are about half way down the quays, probably opposite Guinness's.

Somebody down the back starts screaming:

— Guard, sometin's burnin', I'm tellin' ye, ye better let us out. I'm serious ye stupid cunt, lemme out.

Now the whole van is going berserk. Everybody's kicking and screaming, including myself, because now I smell smoke, and I'm in a small metal box, handcuffed, and there's three good quality locks between me and the outside world. The van stops and the side of my box opens. A big bogman face looks in at me:

— Don't get out. We're just lettin' some air in.

Anonymous voices sound out from the other boxes:

— Guard, are we on the quays, d'ye mind if I run over te de Esso fur a pack a smokes? I'll be right back.

— Guard, run over te Thomas Stree' and get us a qua'ter, I have the money up me arse, I'll take care o'ye when ye get back, ye stupid mullah cunt.

The door of my box closes me into the darkness again. It sounds like an ambulance has pulled up. Somebody's being taken out. The van moves off and I continue my imaginary journey through the streets of Dublin.

Finally we get put in the holding cell in Mountjoy. It's a relief. I'm never happy to be put in a holding cell, but I'm goin' to jail anyway, so the sooner the formalities are over, the sooner I get to bed. There's about fifteen of us in the cell. Everybody's tired and tense, but underneath there's a numbness at the realisation that you've been caught, you're in jail, and there's nothing you can do about it.

I recognise Billy Cox. About two months ago, he nearly took my eye out with a Stanley, in a fight over twenty pounds. I got away with a small scar on my forehead. I hear someone ask him what he's in for:

— Cuttin' up a knacker.

— Whatche do da for?

— He had tree grand sterling on 'im. I said I knew a chap across the fields who'd change it for him. I took out a blade, an' he wouldn't gimme the money so I cut the fuck ou'er 'im. Somebody saw what was goin on, and called the ol' Bill.

Billy is the old fashioned robber. If he had to, he would kill you, but if he has no need to, he won't fuck with you at all. I'm glad I gave him the twenty pounds.

The holding cell is in the base. The base is clean and new. New walls, prefabricated fixtures, smooth. Hi-gloss urethane paint, yellow and green. All the edges are defined and the lines are straight: ceiling, wall, door frame, floor. Twenty cells; four men to a cell and a toilet with a door in each.

It was built for the sick people When they realised that half of the prison was dying of AIDS, they figured it would look bad if it were found out that these people were living in third world conditions. So they built the base, and a new medical wing. Now it's only the healthy prisoners that have to live in third world conditions.

A big, pig-faced, red headed screw comes into the holding cell and calls my name. He gives me a copy of my Rights as a Prisoner handbook and escorts me to cell number two. My two cell mates nod at me.

— Howaya?

— Howaya doin'?

I'm doing great. I'm in jail. *It's all going according to plan*, I think to myself.

I introduce myself to Declan. Declan looks terrified. He's not a criminal, as such. He's in for repeated driving offences. I suppose the judge wanted to scare him, and it's working. He was sent up to B-wing, the main remand wing, and he lasted about two hours before he ran to the Governor, begging to be sent back down to the base. He spoke to me with dilated pupils, of the animals on B-wing.

— They were all on drugs. They just wouldn't leave me alone. I just couldn't stay there, he said.

My other cellmate is an average respectable criminal, in for possession of stolen goods — twenty eight microwave ovens, or something like that.

At about nine o'clock the third cell mate arrives. Skinny and very intense. He grimaces as he lowers himself into a chair. His face accommodates this grimace with ease. He is all pain. I know his face well, from bars and street corners, weddings and roller-discos. It changes from the face of a friend to the face of an assailant, in a moment. And when that happens, when he sees that you are scared, he'll keep on smiling like a friend, because he is enjoying being cruel. Cruelty is not something that he practices occasionally to keep his reputation, it is something he does because he needs to. Monkey's charge is attempted murder; he stabbed a bloke four times. He must have been a very lucky bloke.

— Are ye alright? Says one of my cell mates.

— No, says Monkey, me bleedin' side's killin' me.

— Wha' happened te ye?

— I wen' on fire by accident.

— On fire?

— Yeh, in de van on de way over. I was fuckin' fleutered. I

don' even remember; dey told me I must a bin settin' fire te meself wit' a smoke.

— Ye mean ye actually were burnin'? said the other cell mate.

— Yeh. All me clodes were burned off on dis side. I've no skin left nearly – I'm all ban'ages underneat'. Yeh. I knew I was going down, so I got fuckin' locked. Den – an I don' remember how dis happened – but I wen' over te de Chancery – after I got sentenced!! The fuckin' eejits didn't even notice. I came back and said, take me to jail.

As he talks, his legs cross and his hands wave about. He has forgotten his pain, and it's clear that Monkey is glad to be back. Then he focuses on me:

— You look like yer from a good family, wha are ye doin' in here? Drugs, right! On da fuckin' heroin, are ye? — What's yer charge?

— Possession and supply!

— Whata ya take dat shite for, destroyin' yer body!

At this point it would be honest of me to point out to Monkey, that he is the one who got so drunk that he didn't even notice that he had set himself on fire. But I don't. I don't want to get into any arguments with any attempted-murderers at the moment. I've just noticed that I am getting sick. I lie down and get to sleep easily because it's that yawny beginning of the sickness and there is still some valium left in my body.

I am awake, it's four o'clock. I'm back. Back from the high and its residue. It's just me now, in the dark, in the cell, in my body. There are red lights flashing all over, but I have nothing to use to stop myself from speeding head-on into the sickness. The door clunks open. They all get up. Were they sleeping or not? Had a bleedin' great night's kip. Slept like a log, and all that. They have great appetites. They prowl the breakfast tables hungrily, chewing and swallowing in their imagination – lovely grub ... very tasty ... tasty grub. I drink a lot of coffee. I need to consume something but I can't eat. Back to the cell. Clunk.

Clunk!

— Rec. Anyone who wants to go out to the yard, line up. Fall out!

We make our way though locked doors and stairways and locked doors to a spiral staircase that is the centre of the prison. It runs from the ground floor upwards, with the wings spoking out from it. When we reach the yard I breathe in the air like it's filling my whole body. Everyone walks for a while when they first get out, and they all walk in an anti-clockwise direction.

I see Martin sitting on a bench with some people. Martin was caught with three thousand E's down his pants at the Dun Laoghaire Ferry Terminal. Three thousand little disappointments – sorry kids, ye'll have to just get drunk tonight. Ten pounds an E: one pound for the E and nine pounds freedom insurance: the cost of human effort. We could ask for fifteen a tab to ensure a continuous supply but the competition would cheat. Commerce. He already has six drug convictions, so I expect that no matter how good his solicitor is, he'll be going away for a while. He's a good guy but he never had any idea of self-preservation.

Git's there too. I am glad he's there because he's real hard and he's well known. I have found it very practical, in this business, to have a few friends like Git around me.

Halpo is another one I like. I'm not saying he wouldn't rip you, but he'd want to be desperate to do it, and in that case I'd probably sense it. He's found out that you make more money in the end if most people trust you, and he gets to look like a decent bloke as a bonus. I give him twenty pounds for a Napp that's supposed to be coming down from A wing this afternoon. When I hand him the twenty, my sickness doubles. My gut wrenches and I wonder if I am a sucker.

— Alright, I'll see ye back in the yard layter, he promises.

203

— Kelly, yells a guard. The medic'll see ye now.

I am flooded with anticipation — they're going to give me my Phy, thank God.

I feel like I have a spoon full of yellow bubbling heroin in my hand, and I can smell how good it's going to feel.

— We can't give ye any Physeptone today because . . . and the spoon drops all over the floor of a dirty toilet.

I'm back in the yard when they call me again. Yer goin' up to B wing. C'mon, get yer stuff. I dump my stuff on the floor of my new cell. I'm on my own, thank God.

Back in the yard, Halpo comes up to me.

— It's not here yet. The bloke who was supposed to bring it down with de laundry couldn't get down, because de laundry wasn't done or somtin' like da. But it's alright though, because the laundry has to come down sometime, an' he has the Napp an'all for ye.

It's such a given that these things never work as planned. Who made the fuckin' rules? I hate you.

I'm at my breaking point now, and I'm only two days into the sickness. Being sick has been a part of my life for years now, but I never had to go through it like this before. Now it is a straight two days. If I had a simple heroin habit, two days would mean that it was nearly over and most of the hard work would have been done, but I have a much worse habit than that. I'm addicted to virtually everything. This is not unusual in Dublin. Most of the people I know have a morphine/methadone/valium habit. When I'm on these drugs, I feel normal, so they have become just a good foundation for the other drugs I need to use to get high. To get high from heroin in these circumstances you'd need at least two quarters and there's no guarantee that it'll work and it definitely won't last. Two or three Napps would be a better bet, but it still won't turn you on. And you can drink Phy all day long! So forget about that. In the end you find by drinking and taking more pills you can at least put yourself in a stupor. It's at this stage that you lose all your friends, get barred from everywhere, and hang around either Baggot Street canal, or Ballyfermot.

Two months ago I robbed a pharmacist who, amongst other things, had a lot of barbiturates that he must have been collecting since about nineteen seventy-one. I've been getting high on them since then, so now I have the biggest pill habit in history, along with all the other stuff. The methadone is the other vicious one. It has taken me years to find out what happens when you take that amount of drugs, and two days to find out what happens when you don't take that amount of drugs.

It's seven o'clock and I'm watching a Steven Segal movie during rec. Steven is beating the shit out of a lot of guys, and so everybody is happy. To my left, a few jovial prisoners get their matches out and go to work on some Mullah who has fallen asleep. He catches fire. I'm impressed with how well he burns. He wakes in a violent fit of slapping and spinning and falls over the front row. He sits there in shock, almost looking for comfort from the eyes of the front row. One of the front row gives him a kick in the head and he scuttles back under the TV. Someone offers me a joint and I refuse. All I need now, is to smoke some hash and I'll be on my way to Dundrum in a strait jacket.

I am on my own in the cell. Solitary. I like that. Most of them prefer the company and I agree, you can have a good laugh, but then it's a mandatory eighteen hours a day, with another person. I prefer the company of my dreams, my nightmares: in my sick sleepless twenty-four hour day, these are the places where I live.

This is the end of the second day, and it feels bad. Real bad. Like hell. I burn. I turn towards the wall, the rubber wall, and scream inside, beg and squirm. I hear the door close at eight o'clock, and within about one minute I have lost all patience and I'm ready to scream from the claustrophobia – twelve hours until that door opens up again. I don't scream. I don't really move at all. I have learned that it makes no difference at all which way you lie. Where would you stop if you started shifting. End up climbing the wall. Better go in a different direction. Inside. Find a better position inside.

Skinny hung himself with sheets, from the bars in the window, and it was a success. I look at the window to see just how he did it and estimate how far his feet must have stopped short of the floor. What kind of shoes did he wear? I picture his feet in white Mountjoy sneakers swinging six inches from the floor against the yellow wall.

The glassless iron grid casts bar shadows on the ceiling. The walls have no definition from the countless layers of paint on brick. They look unreal. They look asylum. Victorian. The blue light goes on. I like that. It suits the illness. Peaceful and allowing the mind to wander. Baby nightmare blue. Do you remember floating in the deep end with your breath held. Deep under the sea, motionless, isolated. If you could breathe that water and stay for a while, with big black eyes, looking at the ceiling.

The emptiness is overwhelming. They are only two sounds: the occasional scream from another wing and my heart beating. When I hear my heart beating that way, it makes me think how it's just a thing inside me that does that, like a motor, and so how easily it could stall. I wait for each beat. It makes the silence deafening. Then it sounds like myself. It's my heart doing that. It makes me think too much of myself. I go to places where I seldom go because I get lost there. And when I feel I am going there, I panic and try to think of anything else, and that only makes me more afraid – please, anything else but that old thought, that thing that was in the cot with me, that enormous thing, that was there when I was sick, when I crawled into the bathroom to get away from it. I could hear it coming up the corridor. It was cold in here. I locked the door and I leaned back against a wall that was cool and damp. And when my temperature dropped, there was no one there but me. The mattress is soaked in sweat. My eyes are full of sweat. They are swimming in it. All the pain is going away. My body is numb and soft and moving. There is blood running from my eyes to the floor. It trails off the edge of the mattress into thin strands of red that disappear in the air. My skull is soft. I can push my fingers into it, like I was a new born baby. Liquid is running out of my ears and my pores. I hear it dripping on the floor below. It drips slow, like glycerine from the lowest point on my mattress and falls into a pool. The floor is a pool of this stuff. I am losing all this liquid. It stops dripping and I sit up to look at the floor below. It sits down there, clear and bright and moving around by itself. I run my fingers through my hair and it breaks off, dry snapping. It looks like old spider web in my fingers. I step down into the floor and look at my body. There is no life at all in it. I pinch the grey skin on my arm and it comes off in my fingers like drying putty. I rub my fingers together and bits float off into the air. Some of it goes in my eyes. I rub them and they feel like rusty old iron balls in the scrap yard. Little showers of brittle scales shake from them as I blink, and float out in front of me. I don't want to breathe the bits in. I put my fingers in the crack between the door and the frame and try to prise it open but my fingernails separate from my fingers like the shell of some food that you remove in a nice restaurant. I force harder and the bones snap with a dull sound, inside the putty. I pull them off and shake away the bits, they are no good now. Old dry finger bones, throw them away. I dig the stumps into the gap. I pound on the door with the stumps. I have no arms left now. The bits are in my face, they are going into my lungs. I am suffocating dry. I fall on the floor and try to drink up the liquid, but it runs away from me. Come back to me. Shoot me with heroin. Soak me in valium.

I lie there. My eyes are open, mostly.

Twelve hours later the key turns in the lock.

Twelve hours in my body.

The door is open. There's prisoners out there. I go out. I am a prisoner.

They open the big door at the back of the wing and the wind blows in through the bars. It blows up from the canal, past the traffic and the old people walking. It moved the reeds over the water, climbed the wall and blew through the bars to come to me. It says: you are in here now and only the cold wind comes to meet you in the morning. It brings with it an old sentimental memory of me at twenty-one years of age, walking a girl home, along that canal. When the cold air touches my skin the dirty perspiration in my armpits burns like I am sweating petrol. It burns cold and cruel. I am as cold as the dead. The wind must be getting inside my flesh. It has torn all of the warmth out of me, like a bereavement. It howls into my lungs and comes out colder than it went in.

I have now lost everything that there is to lose. All the little boys have grown up. They stopped coming out to play a long time ago and went home. This one didn't know when to stop. They are safe in warm beds with their girls or their wives: their bodies warm and comfortable. They have the smell of fresh linen and coffee in the morning. Their feet step out of the shower onto a clean shiny tile floor. They are clean. They are good. I am not like them. I turn away from the barred door. I face the breakfast line. I face them. I walk into my role before my body wilts, leaving only a pile of grey clothes on the floor at the back of the wing.

I am imprisoned. They got me. Perhaps it might not be so bad if I were not so utterly sick. I am in the worst place in the world to feel like this in, the most appropriate place, and I have to look like I don't feel like this, like I am strong, like I am hard. And the odd thing is that I do. I am. They don't notice where I came from any more. Babyface, grey leather and dead eyes. I look in the mirror and I see that I have become so different.

— Ye look fuckin' freezin', he says. — Have ye no coat? C'mon, I'll give ye one. I follow him up three tiers, all the way to the back. The cell is warm. He takes the coat off the heating pipe that runs through all the cells. I put it on and for a split second I am freed. Like being born into warm water. Then the escape subsides and the relief becomes moderate. His cell is cosy, homely. Thanks.

Breakfast, they say. What – all those eggs make me scared. What do they weigh? Where do they go? Pushed into hard scarred faces. Chewed in bitter mouths. Pushed back out into steel pots in the early hours of the morning. Slopped out in the same sink we wash our trays in.

I have to try to eat, so I line up and get some cornflakes. Hot jugs of scalding water. Take that in the face. I wonder if they have the temperature control that accurate. A lot of shuffling greybodies, like school, more like school than ever I would have thought. Some went to the university, some went to the bank, and some came here. And they're happy with their choice. They feel important in here. Bad boys. The Dublin School of Armed Robbery.

— Kelly. Ye have a visit.

Niamh stands out from the line of hard faces on the visitors side of the partition. She's young and she's still pretty and soft looking. She will lose that soon, like everybody who uses heroin. They all end up looking hard and cruel, especially the girls.

— How are ye?

— I'm okay.

— What's it like?

— It's alright. It's just that I'm so sick.

— When are ye up next?

— Two weeks.

— And what does your solicitor say, who do ye have, Hanrahan?

— He says I should get bail. It just depends on whether I can get the money or not. I called my parents. I think they'll help if they have the money.

— Is your mother very upset?

— Yeah. I suppose. Does Sara know where I am?

— Yeah, I told her. I'm sure she'll come and see you soon.

— Here, hold onto my hand. I have some valium. I thought ye might need them. I'll bring you in a Napp and some money on Thursday when I get my labour. I'm broke right now.

She slips me about six valiums in a piece of tissue. I put them in my mouth and look at the guard. I chew them. I never thought such a horrible taste could be so good.

She's sliding. For a person from her background, just visiting someone in prison shows this. Soon she will slide a little further, I hear rumours from the girls at the clinic about her. She'll be sitting on this side someday. In fashionable culture, there are all kinds of dabblers, and then there's people like Niamh, who you just know can't stop it from taking them too far. That's why she's the only person to come and visit me. She's just like me.

— I have it for ye! It's gear, though, is that alright? Come over to me cell at lunchtime and I'll give it to ye.

At lunchtime, I go over and get two bags of heroin in my hand.

— Do ye need a works? Hold on.

A young guy comes in. I recognise him as one of the Hutchinsons — an unfortunate family: all thirteen of them turned out to be drug addicts.

— Here!

He hands me two pieces of blackened plastic. This is the barrel and the spike that have been wrapped in pieces of plastic bag and then shrink wrapped with a flame. This makes me think that it's likely that the works has only recently been pulled out of an arse somewhere on this wing, but I don't care, because I'm sick, and anyway, better get used to it, because in here, everything illicit has been up someone's arse, somewhere along the line.

— Be careful of that spike, don't wreck it, they're hard to get in here. He stands there waiting. I cut some gear for him. Halpo doesn't take any.

As I rush back to my cell, I realise that I have no spoon, no citric or cotton.

Having heroin means nothing if you can't get it into your arm. Portion pack jam top for spoon: orange juice for citric; toilet roll for cotton.

I make it to the cell just as the guard is about to close the door and guess what: there's a fucker in my cell. They must have known that I was buying gear and put him in there on purpose as a sick joke.

Put one of those CPAD/criminal/provisional types in there with him, see how he likes that. Cause that's what he looked like to me; like he was going to step right up to me and say:

— Howaye, my name's Christy. I don't care what bunk ye have or what ye wan te do. I just don' wan te see ye doin drugs in this cell.

— Howaye, he says. Peter.

— Howaye, Johnny.

— Yer from the North, I say.

— Aye, Belfast.

— Ye on holidays.

— Aye. He laughs. Just a short visit, I hope.

— Yeah, me too.

I start setting up behind the door, next to the piss pot. That way if a screw looks in, he won't be able to see exactly what I'm doing. As I fumble about on the floor, the awkward conversation I'm making with him gets more awkward. He's saying nothing about what it is that I'm obviously doing, so I say:

— Eh, I think I need to use the table for this. Do ye mind?

— No. Go ahead. Each to his own, is what I say.

I make a little cone out of the metallic jam portion cover. I wipe the jam out of the container and squeeze an orange into it. Pure orange juice, I decide, be on the safe side. I have nothing but warm tea to use to try to clean the works with. I dip my little finger in it and leave it there for a moment, trying to decide if it's hot enough to kill even the most vulnerable of germs. I'm imagining if my finger was a germ, what would happen to it, almost burn my finger, a cell now – very thin walls ... might not survive.

As I pump up my veins Peter continues talking with me as if I were buttering a piece of bread.

The spike hovers above a vein and I say to myself:

— There is HIV in this works. I am sharing a works with the whole prison, but I don't care. I am probably going to catch HIV, but I don't care.

211

The spike is so blunt that I have to stab myself like a murderer to break the wall of the vein. I make many attempts. Blood is running all over me. Then, I draw it back and there it is: blood. Blood and orange juice in the barrel. A direct connection to my heart.

That sweet, dull comfort of heroin, in my legs in my guts in my eyes. Nothing matters now: I might have HIV, so what. I might be in here for eight years, so what. I've ruined my life. So what.

Lana Citron

'THE CRAIC RUN'

Definitely more than a chip on my shoulder that load bearing me down. I picked the four of them up down by the entrance of the Central Bank on the edge of Fownes Street, spilling forth no doubt from some dingy hole of this fair city.

Darrell, Nigel, Richard and John relax back on the comfort of a thin plastic red cushion and mothball tartan rug introducing themselves before they mounted. Very nice to meet yous Lads, lovely to make your acquaintance.

'Are yous right?'

Darrell was the worse for wear, already lipstick marks on his face, Nigel left a stream of his urine racing down the pavement and Richard distinguished himself with fresh blast of beery vomit while John was content enough to sway slightly to and fro and shout out some meaningless obscenity.

Only have to register the Brit twang of their accents to rear off wildly in the long direction. We'll just take a minor detour, reroute to an extra few quid. Call it a guided tour if you will, all part of the service, see clients like to feel they're getting their true monies worth.

The rest of their group managed to hail down a cab.

'Lads I'm only taking four of yous,' said the driver adamant (did they think the eight of them would fit into a Ford Cortina?), putting his foot down and off they raced while nag here trots at little more than walking pace.

To pick up a punter, a loaded oul punter, and they're almost there cause they've broken into 'Molly Malone' intermittently sticking their heads out to cheer on the local talent or anything for that matter and the next thing is they're giving me a rendition of, 'In the Name of Love'. Aren't I the lucky one!

A cyclist jets out to overtake me while I'm already totting up me sweet reckoning and I hoof like heels down Dame Street for me feet are in shreds, I won't be dancing the Fandango this night.

It's gone I am by the clock on Trinity and the city is teeming, steeped in a sea of midriff and a haze of cheap perfume. Tiger cubs are on the prowl and little lionesses purring, hoping to sink their claws into something meaty. Not that I'm one to begrudge anyone a good time, it's just that I'm working so it's kinda blatant and in your face.

Everyone out in search of the craic.

The real stuff.

Soft furry opener.

Do you come here often?

Only when I get lucky.

Legless warriors on the hunt, quick on the draw, inflatable rifles squashed up sweaty ready, to bullet squirt at any given target.

'Bullseye,' shouts Darrell cause he's just gobbed on the window of a parked car.

They've come over for the weekend in celebration of Darrell's last bid for freedom. Stag night and it's an injustice to the animal, I'll warrant there's little grace in their horn play. Darrell's been collared, lassoed into oblivion, she'll have contrived the whole thing. Before he knew it there was a diamond on her finger, the very one she points at him backing him into a corner. I can't tell you how many Darrells I've picked up since I've been doing this, how many best mate's coaxing them on.

He's getting married in the morning, well not quite yet.

Paul say's it's about attitude, humour them, remember they're human after all, fallible like.

'So when's the big day?'

The reluctant groom answers. 'A month from now.'

You have to strike a happy medium see Irish eyes are smiling cause I'm only being friendly.

Doing my patriotic duty for God and for country, you've got to keep the myth alive. Paul says this to me all the time and he's been at it a fair while now, the stories he could tell, he should write it all down, there'd be money in it for sure.

'Having a pleasant ride lads?'

'We hope to.'

'Handsome blokes like yourselves, you'll not have a problem in that department.'

We're heading to, 'where it's at'.

Now geographically speaking it's on every street corner hidden beneath an absorbent cotton gusset. So Lesson Street it is, they've heard about it any-roads. The bargain basement of credibility where they'll be certain to bump into a gaggle — in for it of hens, flappin' their arms to the latest '80's chart toppers. See what's good for the goose is good for the gander. Don't get me wrong, I'm not sexist, the women are as bad, the shrieking out of them, all dressed up to the 99s, flaky characters at the best of times. Tight white mini's, sweaty chaffing thighs, brimming breasts to dip and nuzzle, listen show me a halfways decent filly and I'd buck as good as any boyo no mistaking.

'Look at the legs on that boys,' the vomit one declares sticking his fingers in his mouth to bring up a howling wolf whistle, eh steady now lads or I'll tip yous over and heads turn in unison to a group of pussy pretenders. Looks can be so deceiving these days and the he-girls run over to us, giggling, 'take me big boy', showering flower petals on the blokes in the grand manner of theatrics their lot are so dedicated to. Not to be outdone the lads rise to the occasion, oh yes we have a show on the road for the groom-to-be is now wagging his manhood in their painted faces and they're actually blushing and I'm hoping he's not about to anoint them. Well, well, what do you know but the 'girls' didn't expect that and they've gone all coy their mouths suddenly resembling their pleasure domes, their manicured hands clasping either side of their cheeks, oohing and ahhing like they've never come across a dick-head before and I extend myself forcing Darrell to fall back in the small slipstream I've created.

We leave them squealing, 'bad bad boys, not bad at all,' tottering up Grafton Street to further delights in store, which fortunately we are forced to forego.

They're laughing now pleased with their moment, clocking it so they can tell their mates all about it back home.

'Is it you first visit?'

Turns out they've all been before, Nigel, a newlywed had his stag weekend here eight months back.

'Wicked mate, pisses on Londin dis place does. Luv it.' says Nigel.

'Top craic,' adds Darrell.

Nigel of the weak bladder illuminates further, 'Last time we were ere, we met these burds Aoife and Noreen, had such a laugh wiv em, then today we're walking up wos the name of the street, Clonmel . . .'

'O'Connell Street.'

'Yeah that's right, wiv the piss hag in the baff, I mean we ain't even left our bags in the hotel and who do we bump into, only Aoife.'

'Mental,' observes Darrell.

'Fuckin mental,' Richard clarifies.

'I mean wos the chances of that then?'

In this city probably fairly high.

We approach a gang of glue-sniffing gurriers by the lights on

Nassau Street, plastic bags sticking out of their pockets. It's tragic they're only young, early teens probably drifted down from Thomas Street end. If there's a substance I despise it's that, seen one too many of my ilk die for it. It's gone all quiet in the back, the lads havin' run out of lyrics and conversation, look bored. The thrill of travelling at five miles per hour is wearing thin, Kildare Street not being the most buoyant of people places although culturally speaking it's promising, the Dail is duly pointed out but they're not interested.

They ask if I can shift gear, speed up. The cheek.

Look Lads I cant-er go any faster, I mean carrying the weight of them is no easy thing not at my age.

I round the corner on to the Green, past the Shelbourne Hotel. Jimmy stands on the parkside waving cars in to the empty spaces like he's some kind of corpo attendant. I used to do the runs with Jimmy till his cataracts got too bad, that's when Paul stepped in. Paul is his son, we go back a long way, he has a special fondness for me. Just the other day he bought me a bonnet, for a laugh like, it not particularly to my taste what with the pink ribbon, but it's the thought that counts.

'Are all of yous from London?'

John the quietest of the lot say's he's partly Irish.

And what part would that be?

His mother's mother's mother grew up in Sligo. Whose didn't!

Oirish by default and it's very fashionable these days to be part paddy stock. Denotes a historically acceptable pedigree but what would I know coming from a true bastard breed.

Nearly there, taking the corner, easy does it. Their friends are waiting for them, waving in unison chanting out the groom's name like he's a footie hero, 'Dar-rell Dar-rell'.

I come to a stuttering halt and wait for them to dismount.

'Nice one, lovely jublee, been waiting an age mate, come on.'

They fumble in their pockets but divisive mathematics is slowing them down and it's left to the most sober to sort and be sorted out later.

The damage is done, fifteen quid eased from out of Richard's pocket.

'Have a great time now, enjoy yourselves.'

'We will for shure for shure,' spouts Nigel trying out his newly acquired accent.

A couple more hours down the road and I'll be finished me shift, unharnessed and feeling equine once more.

'They weren't so bad wha?' and Paul pats me on the shoulder.

'You're a fine one,' he says.

I whinny in agreement, one of the best Paul, and he rubs me nose and pops some sugar in me mouth.

Sweetest of reckoning, away into the night, momentarily loadless till another punter hails me services and that's how it goes.

Imelda O'Reilly

'STOVEPIPE'

Possessed, Gonny searches the roads for Stovepipe. He has had shrunken shoulders for months. Day rests on him like a rug he cannot shake off. Night is a dark wind, he fears the bite. Without Stovepipe the world is lead.

Gonny puts his hand in his pocket to find a small round conker, a gift from Stovepipe. He rubs the conker when the ache croaks. 'I always dream badly,' Stovepipe had said. As the conker is wearing thin, he tries to save the 'worryfear' only for the desperate ache.

He remembers Stovepipe. The long journeys at night where they'd talk until the dawn broke, lying together like a pair of fried fish fingers. Spliffs tumbled through the night to stain the moon further. How they quarrelled about sleep. 'That's why I hardly ever sleep,' Stovepipe muttered. 'What's the point, if you always dream badly?' 'I don't remember my dreams,' said Gonny, 'What's the point, if you don't remember?' Gonny would never dream Stovepipe away. Stovepipe had large dark circles under his eyes, two upside-down half-moons. In fact, Gonny didn't know much about him except he didn't feel him to be a stranger.

Stovepipe came into town one Thursday when the sky was a black grey. He headed straight for a little pub buried round the corner of the back street stottle, called the Crooked Rooster. Two large brown wooden doors, barely attached to the hinges, lay at the entranceway. Inside a dim lit area stood to ponder. Stovepipe arrived shoeless with a dark beard hanging. He carried one brown leather satchel. 'I know that head,' Gonny thought. He found himself unusually familiar and comfortable in the presence of Stovepipe. He didn't understand. One look in those eyes and 'yes, I had come out of the cave' Gonny thought. Stovepipe sat at the bar despondently, and ordered a shot of Bushmills whiskey, his voice raw with the crooked dark corners of night. Gonny remembers his green eyes sinister, hidden deep. Gonny felt a smallness he couldn't explain.

Stovepipe opened everything in a different way. His weathered feet cold, bruised neglected abandoned. Stovepipe just shook his head and said, 'I've come a long way.' His hair hung around his face clumsily, in a huge horrible grunt. Gonny liked him. He couldn't imagine not knowing Stovepipe, sitting until light bled through the windows listening to banter between pauses. 'Are there rooms to rent?' Stovepipe asked. 'I have a spare room if you want,' Gonny said. They both understood. Stovepipe kept the brown leather satchel close to his feet like a pair of warm woolly socks.

Stovepipe went home with Gonny on a Thursday night in a black cold grey sky. He lived outside the village down a potholed lane in a small green house. 'Mind the green man,' Gonny mumbled as he ploughed through familiar hedges. Tucked under a bramble of bushes at the bottom of the lane, Gonny's house stood. He had two rooms, a bedroom and a living room. 'It's dark in here, I like the dark,' Stovepipe said. Gonny pulled down a small bottle of whiskey for special occasions from behind two tiny red curtains.

'Even the door is drunk,' Stovepipe grumbled. 'Any chance of a spliff?' Gonny stoked the fire, 'Nah I smoked the last today,' Gonny said. 'If not we can grow some.'

When Stovepipe opened his brown leather satchel, Gonny looked in disbelief. Gonny's eyes peeled as he took out a colourful box. His face changed, the grey lifted and he felt a deep connection to this gesture. Carefully Stovepipe placed the box on the floor. 'Do you know this?' Stovepipe asked. He produced the board game LUDO. 'The object of the game is to get HOME.' Gonny was amazed how he treated the board with careful attention. They proceeded to set up the game and Gonny was given the colour yellow.

Stovepipe scurried in the pits of his pockets for dice. He felt Stovepipe go into a different realm. The game began. It was subtle but he felt the difference. Darkness clawed the curly-wurly of a moon. It was odd, Stovepipe was sharing a deep dark secret. Gonny felt the exclusion of a silly board game. 'No,' he replied, 'you don't understand.' 'What?' asked Gonny confused. 'I used to play this with my old man.' Gonny fixated on the LUDO board.

HOME   HOME

Stovepipe was obsessed with the LUDO board. The board slept at the bottom of his bed. 'On my seventh Christmas I received the game. My old man played LUDO,' he said. Gonny felt alienated by the board as his eyes drifted toward the ceiling. 'Are you listening?' asked Stovepipe. 'I'm listening,' said Gonny. 'I was blue and I won,' said Stovepipe. 'I never remember anything after that. He fecked off, he lived in the same house but he came and went. The kitchen chair became his throne and he only opened his mouth to silence us or shout.' He became haunted. Stovepipe had this horrible dream repeatedly. 'What was the dream?' Gonny asked.

'I dreamt my old man would chase me round the LUDO board and I could never escape. I woke up and he was hitting me.' Gonny's left knee started to shake uncontrollably, he tried to stop but it was useless. Stovepipe stopped. He noticed Gonny's knee and foot, he placed his hand on his knee and arrested the shake. The silence clunked like the tail end of a tin can. Stovepipe continued, 'I'd wake up in a cold sweat screaming and there it would be at the end of my bed, the

LUDO board
staring me blankly in the face. 'It's become a bad wart I can't get rid of.'

Gonny started to walk around the room, fidgeting with dust on the cracked sunken floor. Stovepipe didn't understand. 'What are you doing?' Gonny shook his head limply from side to side, terror covering him. He turned around and saw Stovepipe struggling to hide a tear. He felt overcome and at first it bothered him. He couldn't open to Stovepipe's pain, even though it lay hidden deep.

Immediately Stovepipe started to pack up the game. 'What are you doing?' Gonny asked. 'I cannot play,' he replied, 'I just like to set it up and put it away.' Gonny felt confused although he shouldn't force any kind of response. The brown leather satchel was closed and night bruised white into the morning. The light opened gently and Gonny's hand rested in the hand of Stovepipe.

Gonny never opened his house to a soul. The village thought him peculiar. Gonny kept himself to himself and worked down at Kramers antique shop at the end, the very end of the potholed lane. Stovepipe cooked and cleaned managing to water the spliff plant daily. Quickly they developed a rhythm like two hands of a clock ticking together loud. Stovepipe perfected the details of daily activities. He learned how to make stew and baked odd looking rock buns. They lived together, they dwindled under each other's skin. Slowly they began to pick up habits off one another, Stovepipe always ate with his hands. The use of a knife and fork was foreign to him. Eventually Gonny stopped using his knife and fork. The evenings stretched like two white plump bodies. Gonny left early in the mornings to sell furniture although he was slowly beginning to resent Stovepipe sleeping through the morning. The rock buns became less frequent and activities like hard skin developed as corns.

Days turned into weeks. Gonny and Stovepipe lived together quietly in the green house. Every night, Stovepipe opened the brown satchel and set up the

LUDO board   HOME

only to disassemble it again and put LUDO away. 'No home tonight,' he muttered. Gonny found this very strange, but didn't say anything. It was a quiet occupational custom that comforted Stovepipe in some way. Inbetween Stovepipe would light his spliff and watch the sky become a giant aniseed ball. 'Why don't you ever play LUDO?' Gonny inquired.

'Approaching the board is like opening and closing possibilities, home, death, life, winning and losing, it's a continuum meat and potatoes. Choose or be chosen.'

Gonny stared out the window blankly immersed in thought. 'He saw a round baked potato in the sky?' This question poked at him daily and the more Stovepipe became involved with the ritual of

LUDO

the more Gonny became obsessed with the burning question . . .

LUDO.

Questions gnawed, the dream pressed . . . LUDO LUDO. This discourse between Gonny and Stovepipe became a silent ache. Gonny found himself inside Kramers antique shop dreaming of the LUDO board. He wanted to explore it more. Tonight when Stovepipe was asleep Gonny would go to the board. He left the shop as usual at half five on the dot. Gonny felt happy about this private plan. Stovepipe is lazy thought Gonny. He felt bothered by his indifference to the mess around him.

Come Thursday, Gonny lit the fire and Stovepipe sat lazily watching Gonny move round in a quick scurry. Stovepipe looked out the window. 'It's been raining soft all day,' he said.

'I hadn't noticed,' Gonny replied.

'How could you not notice?'

'Easily, I could not notice easily.'

'It's a dark night.'

'Yes it is,' replied Stovepipe. 'I'm moving on.'

Gonny stopped in his tracks and his face became white. 'Why?' he asked.

'It's time, something is different, I feel it,' Stovepipe said. 'The air has changed.'

Gonny felt strange right down to the pit where all his angst comes from. He became silent. He felt a burning sensation, under his gut. Stovepipe noticed this, and moved closer to Gonny. 'I had this dream last night,' Stovepipe announced. 'You've changed toward me haven't you?' Gonny put his head down in shame. He felt it throbbing. 'I feel like you're watching me when I'm asleep.'

'You're out of your head!' Gonny shouted. Stovepipe took a few steps back. He had never heard Gonny raise his voice in this way before and it surprised him. 'You have become filled with hate and resentment. I feel it,' Stovepipe shouted back. Gonny sat down, 'I have never felt so confused, so stay tonight and we'll sort everything out tomorrow.'

Stovepipe stoked up the fire, put a few more pieces of coal on and began to open the leather satchel. Gonny lay on a blanket on the floor and proceeded to get the bottle of whiskey from behind the curtains. There was no going back now. The concept of betrayal had enveloped his head. He would wait until Stovepipe fell asleep. Stovepipe had a few drags from the spliff, a few glasses of whiskey and he dropped out like a bullet.

It was pitch black outside with the smell of a damp fog. Gonny felt an instinctual thrill. He moved slow at first, hoping not to wake up Stovepipe. Everything seemed far away and a stealing tenacity came over him. He felt very seduced by the leather satchel and the mist of a dark secret about to open created in him a wild sense of confusion. All the lonely dark lanes of bumpy country roads became one, he felt the darkness in a way he never had before and a deep swelling came up from the pit of his stomach. Stovepipe rustled under the blanket, Gonny swallowed a lump in his throat and as he touched the satchel, he had visions of caressing Stovepipe. He imagined he was coming closer and closer . . . Thoughts span round in his head, crazy mad thoughts, of no longer having Stovepipe around. He took out the

LUDO   HOME

board and scattered the pieces about on the floor. Gonny started to masturbate, touching himself slowly at first, brushing up against the Ludo board. He furiously began to fantasise, imagining that the board was Stovepipe. He rustled back and forth and the darkness pervaded him as a giant shield, whacking back and forth crazy muddled images in his head, euphoria, dementia, mountains, climbing toward an inescapable closeness. Suddenly he forgot himself. Stovepipe turned over, disgruntled and disturbed. Gonny surged round, the LUDO board colours began to float, blue yellow red green, red green blue yellow. Gonny opened his eyes only to realise that Stovepipe was coming toward him. They tumbled and grovelled on the floor. 'For fucksake,' Stovepipe muttered. Confusion choked the room like smoke. Stovepipe struggled to stand but he tumbled to the floor. Gonny turned around to see Stovepipe about to hit him with a chair but he moved backwards to avoid Stovepipe and pushed him away. Stovepipe slipped and knocked his head against the stone fireplace. After the thud, not a sound crumbled. The panicked air broke before Stovepipe could breathe or utter another syllable. Stovepipe, motionless lay dead on the cracked floor.

Night blistered wild in the silence. Stovepipe's broken head, a

LUDO BOARD   HOME

Gonny's face burned the crooked sky like a flagrant mop without a bucket.

ACCIDENT BLACK SPOT.

Gonny smashed the small round conker. His 'worryfear' was crushed. LUDO, winners losers home. The giant aniseed ball smacked home.

black
black
black
spot . . .

Robert Cremins

'THE MILE HIGH CLUB'

Of course, none of this would have happened if I'd flown business class. But unlike ninety per cent of my travel, this trip was personal: I was slipping back home to Dublin for what was really a glorified long weekend, mainly to see my mother, whose nerves were getting bad again. It was getting close to push-back time. I was sitting in a window seat behind the wing, looking out at a rainy mid-May evening at JFK. In the aisle seat was this scruffy but teddy-bearish guy in his early thirties wearing a baggy, wrinkled black suit. He looked itchy for a cigarette already on this no-smoking flight. I had him pegged as an out-of-work actor. Not my type, shall we say.

The middle seat was empty. I wasn't sure whether to regard this as a blessing or a curse. I'm a tall girl, and leg room is as much an issue for me as it is for most guys. It would be nice to be able to put my feet up after dinner — I was sure the Bear would be gallant enough to give me the extra territory — and snooze until Shannon, but at the same time I didn't want to give him the wrong idea by tucking my toes right up against his arse. As it was, that empty space between us was opportunity enough for him to start chatting me up (I'd already caught him doing a sly reconnaissance of my figure when I was putting my carry-on in the over-head bin). Talk about being a captive audience. Why didn't the nuns at St. Monica's warn us about the scandalous intimacy of air travel?

When I saw a young woman my own age — her clothes, like mine, casual yet tasteful — coming down the aisle, keeping a close eye on the row numbers but gracefully avoiding protruding bums, feet, and ill-stowed bags, I found myself hoping she was my intended neighbour. I was not disappointed. She opened up our bin and found a niche for her carry-on (the Bear surreptitiously checking her out). Our man then scrambled awkwardly out of his seat to let her in. The captain was on the PA telling the cabin crew to arm doors and cross-check.

'Looks like you just about made it,' I said, gratefully.

She turned to me — I think it was then I felt the first quiver of recognition, something to do with the faint flaws in her well-scrubbed face, like that effect in painting where early mistakes reappear on an old canvas — turned and seemed to be about to give me an easy, pleasant answer when she hesitated. Darts of surprise in her hazel eyes. Quickly followed by the smooth working of her jaw, as if she were sucking one of those boiled sweets they used to hand out before take-off on the flights of my childhood.

Then she said, 'Connecting flight from Dallas was delayed over an hour. How are you, Gemma?'

I think the first thing I said in response was a soft, 'Oh my God.' And then, after a long, uncomfortable moment, I added, 'It is you. Brona Boylan.'

Her smile had become as Americanised as her accent. 'Yes, it's me.' She turned her attention to the safety demonstration.

Suddenly the prospect of sitting beside the Bear for the next six hours didn't seem so bad. I hadn't thought about Brona Boylan much in the last seven years, the seven years since we'd done our Leaving Cert and left St Monica's. When she did come to mind, it was, to be honest, usually as a criterion for social rejection, as in, 'Well, there's the Brona Boylan of this firm,' or 'She's being a bit of a Brona tonight.' Of course, I didn't share this analogy with anyone (although I was sure there were a few charming characters from our class, scattered around the first world, who would). But this sharp, serene, fairly attractive young woman sitting beside me, now deriving some subtle, obscure amusement from the life-jacket lecture, was not the Brona Boylan I had known, or ignored, at school. This was certainly not the Brona Boylan I expected. Her smartly bobbed hair was a small miracle in itself.

Even though I'm a veteran flyer, I have this thing about take-off. When the engines begin their ever-rising whine I never fail to taste my mortality. As our giant plane rumbled down the runway, I never felt more vulnerable. It was all I could do not to reach out and grab Brona Boylan's hand. I glanced at my neighbours. The Bear was busy scratching his nose. Brona's eyes were closed, her face in deep repose, her hands lightly folded on her lap. Was she heavily into yoga now?

When we were up to cruising altitude, and Brona had surfaced from her trance, the Bear began his inevitable chat-up routine. His opening gambit was not very promising, 'So, this plane is headed for Dublin, right?' If I had been Brona, I might have cut him off there and then with the one-word answer the question invited, but she took it as an opportunity to start up a proper conversation, though not one that she encouraged for too long. When the chat reached one of its natural pauses, she began browsing the in-flight magazine. We were now allowed to move about the cabin, and the Bear took this opportunity to slip away to the bathroom. Any woman would have seen what she had done: sent him a clear signal without making him feel like he'd lost face. But not every woman could have done it so well. Her timing was perfect.

We hadn't said another word to each other since take-off, and it was obvious that she was not going to initiate any further conversation, even if that meant crossing the dark Atlantic in silence. So finally I said, 'So are you living in Dallas now, Brona?'

Instantly she put down her magazine and gave me her full attention. 'Fort Worth,' she smiled. 'The other part of the metroplex, as they call it. I can never take that word seriously.'

I smiled jaggedly. 'And what are you working at?'

'I'm an architect.'

'Oh, that's right. I did hear you got the points for that at UCD. Have you been out there long?'

'About a year. I got one of those Conboy visas.'

'Same here.'

I left it at that. This was turning into an interview — was she ever going to ask *me* a question? There had been more give-and-take in her conversation with the Bear. Just when I thought she was going to go back to reading an article about Indonesian basket weaving on the Aran Islands, she finally asked, 'So what brings you back to Dublin at this time of year? I'm more used to bumping into people, old faces, going home at Christmas time.'

'Me too. This is an unexpected pleasure. Actually I'm going back for a party, a house-warming party.'

Brona savoured a smile. 'All the way back to Dublin for a house-warming party?' I laughed stiffly and shrugged. 'It's a big house.'

'Anyone I know?'

Here I hesitated. In the absurd lie I had hastily manufactured it was somebody she knew, or used to know, who was giving the party in their new phantom home. But something compelled me to say the name, perhaps because it was horribly plausible, 'Denise Nelson.'

'Oh,' she replied. Did I detect there the first tremor of vulnerability since she'd sat down beside me? And was there something deep down inside me that got a little thrill from that? It was time for me to ask another question, 'And why are you going home yourself, Brona?'

All her vitality returned in a rich smile. 'I'm not. I'm getting off at Shannon.'

I was still trying to figure out how I might discover what business or pleasure she had down the country without appearing too curious, when I saw the Bear coming back down the aisle. We both saw him, for Brona turned to me and gave me a knowing smile. What we both knew was that the Bear had obviously been doing more in the cubicle than powdering his nose. Or maybe he really had been powdering his nose, or some such similar operation, because he was now walking as if he alone on the aircraft were experiencing severe turbulence. A few heads briefly looked up and took note of him as he stumbled past, checking the row numbers with glazed eyes. They must have assumed he was drunk already. The cabin crew was busy with the drinks trolley at the far end of economy. The Bear collapsed into his seat, leaned forward to give both myself and Brona a goofy, reassuring smile, and then slumped back and slid into a blissed-out condition.

'Lucky for some,' I mumbled, and Brona looked at me and giggled. At last there was something between us, something we could share without complication. I began to relax, if not exactly enjoy the flight.

I'm not usually a big drinker, but when the trolley eventually came to us, I took up the steward's suggestion of an extra bottle of chardonnay for dinner; the Bear was just about coherent enough to pull down his tray and ask for two helpings of whiskey; Brona got nothing stronger than a spicy tomato juice. By now the TV screens had come to life — a documentary about blind scuba divers in Belize was the first offering — and Brona was lost to her headphones. She took them off only to request the vegetarian option for dinner; I hardly touched my chicken, but did manage to wangle another bottle of wine from the steward when the trashy trays were being collected. The Bear had refused dinner altogether and had now fallen into a deep sleep.

It was a tempting state. When the wine began to pull me down into a warm slumber, I did not resist, but instead pulled down the plastic curtain over my window, blocking out the Atlantic twilight, and reclined my seat as far back as it would go; my body was now, for better or for worse, on Irish time; it did feel like the early hours of the morning.

As far as I can remember, my sleep was laced with frequent dreams, but fleeting, insubstantial ones — scuba-diving documentaries. The main feature must have come much later. When it started I found myself playing a surprising role. I was not my younger self, as I should have been, nor anything like her;

I was not typecast as the pretty and competent girl, high enough on the pyramid of popularity for comfort. I was, essentially, Brona Boylan: this dream was based on a true story.

Establishing scenes make it vividly clear that I am — what was the term we used to use? — the class spa. Embarrassments on the hockey pitch and in the changing rooms. Embarrassment in the classroom. Acidic whispers about my hair and skin from Denise Nelson and her clique, who are popular in a certain unloved way.

Then comes the extraordinary morning, the morning of the Mass of the immaculate conception, when Denise takes me aside just before we walk into Spanish class and tells me that the time has come for me to stop being so stand-offish to everybody. What do you mean? I ask. Well, isn't it obvious? she says. You're not going to get anywhere socially, you're not going to be invited anywhere, until you make the first move. What should I do? I ask. That's obvious too, she replies. You have to throw a party, an end-of-term party. Invite loads of people from the class, and we'll help you invite the boys from Berchmans.

So I cycle home after school, thrilled by Denise's plan but anxious that this might all be a scheme to take advantage of me, and delicately put the proposal to my gentle parents after dinner. To my surprise, they take it up enthusiastically, and before I quite know what's happening, invitations are being written and caterers are being called.

Now jump cut to a typical suburban dining room, table laden with seafood lasagna, salads, and garlic bread, chairs pushed back against the walls, and me sitting on one of them, dressed too formally, hair over-done, with a look of bereavement on my face. I know now what's going on, although my parents are still waiting innocently for the first guest to arrive. Denise Nelson has spread the word that nobody, under pain of social death, nobody is to ruin the joke by turning up at Brona Boylan's 'party'. The Berchmans boys have been advised. The real party is happening somewhere else. The plan has been flawlessly executed. Nobody is coming. Nobody.

I woke up feeling confused and headachy, the lingering image of lukewarm seafood making me feel nauseous. There was a chance I was going to be sick. In any case, I had to get out of my seat. Brona still had her headphones on, studying the closing credits of the feature film. The Bear wasn't in his seat.

'Ex*cuse* me,' I said, a little breathlessly.

She didn't hear me, or didn't react.

'Excuse me.'

She heard that for sure, and let me out into the aisle most graciously.

Five people stood in line before me outside the toilet: I had hit the post-film rush. And while the threat of throwing up subsided greatly once I was able to move about, I now had a poignant need to go to the bathroom. But I found that every time I took my mind off my nagging bladder, I started to think about that bad dream I'd just escaped from. The physical discomfort turned out to be preferable.

But only just. Mutterings soon began up the line, ones that I readily concurred with: whoever was in there was taking their own sweet time. I had a feeling who it was and — after a lot more swearing and door banging and threats to call the cabin crew to forcibly open the door and at least three more minutes — I was proven right: the Bear emerged, looking as if he'd just experienced a religious vision. He proceeded serenely down the aisle, immune to the sniping and contemptuous glances of those he'd kept waiting longest. As he floated back to his seat, the woman in front of me turned around and said, 'That fella looks like he's on drugs. Terrible what goes on in these aircraft toilets. And then decent people have to go in and use them afterwards. They should really do something about it.'

'They should,' I nodded, trying not to smile as I envisaged separate toilets marked Decent and Deviant. But then I remembered Brona, and felt the queasy pulse of my bladder again, and there was no further danger of me laughing.

I took my time in the bathroom too, spending most of it looking in the smudged mirror and thinking. I had to say something to her.

This situation was absurd, outrageous. How long could we go on pretending that the past didn't matter, that we were creatures of the present only? Soon we would be landing in Shannon, and I couldn't let her get off the plane without us having really recognised each other in the first place. I had to say something to her. It would make me feel better.

When I stepped back into the cabin, the lights were back on and breakfast was being served. Back at our row I found Brona deep in conversation with the Bear. Or rather, she was listening sympathetically as he tried to explain something profound in a slurred, slow-motion way. It took several moments to get their attention, and in the end I had to virtually climb over their legs since the Bear tried and failed to get up.

Back in my seat, I raised my plastic curtain and was hit by the sharp light of the fresh sun we'd found; I lowered it most of the way again. Neither Brona nor I ate much of our breakfast; I drank the orange juice in one go, parched after the wine, but couldn't touch the food; Brona donated most of hers to the Bear, who was now seized with a serious case of the munchies. Whatever he had been taking in the toilet, I wanted some.

Finally, with the trays cleared away once again, and the captain coming on the PA to wish us good morning and tell us how close we were to the Irish coast, Brona ended her mission of mercy to the Bear and got herself ready for landing. Now was obviously my chance.

'Brona,' I began gently.

Once again she was instantly all ears. This made it more difficult for me. I looked away from her momentarily at the rectangle of blue light on my other side, then back at her, though not quite making eye contact.

'Brona, I'd just like to say that I know it must have been difficult for you, very difficult at times, when we were in school. Especially the time you gave that party and . . . and I was giving another party that same night. I guess you knew about that.'

She turned away and looked at the headrest in front of her. For the best part of a minute I thought she wasn't going to say another thing, that she was going to freeze me out, and that this was how we were going to part. But then, not quite looking at me, she finally replied, 'Of course I knew. Of course I found out.' Now there was a voice I recognised. 'And I don't have anything more to say about it. Unless you do.' Without really thinking about what she was saying, I replied, 'Oh, no. No I don't. That was it.'

Now we made eye contact, as she smiled confidently again, the smile of a successful young architect from Fort Worth. 'Well then we won't say anything more about it.'

We hardly said anything at all after that. When we landed at Shannon there was some small talk about the weather and the greenery, which even the Bear contributed to; he now appeared to have been restored to something approaching normality by the miracle of a double airline breakfast. Brona was on her feet as soon as the seatbelt sign was off, part of the small minority not going on to Dublin. She didn't turn to look at me until she'd got down her hand luggage. Once again, the American smile.

'It was so nice to have seen you again, Gemma. I always really enjoy bumping into people from St Monica's.'

I didn't know quite what to say in response.

'And it was great to see you too, Brona. Enjoy your . . . holiday. Hopefully we can stay in touch.'

'Oh, don't worry. I'll be back in your life.'

She turned around as soon as she said that and started walking down the aisle. I looked over at the Bear. He shrugged, as if to say he had been soberly analysing her throughout the entire flight and still couldn't figure her out.

An elderly man who did not remove his flat cap took Brona's vacated place. The flight over Ireland was quick and silent. My mind finally turned to the reality, the private reality, that would be waiting for me on the ground. My father was coming to meet me, possibly my sister, definitely not my mother, though she would certainly be awake already and waiting at home. At least I had got some sleep.

I had come home so often that the ritual of arrival in Dublin made only a muted impact on me. Up until baggage reclaim, I was on automatic pilot. So when the Bear came up beside me and said hello, I almost jumped. Back on the ground, he was looking no more disreputable than when he had got on the plane at JFK, with the exception of slightly longer bristles. Maybe he'd had much practice crossing the Atlantic in oblivion. Maybe, just like Brona, his timing was perfect. He was making me feel like a novice traveller, an unaccompanied minor. Just as I saw my suitcase, he reached down and grabbed a bulky black bag.

'Well,' he said, 'maybe I'll see you in the air again.'

I made an effort to smile. 'Yes. It was nice to have met you.'

He seemed happy with that non-compliment, and walked away. I turned back to the carousel just in time to catch my case. The Bear didn't see how close I was behind him as he walked through the green channel of customs unchallenged. For a moment I was sure he was going to be, for standing behind one of the examination tables was a very serious and alert trio of officers.

What happened after that I can hardly bear to think about, though I can't stop thinking about it. I suppose that was the point, *her* point. When one of the officers asked me to stop, it simply didn't register; I assumed he was talking to somebody behind me. That, I'm sure, made things worse, made them even more suspicious, substantiated their hot tip. At first I thought I was going to have to suffer the hassle and humiliation of having my luggage opened on the examination table. But no, the officer who politely stopped me in my tracks asked if I wouldn't mind following them. My luggage was carried for me. I was brought to a small room with pitted plywood walls. Waiting there was a short female officer. The nausea returned. I'm not sure if it was caused by the woman, or the ranks of small black holes, or the fear that I might indeed have something to hide.

They were very professional, if professional can mean both tactful and ruthless. They examined everything that could possibly hide something else, and that meant *everything*, including myself.

At first it was almost ridiculous how anything at all connected with my sex was left to the female officer. I was mainly irritated as I watched her take apart my make-up and scrutinise my toiletries, even my birth control wheel. But as she sifted through the plastic bag of dirty laundry I was uncharacteristically bringing home, I could fight off the advances of humiliation no longer. Later, towards the end of the forty minute ordeal, when they informed me that it was regrettably necessary, she was naturally the one to administer the full strip search.

When I finally emerged into the arrivals hall, my absolved suitcase packed more neatly than when I had left New York, I found my despairing father still waiting. It was then that I burst into tears, knowing that I would have to give some explanation of the injustice that had been done to me, without revealing the name of the girl guilty of setting me up.

P-P Hartnett

'GOD LOVES YOU'

Eire
West Europe
Initials: IRL
Time: GMT
International Access Code: 16
International Country Code: 353
Language: Gaelic, English
Area: 70,284 km² / 27,137 sq mi.
Population: 3,547,000
Capital: Dublin (Baile 'Atha Cliath)
Religions: 88% Roman Catholic
Climate: Mild but wet.

The concrete bar and surrounding austere slate-grey tables received a blast of machine-ice smoke. For atmosphere. Intricate designs of laser beams and neon, reflected in the mirrored walls, lit faces that receded into infinity.

It was packed. Packed. Like a deathtrap firetrap. Some great-looking fairies, tanned to all tints of bronze. The music was too loud, talking was not worth the effort, so they stomped in a uniform, pulsing undulation, doing all variation of aerobic — but nonchalantly. Stomped, all in the same kind of mood, hardly looking at one another but eyes everywhere — swivelling chunkily to the left and right in a tight fashionable style they'd all picked up somewhere. Maybe there. Every bit of the nonchalance was fake. Fake as the coated denim, misted PVC, rip-stop nylon and light-reflective tape.

While heads swayed (hair slick with a jar-load of gel), while heads bobbed and jigged, while heads veritably bounced with all that jogging on the spot . . . so itchy-footed . . . dilated eyes hunted. Waiting to see, waiting to be noticed. Working every jackboot beat like they had some kind of investment in the music industry. Clownishly intense animals in mating desperation, all puffed up and on display. Few seemed to be genuinely enjoying themselves. (This is normal.)

Occasionally two nineteen-year-old boys looked into each other's eyes and smiled. All they knew about each other was how the other looked. It seemed enough.

Each had noted the other's pierced right eyebrow. Each had spotted the similar (almost identical) designs scratched with ink into the other's bulging right bicep. Each was rather tall, almost six foot, with deeply-etched, masculine but highly sensitive features. From close-cropped skulls to whitest smiles they were . . . could've been twins. As a snapshot it could hardly have been more beautiful, one of the two of them thought. Unless, of course, one of the two of them thought, a camera could have got an aerial view shot of them hours later: asleep together in sunlight. Like brothers, little urban brothers.

Getting to know each other between glugs of . . . *Spa* . . . they would 1) whisper into each other's ears, then 2) laugh outrageously.

As I held him I could squeeze the sweat from his vest where it clung down the channel of his back. So I took his drink from him, and pulled it over his head in one.

PJ: Got any diseases I need to know about?
Jim: No, just crabs.

Together: Ha ha ha.

PJ handed Jim his bottle. He unscrewed it slowly, with a grin, looked away. Looked down along and through the transparent plastic of that bottle toward the dance floor and then, swallowing, gave — too close to be in focus — a look of tenderest trust.

Good bod. Hard bod. Gym bod. Not bad.

Of the two, PJ was the more experienced. Jim was just a lad. Maybe, PJ thought, maybe I've caught myself a virgin. A virgin who needs to be shown the ropes, step by step. A young fella who needs to be handled gently. Fat chance.

PJ was surprised when Jim paid for the cab back to PJ's place. Made a change, made him cuter still.

The sex wasn't bad: they'd both got goosebumps at some point. It was memorable. One of those real scenes, though a bit on the quick side. Showbusiness, but real.

They did it in the shower. Within seconds of HOT being perfectly mixed with COLD, PJ's throat had been stripped of its soft, protective mucus. It'd be sore by tea time.

Jim had come quickly. Too quickly. Shame. PJ had wanted that cock up him, up his mancunt.

On a double mattress, between white sheets, they lay side by side. Together. Almost identical. Both tall, both slim, each with a knee dragged up sideways — face to face. Like a couple of queer honeymooners. Balls slipped over each other kind of thing. Cocks slid across dark curls kind of thing. Icily regular. Peaceful. Peaceful tanned flesh. Photo by Bruce Webber kind of thing.

It would be a while before they awoke. Both had taken something stronger than glue exactly an hour before they met. Swallowed with the same bored know-how in the same bar. Same cute bar boy, same pimply-faced dealer. PJ would change position once, being face down for an hour before waking.

At one point in the night I think he was having a falling dream because he suddenly jolted as if he'd caught himself just in time.

PJ remembered the hand at the base of his neck which was cool. He'd been having one of those falling dreams where you jolt awake before ... Splat. That hand had given him a soft, little clock-wise rub which said everything was okay, that someone he'd just met cared. Probably not the case, PJ thought, but a nice touch.

What PJ didn't remember, something he had no recollection of at all, was the touching that had gone on while he'd slept — in the last hour. Touching that was so soft it would have almost tickled had he not been stoned. Touching by fingers, detached from hand, detached from wrist. Fingers which as they had started to run up and down his back had almost scratched initials — a name that would have sparked a small moan.

PJ

There he slept, still and content. Jim felt left out. No cuddle.

Fingers attached to hand, attached to wrist — controlled by a sudden impulse — pulled that covering sheet right down. Off.

How very trusting he was, Jim thought, fast asleep with a stranger. Wallet on the table, keys in the front door, car keys on a hook marked **CAR** in the kitchen. How very trusting. Happy enough after the slapstick sex. Naked, face down, as if ready for a rectal examination.

Propped on an elbow, Jim scanned that body beside him without blinking. There was too much of it to see, to touch. Too much information, so he began fixing on details. All those bits and pieces which are usually forgotten — ignored in favour of eyes, teeth, nipples and cock. What his eyes zoomed in on was the little fold of flesh at the armpit. Then a mole. A scar, base of spine. Little op by the look of it, maybe three years back. A silvered scar.

Again Jim got up, moved. Like a thief.

It was almost a push up position he was in, above the sleeping body. Lowering his left ear down, Jim listened to the beating heart, then the intestinal music of rising bubbles in PJ's stomach and the slow, deep breathing of those lungs.

It was a much fingered textbook arse: rock hard and boxy (with the edges rounded off) inward curving dips creating cute shadows on the sides. Empty eye socket of an arsehole. Bullet hole of an arsehole. Corrupt belly button of an arsehole.

'What's a nice hole like you doing in a boy like this?' Jim whispered, his joke of the moment.

Jim imagined his tongue disappearing up that arsehole. One finger, two fingers. His cock. Three fingers, four. His fist. Forearm. Launching up after a perfect pike dive, with snorkel and flippers, to explore the soft insides.

I'd probably need a torch, too.

Jim wanted to lower his tongue down. Force in. He began to grind the sheet.

How many people had fucked on that white cotton sheet beneath them? he wondered. The mattress underneath felt penetrated with the presences of many. Sweat, saliva, sperm. All those bodies, jerking off. Gasping. Farting. There was more than a hint of CK and spilled poppers coming off it.

'Hey,' Jim whispered.

Once again fingertips started a touching that was so soft it would have woken PJ had he not been so out of it. Touching by fingers, detached from hand, from wrist, from mind.

PJ

Like someone wanting to cover up an incriminating word with a mass of graffiti, Jim wrote in meandering squiggles:

GOD LOVES YOU

Smiling, Jim put that finger into his mouth. What he tasted was PJ.

LIKE FUCK HE DOES

What if each letter erupted in sunlight like a tattooist's most colourful inks? Jim thought.

The saliva soon dried.

Jim began to shake the bed gently with a silent fit of giggles.

GOD LOVES YOU

The rectal mucus soon dried.

Again, the bed began to gently shake.

LIKE FUCK

The silently spurted semen took a while to evaporate up into the air.

That finger tasted more of Jim than his sleeping playmate. And, in the silence, that finger tasted delicious.

Skin more used to tingling with sunburn and dried sea salt was tightening with neat coats of spunk, rectal mucus and glittery spit. It was the tightening of that precious skin which woke PJ.

'Penny for your thoughts,' Jim whispered.

PJ smiled, said nothing. Winked. Made for the bathroom. Jim's eyes closed. Alone, he'd be able to sleep. Snatch five minutes worth.

PJ knew it had to happen, knew it was going to happen some day and — late on a Sunday morning — there it was. Happening. All over his head. Just the way it had with his father back in 1968. He was going grey. There. Look. 1-2-3 . . . Shite. Loads. Like guitar strings, they were. Poking out.

His brow knitted up in the shape of an anus. (He'd never have done that had he known.) Going grey: at nineteen. Nineteen! It felt like a good deal had come to an end, like cheap rent or free food.

'Age does worse things to a queen than it does to a woman,' he confided to his reflection.

Nine out-of-nowhere silver hairs, all a precise three millimetres in length, were carefully plucked with rusting tweezers. Sometimes PJ pulled a perfectly good black hair with the offending new growth, and when he did that it hurt.

PJ turned on the HOT water tap and began shaking a near empty can of shaving foam. Abiding by the rules he'd set down aged sixteen, PJ obediently half-filled the sink with steaming water, then began splashing his face. Chances were that in half an hour he'd be shaved and showered and in a fresh shirt. His day was, of course, ruined: going grey at his age. Not for the first time he cursed his genetic inheritance.

After a few seconds his face was white — very Father Christmas. He'd long since mastered the tricks of wetting the face, angling the blade and arching cheek with tongue. His father had never shown him. No, and he'd been too embarrassed to ask that busy busy businessman. Uh-uh. He'd picked up tips galore from the shiny pages of magazines such as *GQ* and *Attitude*. All the dos and don'ts. Techniques so beautifully illustrated with the aid of bright-eyed, smiling, nipple-chewed models in snug-fitting boxer shorts.

Bristles softening, he began to pee. It was this almost musical tinkling that woke Jim.

PJ cut himself in that first contact of blade to skin.

'Christ all fuckin' mighty!'

With a splash and a few seconds firm pressure that cut became nothing more than a scratch which had given up bleeding.

Two scrapes down, bang bang against the sink.

Two scrapes down, bang bang against the sink.

Rinsed in the blade's wake, his cheeks tingled — were smooth. Felt good. PJ took a long look at himself in the mirror. The relationship he had with his own reflection ran deeper than anything ever experienced with another person. He hadn't noticed Jim, standing behind him in the frame of the door.

Again, he rinsed. This time with cold.

Yes, PJ thought: done. Then he spotted Jim, and that look in Jim's eye.

They kissed, breathing into each other. PJ's face was a delight to lick. The tip of Jim's tongue briefly probed that tiny wound for a moment. PJ's mind was already on the journey over to Dollymount within ten minutes of this guy's departure. Jim's fingers were heading toward an arse suddenly yawning for cock.

PJ turned. Bent in front of the mirror. Looked at his (almost) twin.

'Go on.'

'Not without a condom,' Jim roared.

PJ sniffed hard and flounced off to put on a pair of fresh, snug-fitting paisley boxer shorts. Paul Smith. Ugh, he whined internally, he's too — much, you know? He hoped he wouldn't have to suffer the usual smalltalk.

PJ sniffed again. Three weeks is a long time to have a cold, isn't it? he half-thought.

Breakfast was coffee. Black coffee.

'Sorry,' PJ said, 'outa milk.'

PJ didn't take milk. Dairy products, he'd read somewhere, slow you down and he was watching his weight. He didn't want to gain after the sudden recent loss.

Black coffee was sipped in silence.

They shared Jim's last cigarette.

PJ didn't talk about film school. Jim didn't talk about his father's shop in, oh, wherever it was. Absolute silence — except for that brief exchange when Jim stood by the window.

'That your car down there? The silver one?' Jim had asked.

'Yep,' PJ had replied. Bored/pleased/bored.

'Lovely.'

Within just one disco beat of saying that, Jim's brain was spelling out D-I-C-K-H-E-A-D.

Phone numbers were exchanged out of decency. PJ's were on a card, Jim's in a scrawl on the back of *GCN*.

Within a minute of the shopboy being out of the place — history — PJ was dumping the body temperature paisley boxers in the laundry basket, an item of clothing which landed on the night's Levi's and vest. Faint traces of makeup were on the neckline. Something PJ defiantly/defensively referred to as bronzing moisturiser.

The bed sheets were hauled toward him like fishing nets, towels retrieved from the spacious bathroom as if on fire. Then he dusted, hoovered, douched in the shower.

Wearing a grey ribbed t-shirt tight enough to show the tone and definition he'd worked hard to gain in a number of gyms since the age of fifteen, PJ looked in the mirror. A familiar, dull ache somewhere in his bowels was starting up again, as if a well-trusted anaesthetic were wearing off. Maybe he'd pick up in the dunes. If not, he'd hit The Boilerhouse or Incognito around four.

PJ decided against jeans. He slipped into a little something from GAP with pockets on the side of the leg.

Brief attention was paid to something he hadn't noticed before on his right foot. On his big toe. A spot, small, like the stain of a crushed grape — purple. Must've banged it, he thought, as he pulled on mountaineer-style socks. Done it dancing.

Q: CATs, trainers or Timberlands?

A: Trainers.

Q: The new over-complicated Nike ones?

A: The new over-complicated Nike ones!

Again the mirror helped PJ with his all important full-frontal inspection. Standing back he checked himself, wolf-whistled. Blew himself a kiss.

Arena is so fat this month it looks like a phone book.

Eyebrow brush.

Wouldn't it be great to do a porno of nothing but good-looking carpenters from Cork. Or Sligo.

Aftershave.

'Sligo,' he sing-songed. '*Schli-go.*'

Just for a moment he wanted the new Ultra Naté track on, but couldn't be bothered doing all the things that had to be done before sound filled the place. So he hummed to himself a while.

Just a short while.

Alan's really good about throwing things out — if he buys five new shirts he throws five old ones away.

Final check.

'Accessorise!'

On went a thick, black leather belt and a small, worn silver crucifix.

'Yeah. Nice touch. A cute old-fashioned detail.'

Oh, New York New York, where the parties were great. Where everybody was somebody. Once again he'd gone everywhere and had lots of fun. Fun fun fun. Except that last night, at his sayonara party, where he — the host — had asked the most beautiful boy in Belgium to dance. The pretty, spoiled cute kid, just adorable, had said no. Had said N-O. Just like that. In capital letters. Such rudeness. Didn't he know whose party it was? Didn't he know *who* he was? Who his father *was*? Retard.

The first dish was fresh liver. The goose was just killed in the kitchen and the liver was taken out and cut into slices and warmed up — half-warmed by a gentle gas, and half-warmed by the goose. It was delicious.

Teeth.

Just white walls and a clean oak floor, that's all I want. The only chic thing is to have nothing. I mean, why do people own anything? It's really so stupid.

Then teeth paranoia. He'd read in *Boyz*, *OUT* or *Gay Community News* that flossing before a blow job is a no no. Even brushing your teeth. *Urgh-yuk!*, PJ thought, the very idea.

'Zip me up, before you go go . . .' he sing-songed for the ?th time.

The mirror reminded him gently: rucksack.

Maybe I won't need the umbrella, he thought. He hated the extra weight. The weather forecast was good, but he left the brolly there, lodged somewhere between sunglasses, factor 14, ready-rolled joint, CD player, pool-warped copy of The Spell, poppers, pack of three, pack of tissues and all essential mini lube.

Nothing worse than being drenched on Dollymount or Forty Foot.

Then he was all set. But he couldn't find his car keys. Anywhere. He was sure he'd left them on the hook marked **CAR**.

Standing alone by the window, PJ's forehead knitted up in the shape of an anus for the second time that day.

Colum McCann

'AS IF THERE WERE TREES'

I was coming home from The Well when I saw Jamie in the goalmouth. The sun was going down and there were shadows on the ground from the flats. Jamie had his baby with him. She was about three months old. She was only in her nappy and she had a soother in her mouth. They were sitting together on a horse, not Jamie's horse, he'd sold his a long time ago to one of the other youngsters in the flats. This one was a piebald. It was bending down to eat the last of the grass in the goalmouth. Jamie was shirtless and his body was all thin. You could see the ribs in his stomach and you could see the ribs in the horse and you could see the ribs in the baby too. The horse bent down to the grass and it looked like all three of them were trying to get fed. There's nothing worse than seeing a baby hungry. It makes their eyes much bigger. None of mine ever went hungry and I've had three so far. The baby was tucked in against Jamie's stomach and he was just staring into the distance. The sun was going down and everywhere was getting red. There was red on the towers and there was red on the clinic and there was red on the windows of the cars that were burned out and there was red on the overpass at the end of the field. Jamie was staring at the overpass. It was half-built. The ramp went out and finished in mid-air. You could have stepped off it and fallen forty feet. Jamie used to work on the overpass until he got fired. They caught him with a works when he was on the job. He complained to the Residents Committee because he was the only one from the flats on the overpass, but there was no go. They couldn't help him because of the junk. They wanted to but they couldn't. That was two weeks ago. Jamie was moping around ever since. Jamie started nudging his heels into the side of the horse. He was wearing his big construction boots. You could see the heels making a dent in the side of the horse. I thought poor fucking thing. I was standing by the lifts and every time the doors opened there was a smell of glue came out and hit me. I was thinking about going home to my young ones who were there with my husband Tommy — Tommy looks after them since Cadbury's had the lay-offs — but something kept me at the door of the lift watching. Jamie dug his heels deeper into the horse and even then she didn't move. She shook her head and neighed and stayed put. Jamie's teeth were clenched and his face was tight and his eyes were fierce as if they were the only things growing in him. I've see lots of men like that in The Well. They get that look like the only thing alive in them is the eyes. Jamie's eyes were fierce like that. He was kicking no end and his baby was held tight to him now and the horse gave a little bit and turned her body in the direction of the overpass. Jamie stopped kicking. He sat and he watched and he was nodding away at his own nodding shadow. He stood there for a long time just looking at the men who were working late. There was four of them altogether. Three of them were standing on the ramp smoking cigarettes and one of them was on a rope beneath the ramp. The one below was swinging around on the rope. He looked like he was checking the bolts on the underside of the ramp. He had a great movement to him, I mean he would have made a great sort of jungle man or something, swinging through the trees, except of course there's no trees around here. He was just swinging through the air and pushing his feet off the columns and his shadow went all over the place. It was nice to look at really. The ropeman was skinny and dark and I thought I recognised him from The Well, but I couldn't really see his face I was so far away.

A lot of the men from the overpass come into The Well for lunchtime and even at night for a few jars. Most of them are Dubs although there's a few culchies and even a couple of foreigners. We don't serve the foreigners or at least we don't serve them quickly because there's always trouble. As Tommy says The Well has enough trouble without serving foreigners. Imagine having foreigners, says Tommy. He says there's problems enough with the locals. Not that Jamie was ever trouble. Jamie when he came to The Well he sat in the corner and sometimes even read a book he was that quiet. He drank a lot of water sometimes, I think I know why but I don't make judgements. We were surprised when we heard about him shooting up on the building site though. Jamie never seemed like the sort, you know. Jamie was a good young fella. He was seventeen.

I looked back at the field and all of a sudden the sun went down behind the towers and the shadows got all long and the whole field went much darker. Jamie was still watching the ropeman on the overpass. The horse didn't seem to mind moving now. Jamie only tapped it with the inside of his heel and the horse got to going straight off. She went right through the goalposts and past all the burnt-out cars and she stepped around a couple of tyres and even gave a little kick at a collie that was snapping at her legs and then she went along the back of the clinic at the far end of the field. Jamie looked confident riding it bareback. Even though it was going very slow Jamie was holding on tight to his little girl so she wouldn't get bumped around. In the distance the ropeman was still swinging under the overpass. It was going through my head who the hell he was I couldn't remember. People were getting on and off the lift behind me and a couple of them stood beside me and asked Mary what're you looking at? I just told them I was watching the overpass go up and they said fair enough and climbed into the lift. They must have thought I was gone a bit but I wasn't. I hadn't had a drink all day even after my shift. I was thinking Jesus Jamie what're you up to? He was going in rhythm with the horse, slow, going towards the overpass, the baby still clutched to him only in her nappy and maybe the soother still in her mouth I couldn't see. There were a couple of youngsters playing football not too far from the overpass and Jamie brought the horse straight through the middle of their jumpers which were on the ground. One of the jumpers caught on the hoof of the horse and the goal was made bigger and the youngsters gave Jamie two fingers but he ignored them. That was where the shadows ended. There was only a little bit of sun left but Jamie was in it now, the sun on his back and the sun on his horse and — like it was a joke — a big soft shite coming from the horse as she walked. Jamie went up to the chickenwire fence that was all around the overpass to stop vandals but the chickenwire was cut in a million places and Jamie put one hand on the horse's neck and guided her through the hole in the wire. He was gentle enough with the horse. He bent down to her back, and his baby was curled up into his stomach and all three of them could have been one animal. They got through without a scrape. That was when I saw the knife. It came out of his back pocket, one of those fold-up ones that have a button on them. The only reason I saw it was because he kept it behind his back and when he flicked the button it caught a tiny bit of light from the sun and glinted for a second. I said Fuck and began running out from the lifts through the car park into the field towards the overpass. Twenty smokes a day but I ran like I was fifteen. I could feel the burning in my chest and my throat all dry and the youngsters on the football field stopping to look at me and saying jaysus she must have missed the bus. But I could see my own youngsters in Jamie that's why I ran. I could see my young Michael and Tibby and even Orla, I could see them in Jamie. I ran I swear I'll never run like that again even though I was way too late. I was only at the back of the clinic when Jamie stepped the horse right beneath the ramp. I tried to give a shout but I couldn't, there was nothing in my lungs. My chest was on fire, it felt like someone stuck a hot poker down my throat. I had to lean against the wall of the clinic. I could see everything very clearly now. Jamie had ridden the horse right underneath where the ropeman was swinging. Jamie said something to him and the ropeman nodded his head and shifted in the air a little on the rope. The ropeman looked up to his friends who were on the ramp. They gave him a little slack on the rope. The ropeman was so good in the air that he was able to reach into his pocket and pull out a packet of cigarettes as he swung. He flipped the lid on the box and negotiated the rope so that he was in the air like an angel above Jamie's head. Jamie stretched out his hand for the cigarette, took it, put it in his mouth and then said something to the ropeman, maybe thanks. The ropeman was just about to move away when the knife came and caught him on the elbow. I could see his face. It was pure surprise. He stared at his arm for the second it took the blood to leap out. Then he curled his body and he kicked at Jamie but Jamie's knife caught him on the heel. Jamie's baby was screaming now and the horse was scared and a shout came from the men up on the ramp. That's when I knew who they were. They were the Romanians. They were shouting in their own language. I remembered them from The Well the day we refused them service. Tommy said they were lucky to walk, let alone drink, taking our jobs like that, fucking Romanians. They didn't say a word that day, just thanked me and walked out of The Well. But Jesus they were screaming now and their friend was in mid-air with blood streaming from him, it was like the strangest streak of paint in the air, it was paint going upwards because his friends were dragging on the rope, bringing him up to the sky, he wasn't dead of course, but he was going upwards. I looked away from the Romanians and at Jamie. He was calm as could be. He turned the horse around and slowly began to move away. He still had the baby in his arms and the cigarette in his mouth but he had dropped the knife and there were tears streaming from Jamie's eyes. I leaned against the wall of the clinic and then I looked back towards the flats. There were people out in the corridors now and they were leaning over the balconies watching. They were silent. Tommy was there too with our young ones. I looked at Tommy and there was something like a smile on his face and I could tell that he was there with Jamie and, in his loneliness, Tommy was crushing the Romanian's balls and he was kicking the Romanian's head in and he was rifling the Romanian's pockets and he was sending him home to his dark children with his ribs all shattered and his teeth all broken and I thought to myself that maybe I would like to see it too and that made me shiver, that made the night very cold, that made me want to hug Jamie's baby the way Jamie was hugging her too.

Gavin Patrick Carville

'HANRATTY'S TIME CAPSULE'

Summer heat cracked the earth around the home of Bob Hanratty MP. Spike and Cathal, after ten minutes of cautionary inspection by security at the gates, sped up the driveway, eager to start. They had one hour to film the feature.

It was a peculiar idea for a television show: go into someone's house and determine their character from whatever hatstand stood in the hallway, but it's viewing figures were consistent. The house was an elegant, Victorian structure, outside of which the European flag flapped steadily against the North Antrim sky. As Spike lit the bathroom, Cathal filed through something witty to say about the marriage photo hanging on the wall. Above the fireplace a portrait of Hanratty, proud and demented, surveyed the team with contempt.

The morning had been agreed after a week chasing the old man's wife, Nessa. She was concerned over security implications and insisted they were given a directory-sized volume on areas not to be filmed, in case any paramilitary was around to catch the late night show. It left only the garden, kitchen and lavatory open to inspection. Nessa thought this agreeable, Cathal thought it restrictive. He wanted her to know that Bob Hanratty was appearing on *Let's Scope The Joint* only because Su Pollard had pulled out.

Hanratty floated on the outer fringes of Newsworthy. His recent, supposedly liberal, stance alongside his love of showmanship (coming on stage at Party Conferences to 'Eye Of The Tiger') made him charismatic on a political catwalk of beige leather jackets and grey cords. Cathal had hoped to meet him and was disappointed when Nessa announced he would be away in Spain that day, while she went shopping in Belfast.

All the rooms had been censored. They hid the alleged wife-battering rumours and coke habit. Any hint of character was burgled in furtive embarrassment. Copies of *The Prince* and *The State We're In* sat on the coffee table with their receipts still inside. There was a battalion of war memorabilia, bayonets, cudgels. A dummy dressed in Navy uniform overlooked the kitchenette. Behind bullet-proof bay window the North Sea view was bereft of sound.

'How charming.'

'He has the modesty of Zsa Zsa Gabor,' said Cathal.

'Well, whaddya know?'

Spike held up a picture of Bob greeting a clearly bewildered Daniel O'Donnell that had been placed amid family holidays and graduations.

'Classy.'

The house was producing empty responses to Cathal whose viewers expected some narrative flair. He soon realised that Hanratty's true character would be found in his Westminister apartment. Free of surveillance, of wife, the place would be scarred with poisonous details. It would be his relinquishing of power pad, cleaned by a call-girl in SS uniform and then wrecked by junkies and their dealers. This house was the ruse of gentlemanly intellect. There would be unnoticed blood in Westminister.

Out on the lawn, Cathal had a pre-rehearsal cigarette. This was the garden Bob had been filmed sauntering through the previous summer when one of the proliferating rumours of misbehaviour actually broke out.

It was reported that Hanratty had a nervous breakdown during a committee meeting. There were stories he had urinated over the desk before trying to climb out a window. The PR exercise with his wife was their way of cornering the gossip, branding it malicious, and hauling it's carcass into the night. The couple's hurt at the accusation became embodied in Nessa's one finely choreographed tear. Hanratty was of strong character and could never fall under something as weak as mental illness was the clear message. Besides, he adored the few committees he sat on. The kind that have long discussions on global catastrophe that end in battles over golf handicap.

Cathal remembered being disgusted by that, its manipulative insincerity, way back when politics here interested him. He came in from the ghosts on the lawn, their tawdry sound-bytes blown briskly away by the wind.

Cathal had sold out now, he knew that. At Queen's University this was the stuff he threw beer cans at in disgust. The tacky pap his media career was going to kill off. Somewhere, probably in Dublin where he had trained, that vocation quickly disappeared.

They did a few takes. Cathal eased into his TV double, his soft brogue the tone of a laconic navigator through low culture, picking it apart half-seduced, half-repelled. The stars taking part like the self-deprecating honesty of being made arseholes of. Their managers sweat abundantly under tunnelpaths with researchers intoning in a mantra, 'They want to appear human and interesting.' The £500 fee was so pitiful that only those woken with Butlin Bank Holiday nightmares usually appeared — or politicians looking at the everyday bloke card.

'This is out of this wo-o-rld,' sang Spike as the sun, acting as spin-doctor, tactfully draped the hedges and grass. Cathal wandered in circles, mouthing his scribbled lines. They then did the final rehearsal so Cathal said what he liked,

'This is a relaxed man, a man who likes his home comforts. I picture him snorting coke bought from a paramilitary golf buddy, or holding his legally held shotgun to his head and sobbing into the mirror before inserting a hamster in his—'

'Okay, Cathal. Let's do it for real.'

'That was for real.'

Then came the gunshot.

Spike dropped to the ground and Cathal fell behind him. Another shot sent Cathal scurrying across finding more grass but no shade. The shot's echo was drifting now with the last cries of startled birdlife.

After some moments Cathal untightened his eyes and looked past the purple spots and across the slanted landscape. From behind the long barrel of a swaying shotgun Bob Hanratty stood muttering, 'We're going on, we go forward . . . and bring the fucking camera down with you.'

Cathal and Spike were frog-marched into a nearby field.

'Move on there, fuckwits,' Bob ordered.

The seagulls cried and circled above them. Bob then told both men to stop before edging ahead. With the rifle still trained on them he kicked back grass and dirt from the ground until the sharp scrape of metal was heard. He then reached down to lift up a door set into the ground. He beckoned Cathal and Spike forward. Cathal came first to the mouth of the hole and dragged his eyes down to what he feared was his grave.

'Walk on down, now, and none of your funny business,' said Bob.

Wooden steps led into black and stench. Cathal did as he was told. The darkness seemed physical and attacked his knees and nerve. He was soon engulfed. Spike followed with Bob behind.

'Stop, now, or I'll use the gun my Father had in the war.'

The three stood in a small, terracotta-hued room. Makeshift wooden beams held the ceiling that rested inches from their heads. Bob brought the door down and drew six bolts across with a grim, puckered face and air of finality. They were sealed in and the air began to boil.

'Throw your watches on the floor.'

Cathal and Spike did so. Bob brought the gun's butt down with a splintering sound before smiling,

'Time is of no consequence.'

The floor was carpet-lined, it lead onto one more larger room that was darker still. Candles and gas lamps lined every wall, the heat and cold vying for status against the general seesawing of emotion. They stood still, no breathing. Bob's movements were unsure of direction, head hung below his arched back so his brown eyes were fixed upwards looking pained and anxious to share it. The wellies he wore looked misplaced with his tweed three piece and were plastered in mud. His hair had missed the grooming from his personal secretary and revealed his previously shy bald patch.

'Sit down, men, and take in the splendour around you.'

He pointed to Spike and the camera,

'And turn that godforsaken thing on and film something decent for the first time in your career.'

Spike took a minute to arrange his limbs in a confident way. He fiddled with the camera dumbly, stopping to inhale a sob-defying breath.

'Take your time, we've got a few years ...'

Through the view finder Spike framed each wall. There were old political campaign posters, newspaper headlines in stern, inch thick lettering. On the floor, arranged in pattern, were tins of frozen food and crockery wrapped in *The Irish Times*. Thousands of magazines and banks of labelled video tapes lined the freshly plastered wall.

'This is my time capsule, feel dizzy? By the time we're unearthed the motor car won't exist and your grandchildren will have snuffed it.'

He placed the rifle against a battered stove.

'So what's your names, then?'

'Cathal Moore ... and that's Spike.'

'I'm pleased to meet you. I'm not familiar with your work, though I'm sure I ain't missed much. I've a problem with your crowd, which I'll go into later.'

273

A media grudge, Cathal thought, he'd gone insane over that?

'Point that camera over here, now ...'

Spike turned the camera to the seated Bob,

'Got a good close up? Nice, aren't I? Right ...'

Before speaking, Bob coughed into an old, yellowing hanky, dotted with black spots.

'Now listen in and listen good. We've tried everything for this country, been to South Africa and watched their peace jealously and I've had enough of it.'

Bob coughed again densely and moved forward.

'I've seen it all. Tiny children bursting with sorrow for their missing father, who's hung upside down with his head punctured, dying as slowly as time lets him. I've shaken hands with killers who don't understand guilt or pain. Dined with clergy who've raped people. Well, this is my project now, away from those stomping feet above who are sure to crack pavements and skulls until some side feel vindicated.'

He brought up a long, brown strand of spit to drop onto the floor before resuming,

'And it all piles up, doesn't it? Imagine the funerals you've got on tape. Tonne upon acre of slow death marches, the grief as similar and paltry as the next, all eaten into the lens and the slow, revolving tape, into blackness. Each hour, every day, over these endless fucking decades — bullets sinking into arms, legs, pregnant bellies. Guns emptying their chambers into the same blackened head ...'

He halted, waved the camera to stop and rose long, craggy fingers to his red eyes. Spike looked up from the camera, then glanced at Cathal. Bob had lowered his head further. Spike took his chance and swung the camera down on him but missed. Bob leapt forward and pulled him back. They both toppled to the ground. Cathal got up and moved in. Then Spike screamed, backing off, his stomach unloading blood in quick spurts.

Bob held up a knife,

'Well and truly spiked ...'

With a thud Spike fell and crawled into the corner, comforted by futile hugs from Cathal. Sometime after that he died.

Cathal slept for an hour of strobe-lit dreams. Upon waking he sensed the room to be swaying, maybe sinking into the core. The beams twitched with time-strain. The walls had turned colour from parched reds to ancient and ghostly greys.

Bob was speaking,

'Now there's enough food to eat for six months, so don't worry on that score. I've candles, I've reading materials . . .'

'Spike is dead,' said Cathal, hoping to hear someone refute it.

'I know, but he was capable of hurting the capsule and I couldn't allow it. Listen, though. People's grief is an intermittent thing. Revulsion spreads and disappears like a hangover, it's easily sated.'

Bob dipped into the dark corner. Only forehead and cheekbones remained as light islands marooned against black.

'Look at Spike over there. A victim of a brutal attack but you don't seem concerned, Cathal. He was just another colleague who you bitched about over your coffee.'

'No, Spike was a friend.'

'You know his favourite song?'

'Let me go.'

'You know where he lived? Who his parents were? No. You didn't care, you didn't want to know.'

'What's your point?'

'Why do you want to go back?'

Cathal opened his mouth but no words followed.

'I want you to record all this, Cathal, our protests down here in the dirt. I've spent a year planning and building this thing. Gathering up papers, randomly taping the telly, as record, as evidence. It was hard keeping it from Nessa, lying to her face all that time, but she will come to accept my disappearance. She'll be glad I've finally done something to change the world and that's what we're at, Cathal. We're going forward beyond this rut. Eventually we'll be found, maybe in ten years, maybe in fifty. We may survive to give an oral account, if not, they'll have all this stuff as data. They'll be dressed in silver suits and haul us out as a reminder, as a document, so you must keep filming.'

'We'll be dead in a few days, Bob. Police will be on the scene here soon. Give up.'

'There will be no peelers coming here. This is the last place anyone will think of. We'll be found much later on and just think what they'll see, Cathal. When they unearth us from the ground what will they make of this documentation, our sacrificed bodies?'

'They probably won't give a fuck and mark it off as gay lovers or two nutcases.'

'Gay lovers? How beautiful,' he smiled. 'Just think of their interpretation, the quick spread of theory and thought, link to link as chains of conception are formed. They'll be free from traditional thinking, no pre-determined opinion to buckle or hollow out their response. Think of the new ideas rattling over our dust. This will be fresh and open reaction, like a child's. When they open this capsule we'll have recorded a testament that will speak a new language. What do you think Cathal?'

'I think too many people have sacrificed themselves. I think there is no cause worth dying for, only causes worth living for. This place has always had a despicable, romantic streak to it's politics. Big, noble gestures that are in fact macho and facile and unthinking.'

'That's good, that's a debate already, you see? A fuckwit like yourself has never spoken like that before, am I right? It's so refreshing, Cathal. These ears of mine are congested with words that feel like dead bugs, blocked with insects of passion that seemed so relevant at so many times.'

'But I can't breathe properly . . .'

'And you can do up there? Bollocks, son.'

'Bob, you're sick. You need help.'

'Why do you want to go back? Come and see the sights with me, years from now. It'll be like utopia to us lot. Why would you want to go back?'

Cathal leaned against the wall. Above, on the fiftieth floor, his editor pads across fresh fibres in the office, breathing in yawns and warm ventilation as the electro-light unpicks his migraine protection. His screams of abuse, slowly turning everyone to tears, are as plastic as the material holding him up in the air.

'*Where the fuck are they Janice, you silly mare?*'

In and out, constantly this movement through doors into scenes that seem like the previous scene.

'Bob, let me go.'

'But why? Explain to me.'

Cathal, prematurely balding, paid three quid a month to mouth banalities Royalty would think insincere. He knew he wouldn't have to do this kind of work for long. He would show his mettle, offer ideas, do something intelligent on Irish history. There were things he could do in this country that could be useful. That was a good enough reason.

'I love my life.'

'You don't, you couldn't love any existence like that. You've just conned yourself into thinking there's only so many moves. You've shed any hope for the better but I'm offering you a chance to do something, Cathal, to be a noble part of this great plan.'

Cathal croaked a final, 'I want to go back.'

But the words were numb on his tongue, they fell out like unwanted food. He had been trained to gloss over, to sanitise into agreeable commodity. Difficult words were expendable. Anything intricate could be jettisoned. Cathal had never stared into a problem's eyes and all this was panoramic, he couldn't make out its size.

The remaining space still caught in light narrowed to a small stage.

Cathal bit into the salami and chewed, thoughtful, aware that he was no longer scared of the increased dark or the mad man in the corner. Dim candle lights flickered, there was no sound able to reach them. Even the air had cooled.

'Who was the last person killed here, Cathal?'

'Spike.'

'No, above us, in the terrible troubles.'

'I don't know.'

'You ignored it, then. Well, I'll tell you. It was a twenty-year-old man in my constituency called Paul who, if you pardon the newspeak, was attacked yards from his home and beaten savagely. When they say beaten savagely they mean he was tortured for a while, they used hammers to break his legs so he couldn't run, then smashed his ribcage and left him to die in agony.'

Cathal hoped a long exhale would do as way of response.

'And, as required, my colleagues and I went through condemnation corner but you know how it is; who was this man, what was he up to? We all heard the gossip about his family and friends. He was from a fairly shitty area, his sister was in jail. Could he have warranted it? My colleagues still fall back on these speculations but I know Paul was just another innocent. I know Paul was killed because of his religion, Cathal. How vulgar is that?

'And the killers will not be caught. Dixon of Dock Green will fail to swoop down. The blood in their bathrooms will not be swabbed and used as evidence. His father and mother's days will now be dogged with their imagination. They will hear his screams repeated everyday, see his arms fend off hammer strikes uselessly. Paul's mother told me that her only hope, the thin thread of hope that keeps her from falling into insanity is that Paul would have died from the first blows. Think of that. What a hideous thing to have as a buffer against total breakdown.

'The killers' own vision of the death will be so much more awesome. They will remember his struggling fondly and with a clarity none of us could fully envisage. Two versions of that one death struggling together in the night. What do you think?'

'I don't want to think.'

Bob moved close to him,

'You must think, you must think. You mustn't let it drift, be consigned, written off with complacent words of sorrow. Something like that can't be let go of and form some vague feeling of frustration, another momento to suffering, another example on file to be glanced at. Stop scanning it and see his death, hear what the killers screamed at him as he flailed down that fucking alleyway. Think of his family's own long deaths, Cathal.'

'I don't want to think. Fantasising about that man's death won't alter things, it's morbid, it's stupid—'

'No. Paul's parents imagination will destroy them eventually. Our imagination can fight against that.'

Cathal didn't speak.

'It's the only escape route, Cathal, to confront all possibilities, to know about it. Don't you get it? Say you hear me.'

Cathal heard him. The capsule could be found and it could mean something or it could be forgotten and lost. His country suffered a disorder no psychiatrist or surgeon could cure. Blinded by the past. Deafened by the present. They stagger clutching trophies dug from the ground as guide, as God. The trophies their fathers had buried, wanting no more of them, now unearthed as traps for their children. So what if they dug up this?

'Cathal, there is nowhere for them to go. We can sink into the ground and wait; a living document, a blast of new extremes. We are too well practised at grief, every atrocity is forgotten, never seen as the last; blood ongoing, unstoppable death. This country is built on mass graves and the promise of more blood to deepen the reddened soil. Unless someone draws a full stop and starts something new—'

'What exactly?' Cathal asked.

'This.'

Bob did not say more. Cathal let his eyes fit and then love the few remaining colours trapped in the dark, let the dead air transform and tingle on his tongue and settled into the corner. Cathal raised the camera, a red light appeared, and Bob began.

Nicholas Kelly

'THE CONTINUING ADVENTURES OF GURDY O'GRADY'

My name is Gurdy O'Grady. You don't know me yet, but I suspect you soon will. In fact, if I were a betting man (which I'm not), I'd say there's an odds-on chance of me achieving moderate fame within the next twelve months. I've recently embarked on a very interesting project, you see. Those nice men and women in RTE have kindly given me the sole responsibility of producing and directing a low-budget video-documentary on the state of our beloved nation; and in particular, I'll be examining the vibrant club scene around Dublin. I've been entrusted with a Sony Handicam and I am supposed to present the commissioning editor David Barker with a fifty-six minute final cut by September 30. The video will be made up of footage in clubs, interviews with prominent people, and hopefully a little sociological analysis. I'm a one-man team and I'll be editing the project myself. Needless to say, this a very exciting time for me, and I hope it is for you too.

For my money, there are only two venues in Dublin worth a visit: Cookie's on Poolbeg Street, and the Sauna in Temple Bar. Cookie's, if you haven't been there already, caters generally for the handbag crowd, and seventies disco is generally the norm. The Sauna, however, takes things far more seriously, and prides itself on being Ireland's premier venue for drum 'n' bass, acid jazz, speed garage, and a pot-pourri of exotic dance music you probably haven't even heard of yet.

I've got permission from the management to tape at both venues, which makes my job a tad easier. I shot some preliminary footage of Cookie's the other night. The DJ, hooked up a sixteen-millimetre film camera in the upstairs bar and screened *Conan the Barbarian* on the wall near the emergency exit. The speakers pumped out Boney-M's classic 'Rasputin', and on the dance-floor, hoards of beautiful people raised their arms and cried out 'Russia's greatest love-machine' in unison. I was mesmerised.

Two American actors, Jimmy Stewart and Robert Mitchum died recently of old age. They were both in their mid-eighties and seemed totally incapacitated. A thought struck me (I frequently have such insights): we will all turn to dust. Death is the end of all parties. It is therefore one's duty, regardless of any religious beliefs you might hold, to live every day as potentially your last.

I have made a pledge to do so.

LOLA: I love it here, you know. I come every second night, and sometimes even on Sundays. It's all to do with style, you see. Style's not anything you read in The Face. *Style is feeling comfortable and looking good. Style is the confidence to admit you're a sexual being. I bought this leopardskin top in the Portobello Market when I visited my friend Natasha last April. I think it's dead chic. And, oh, I can't wait 'till the end of the month. I'm getting my labia pierced.*

I graduated with a degree in Communications three years ago. I was an exceptional student, primarily due to my off-beat sense of humour coupled with a practical academic know-how. I've been unemployed ever since. Officially, I mean. There's no excuse for someone like me to do conventional work. There are other people to take jobs like that, to fill all those carrier bags with food. I'd only be depriving people with no ambition of gainful employment. Instead, I've spent the last few years developing a number of diverse, but equally fascinating, media projects. This will be my second film. I was commissioned to make a video-diary about my love life last year, but unfortunately it never got broadcast. I've also directed a few rock videos (and a couple of weddings) for a number of Dublin underground rock groups. I even played bass with The Skullfuckers for a while. You might have heard of us. Our music was an eclectic fusion of African rhythms and the tortured pedal steel of Gram Parsons. We had some minor success and received favourable reviews from the majority of free-sheets in Dublin.

I'd never played bass guitar before The Skullfuckers but that was hardly a drawback. I soon picked it up. I believe every man (and some women) are capable of playing the bass. It's not a complex instrument. There are only four strings. Music is made up of eight notes, which are repeated several times on the fretboard. Eight notes make an octave. Once you grasp this simple fact, you're halfway there.

Similarly, I think every living man, woman, or child is well capable of making a documentary film. After all, what is a film but life compressed onto a screen? What is salad but lettuce? What is ketchup or mackerel? The world is a very complicated place, but recording it is not. You do exactly what it says on the tin: stick in the tape and the red light goes solid.

DR MARTIN J. BRANAGH: *What, I think, in essence, we're talking about here is shamanism. The entire notion of dance culture is an unconscious return to a primeval desire for hedonistic worship. It is not based on sky-cult but earth-cult. This is a very important idea, Gurdy, and has a long tradition in Western thought. The transcendental notion of the anthropomorphic deity has lost favour with today's youth culture. The need to express worship is now much more immediate. If you look at the visual iconography of the dance culture, you'll find it bears a remarkable resemblance to primitive rites of religious worship. Frazer's* The Golden Bough *is a particularly good source on such matters. So-called hallucinatory drugs have been used throughout history by man in an attempt to reach what has been fancifully known as a 'higher state of consciousness'. There is nothing original, or particularly inventive about this trend. The paraphernalia just serve to give the cult its immediacy.*

I live in Phibsboro, Dublin 7, which is fast becoming a Mecca for those seeking the counter-culture. I've been there for two years now, and it's really quite depressing to witness the onslaught of shaven-headed blow-ins who descend upon the Hut every Friday night. Not that there's anything wrong with a shaved head. With the right profile, and a decently shaped skull, it can really be quite striking. On a man, of course. I draw the line, though, at women. This is one thing the general public has never quite understood. Beautiful women have beautiful hair. This is a universal truth, like Trotsky or the genius of Jack Keroauc. There is no room for debate.

Emma, to be fair to her, has always done the right thing. We've been romantically involved now for thirteen months, and I must admit, she really is quite a stunner. In an understated way, though. Blonde hair and blue eyes that flutter when she's nervous. Emma has an innocence, a timidity, that a man like myself cannot help but find touching. I met her in the Attic last January, where The Skullfuckers played to a packed audience of friends and relations. Emma was working freelance for The Kleg at the time, and had come along to review the show because her cousin was the drummer with Cannibal Kennedy, our support band for the night. After the gig, I took her aside, to see what she thought. She told me we were the sloppiest band she had ever seen. I've always admired honesty, even if it's misguided, and that's the way it happened. The romance, I mean. Our sex-life is not particularly exciting, but she has very nice legs.

DJ FROG: I like playing music, because music's my life. It's mostly trip-hop, jungle and ragga in here, and that's what the crowd seem to be into. Sometimes I experiment. I've started using The Omen soundtrack a lot, and that's pretty cool. Snatches of Abba, The Carpenters. Some jazz now and then. Miles Davis. Coltrane. My tastes are diverse but I draw the line at guitar rock. That stuff is for shoegazers who can't get on down. I won't have it.

I'm very excited. Having run into Lola again, she's very kindly invited me along to witness her 'operation'. I can't wait, although I'm not exactly sure how it fits in with my current project. Nevertheless, I must admit, Lola's rather intriguing. She has black hair cut into a stylish bob, vivid red lipstick, and on Friday was wearing a Sesame Street t-shirt cut tightly around the bust, leaving just enough room to reveal a small gold ring sewn into her belly-button. She explained the technicalities of the piercing to me in great detail, which, apparently, is not for cosmetic effect, but a necessary appendage to 'heighten her sexual passion'. I can appreciate that. Any red-blooded man cannot help but respect a red-blooded woman.

I've also learnt that there's a 'back-room' at the Sauna. In order to gain entrance, one has to be in possession of a Gold Card, which are given out by the management to some of their more exclusive clients. Rumours abound that Jack Dillon (soap opera star), Barry Coogan (celebrity journalist), and assorted members of No Sweat (defunct AOR band) are all regular proprietors. I've yet to get my hands on a card, but I'm working flat out on it. Frog, the club's resident DJ is an old acquaintance of mine, and he's promised to pull a few strings. In the mean time, I have to resort to interviewing the general public.

A word on the drugs. I don't do any. This might come as a surprise to you, given my free-thinking attitude, but they do nothing for me at all. I can empathise, and see how ecstasy (or 'yokes' to use the vernacular) leads to a sense of communal well-being, helping to foster what Dr Branagh calls the 'shamanic experience', but I have to say I've always considered myself above all that. I took half an E once, when my friend Thomas went off to India in search of a guru. It was a conciliatory gesture, and I must say, despite having felt like I'd just run up ten flights of stairs, I was singularly unimpressed.

David Barker, my editor, is very interested in such matters, however, and wants me, if possible, to infiltrate the 'drugs culture'. I have consented, albeit reluctantly. The other night

Lola directed me to a gentleman called Jimmy who was dealing ecstasy and wraps of speed in plain sight. He also sells bottles of Evian. I tried striking up a conversation, but I think the camera put him off. I paid for my water and left.

I don't think Emma approves of what I'm doing. But then again, she never does really. Emma's always been jealous of my success, as she's now working as a webmaster for an Internet design company in Ballyfermot. Like many of my peers, she feels she is 'underachieving'.

Incidentally, the homosexual American writer, and reformed drug-addict, William S. Burroughs died today. Several years earlier, Mr Burroughs shot and killed his wife in a bizarre William Tell re-enactment. Apparently, the event helped to launch the author's career on a world stage.

CATHAL: Now, I'm just going to put my two fingers here. Is that alright? Now. Okay. Now, relax. There's nothing to be afraid of. Everything's under control. Now, you'll feel a bit of a twinge, like.

Up three flights of stairs, over a place that sells second-hand records, resides one Mr Cathal MacManus. Originally from Cork, Mr MacManus now runs Dublin's finest body-piercing emporium, specialising in what the advertisement in *Buy and Sell* called the 'intimate zones'. I'm not usually squeamish, but watching a tattooed mustachio make an incision with a sharpened scalpel at the base of Lola's clitoris was enough to put me off vaginas for life. Lola gripped my hand all through the operation and at one difficult juncture — when the stud went in — she dug her long fingernails into the sweating flesh of my palm. This, I imagined, is what childbirth must be like.

The operation was successful. Unfortunately, this means Lola will be out of action for the foreseeable future. Cathal has advised her to rest for at least eight days and not to walk anywhere further than the bathroom. Lola, however, in her infinite kindness, has arranged for me to meet her friend

Geraldine, and we're to rendezvous for the first time tomorrow at Jake's Dungeon, a night-club of dubious merit on Parnell Street. Geraldine's apparently a reformed manic depressive who received shock treatment three times in the mid-eighties. I must say, I'm looking forward to it.

GERALDINE: I hate this. I fuckin' do. Why do I come here? I don't know. What else would I do? Sit at home by myself? Look at me. Do you know how old I am? Take a guess. Wrong. I'm thirty-five. Thirty-five years of age. What kind of age is that? In a place like this. Look around you, go on. That poor boy over there can't be more than sixteen. Look at me, drinking cider, getting old, fat, and more boring by the day. My one pleasure in life is headbanging to Whole Lotta Rosie *by AC/DC. This is the only place in Dublin where they still play it. I don't have a choice. I am what I am. And Bon Scott is dead.*

I don't think I'll be going back to Jake's Dungeon. The venue was dark, inhospitable, and almost entirely devoid of humour (a.k.a. the happy buzz). The people who resort there fall into two camps, and I'm not sure which I find more distasteful. In the black corner were the straggling metalheads, still finding inexplicable novelty in bands like Cryptic Slaughter, Entombed and Carcass. In the other black corner, and actually making somewhat of a comeback in the final round, were the white-pasted little children that frighten old ladies in shopping centres. Geraldine, to her credit, seemed to act largely as an arbitrator, finding inspiration both in Black Sabbath and The Sisters of Mercy. I wasn't very taken with her, however. I watched her sit there as she fiddled with her split-ends, not really saying much. Wrapped in a seemingly infinite number of shawls, she was just like a big black hole, sucking all the life from me. Geraldine's writing a vampire novel set in Finglas, but before she got time to tell me about it, another testosterone-fuelled rock-anthem blasted out through the speakers, and she lumbered over to dance with a spotty Spanish student.

I had a look at the footage this evening, and I've decided the entire shoot was a waste of time. I'm not going to use any of it. Dark matter is the mortal enemy of all life in the universe and those people wouldn't know cool if you cryogenically froze the whole sorry lot of them. I really hope Lola's clitoris heals up soon. After all, she's most likely my ticket to the back-room.

I'm also more than a little concerned about the validity of some of my interviewees. I spoke briefly to Doctor Martin J. Branagh on the telephone today, just to make a casual enquiry about the cultural significance of lozenge inhalation in the larger spectrum of things, and the good doctor admitted, with some embarrassment, that he hadn't set foot in a night-club since 1978. This puts me in a bit of quandary. Martin J. is senior lecturer in Cultural Studies at Marino University, whose research is considered by many as the finest in Western Europe. His ethnographic fieldwork, however, leaves much to be desired. I explained my position to the good doctor, but he didn't seem at all phased by my argument. As a compromise, I suggested he accompany me, at the next possible juncture, to the Sauna, where he could observe the phenomena of bodybeating firsthand. He said he would consult his desk diary and get back to me forthwith.

On a completely different matter, I'm supposed to meet a man who sells horse-tranquillisers next week.

EDDIE: I like men. I like fucking them. I like fucking them with my cock and sometimes with my fist. I fuck them as often as possible. I once fucked ten men in one night in the gent's toilet here. I give magnificent blowjobs. I have a very long tongue, and if you wanted me to, I could stick it right up your anus and lick the cum out.

Today was Saturday. I couldn't shoot anything because I had to go out with Emma. Her older sister was having an engagement party out in Ranelagh and she dragged me along as the 'boyfriend'. I explained that I had work to do, and had an appointment with the man who sells horse tranquillisers, but she insisted that I cancel it. She says I have no time for her since I started the video, and that my disinterest is beginning to upset her. So I had no choice really, but to concede.

Foo-Foo, Emma's sister, is a goofy blonde with no class. Her real name is 'Fiona' but she insists that everyone call her Foo-Foo. Her friends, who formed an orderly queue to present Foo-Foo with candlesticks, brightly coloured picture-frames and ashtrays in the shape of tropical fish, all seemed to work in the computer industry editing 'content'. Their boyfriends were accountants that played weekend soccer for suburban teams, and the conversation alternated between the soaring cost of house prices in Dublin and the destruction of the Glen of the Downs. I tried putting on my DJ Babel CD to liven things up, but nobody seemed to be interested. Some people have no taste whatsoever. Resigned to my fate, I had ten glasses of Jacob's Creek and suffered Michael Bolton's *Soul Provider* instead.

Afterwards, in the taxi home, Emma told me I wasn't taking her seriously enough. She said after thirteen months, it was time to take our relationship to a different level. What would this constitute, I wondered? She suggested that we move in together. I don't need to tell you what I thought about that.

EMMA: What are you asking me for? You know what I think. You know I don't like it. It's all a pretence, isn't it? Rave. Ravers. Knackers, Gurdy. Knackers in cycling shorts rubbing cooking oil into their thighs. These are the same people who bought yo-yos when they were kids. They've never grown up. They want to pretend they're sixteen for the rest of their lives. What? I'm not blinking. No, I'm not. Don't tell me I'm blinking. Did you tape that?

On Wednesday evening, in the pouring rain, I found myself standing in a cement clearing, surrounded by the Ballymun flat complex. I could hear the planes descending overhead, and in the distance packs of young boys scavenged the area like wolves. Luckily, the Sony Handicam is relatively compact and I managed to conceal it in the inside pocket of my yellow Firetrap jacket.

After about fifteen minutes, a young man arrived astride a white horse. He came galloping out of the rain, circled me a few times and then brought the beast to a halt. He was a thin, wiry man with a pockmarked face. Tranquillisers, he told me, are very popular amongst those weaning themselves off heroin. Unfortunately, usage can often be fatal. He took a dark green vial out of his pocket and said it would cost me ten pounds. He never dismounted. I asked him whether it would be possible to interview some of his friends, to which he demanded the entire contents of my wallet. I had no real choice but to agree. The horse deposited a steaming load inches from my feet and the thief then departed.

I also slept with Lola last night. She was quite eager to try out her modified vagina, and I saw no reason not to assist her. I must admit, the intercourse wasn't as spectacular as I might have imagined. The clitoral ring obviously serves its purpose all too well, as the whole thing (foreplay, penetration, consummation) was over in less than two minutes. Having watched Lola grunt in what seemed like pain, I lay there, rather perplexed, as she sat straddled over me, panting, beads of sweat running down her face.

I also learnt, to my surprise that Lola actually works for a living. Her real name is Cathy O'Reilly, and by day she's a secretary in a solicitor's office on Ormond Quay. After the orgasm (one presumes), she climbed off me with great urgency, and shut herself into the bathroom. I lay there, uncertain of my next move. It was strange to find the tables so turned in this manner. I was still in an obvious state of arousal, and here was Cathy/Lola preparing for bed! Perhaps this is the real nature of the clitoral piercing: a revenge against the dominance of the male orgasm. I have made a mental note about this, and will discuss it with Doctor Branagh at the next available opportunity.

When Lola came back, she told me that Geraldine is thinking about killing herself again.

The Italian fashion designer, Gianni Versace, was assassinated this evening outside his luxury home in Miami. Police suspect a crazed gunman was responsible for the murder.

DR MARTIN J. BRANAGH: To be completely frank, I feel entirely out of touch with that kind of recreational practice.

I made a mistake. I don't make mistakes very often and this is a difficult thing to admit. I made a tactical error, and I should have known better. It hurts even to tell you. Dr Branagh very kindly agreed to accompany me to the Sauna on Monday night. I had hoped that this would be a learning experience for both of us, as we had much to discuss, but alas I was wrong. Because Monday, as I neglected to remember, is in fact gay night.

This simple fact caused all kinds of problems I had not really anticipated. Dr Branagh, despite the iconoclastic nature of his research, is married with two children, and by all accounts is very devoted to his wife. He is also remarkably good-looking for a man in his mid-fifties, and with his slim build and shaven head he appeared very handsome in his Calvin Klein suit. A series of highly amusing incidents were recorded on camera, the most memorable of which involved Eddie, a Canadian body-builder I know, who very kindly offered to 'felch' Dr Branagh in the gents' toilets. Felching is a sexual practice I feel is probably not a fit subject for a television documentary, so I'll say no more about it.

Dr Branagh, however, did not see the humour in these boisterous episodes and has demanded that I return the tapes to him immediately. Although a little drunk, and probably still reeling from shock, Dr Branagh even went as far as to threaten me with legal action. I'm unsure of my next move. Perhaps some kind of compromise can be reached. To make matters worse, I returned home to find a telephone message from David Barker, informing me, in case I wasn't already aware, of a VIP Room at the Sauna. As the man says, when it rains it fucking pours.

LOLA: There are three kinds of buzzes and they depend on the atmosphere. The happy buzz. The mad buzz. And the love buzz. There's a love buzz tonight. Can't you just feel all that love, Gurdy? Look at the love. Look at the eyes. They all love you. We all love each other. Everyone is the same here. Everyone's on the love buzz. Let that love sweep you away, Gurdy. Let that love take you higher. Into orbit.

I had a dream last night. I must say, I was rather disturbed. In the dream I'd finally gotten access to the back-room in the Sauna. I glide through the door, expecting to be introduced to all five members of Def Leppard, including the gentleman with one arm, but instead I find myself surrounded by statuesque blondes, in varying states of undress. Naturally, I'm terribly aroused, and I allow them to lead me to the raised concrete slab on the middle of the dancefloor. I'm tied down with silk scarves, and I'm thinking *this is going to be really great*, when the knives comes out. Ceremonial daggers, you might say. I now notice the six women surrounding me have become hideously ugly, with a thick green fluid pouring out from their eyes, and they commence stabbing me, each in turn, all the while murmuring a prayer I can't quite make out.

I know what the dream means, of course. It's a kind of warning. It's telling me, be careful. There are people out there who will want a piece of you. There are people who will exploit your new-found success for their own invidious intentions. There are money-grabbers and leeches and worms, and all of them will use you. Be careful, Gurdy, you are entering uncharted waters.

Diana, Princess of Wales, died this morning in a tragic automobile mishap in Paris, France. I must say, I almost shed a tear. It was something about her innocence (not to mention her heroic attempts to single-handedly rid the world of landmines) that touched a chord deep in my soul. I bet she fucked like a maenad.

I was very disappointed with the paparazzi, however. Having spent the best part of twenty years chasing the Queen of Hearts across five continents, you'd think they'd have the professionalism to get a decent shot of her closing moments of life. An epitaph, as it were. The entire world appears grief-stricken tonight. BBC have even cancelled a screening of Oliver Stone's bio-pic of Jim Morrison and have replaced it with a film about a loveable otter. As a mark of respect, I've decided not to go to the Sauna. Feeling a little sentimental, however, I give Emma a ring. She's calling over at ten. We're going to split a pepperoni pizza and watch *A Tribute to A Princess*.

EMMA: I don't ... I don't understand you. How can you be so callous? I'm talking to you here. Switch that off, Gurdy. Switch that off. This is you and me. This is not for your fucking programme. This is a private moment between you and me, Gurdy. Can't you understand that? I don't want to talk to your camera. I want to talk to you. I'm saying I don't love you. That I can't love you if this is what you are. Does that make any sense to you? Can't you give an opinion? Is there a human bone left in your body?

Anyway, I end up in Jake's Dungeon again. It's a little more interesting this time around, because Lola is with me, and wearing a stunning turquoise kimono an old boyfriend brought her back from Tokyo. It turns out Geraldine's finally decided to snuff out the candle, and Lola's very kindly persuaded her to allow me to record this dramatic event. I think she's secretly pleased that Geraldine will finally be out of her hair.

Geraldine washes down a handful of unidentified pills with a large G & T. She then begins her version of Ophelia's mad scene from *Hamlet*, a play by William Shakespeare that was made into a very successful three-hour motion picture recently.

Geraldine's hair is astray. Her fingers are stained nicotine yellow and her nails bitten ragged. I can't look at her face. She hands Lola the only copy of her novel, *The Secret Fetishes of Jack Maguire*. We're to leave her alone now, she tells us. She wants to be by herself in the darkness. The DJ has promised to play Black Sabbath's *Iron Man* at exactly one-thirty am. She thinks the spasms will begin then. No one will see her sitting alone in this booth in the dark. No one will care. She can die, happy, alone.

I'm quite anxious to tape the scene to the bitter end, but Lola won't allow it. I'm a little disappointed, but have a hunch that a quick fade-to-black after the closing embrace might work equally as well. Sometimes the subtle approach can be highly dramatic.

Lola embraces her friend for the last time, and the pair of us walk out onto the pavement. I feel a soft rain and a cool breeze on my face. We stroll hand-in-hand down O'Connell Street and over the bridge. I feel curiously exhilarated, not least because it appears we are now 'seeing' each other. We bump into the man who sells horse-tranquillisers outside a fast-food restaurant, and he offers to sell Lola some speed at a thirty percent discount. She laughs in his face. A seagull, as if on some kind of kamikaze mission, narrowly misses colliding with my head. We laugh again, speculating on who will die first — the seagull or me. I suspect it will be the bird.

We have sex at my place, and once again I'm ordered to stay still. The event, though short-lived, is tinged with a curious sadness. Melancholia, I suppose

GERALDINE: Have I ever had a moment of happiness? I don't think so. Has there ever been a second when I could say 'I fit right in here; I belong'? Of course not. I've always been alone. All of us are. But the little things that bring other people together have never held an appeal for me. No matter what I wear, or the music I listen to, the books I have read. I am still alone. Not even the drugs help. None of it. Some people say the soul can die before the body does. Maybe that's what has happened to me.

Time is running out now. I've reviewed all the footage so far, and I must say I'm very impressed. Geraldine's suicide is certainly poignant and serves as an effective counterpoint to the bulk of the programme's mainly light-hearted content. Dr Branagh has agreed to give his consent to the 'felching' scene, providing I take his class for two weeks while he and his wife go through some counselling.

All is well. However, there is still one vital piece missing. I have yet to gain access to the 'back room'. Despite persistent telephone calls to the management, the heroic efforts of Lola, and even a promise to allow Eddie to fellate my virile member should he get me inside, I have still garnered nothing. I'm reminded of an episode in a book by Franz Kakfa, a rather irritating Czech writer who was obsessed by his small penis, and wrote lots of short stories about it. There is an anecdote concerning a man waiting outside a door, who persistently requests entrance. He is constantly denied and yet remains standing there for the remainder of his natural life. He eventually dies; realising the endeavour was a fruitless pursuit.

I do not think this will happen to me. In fact, if I were a betting man (which I'm not), I'd say I should have my Gold Card by September the fifth. I imagine I'll be drinking champagne with Dublin's social elite very soon.

Any day now.

Colin Murphy

'RED ISUZU'

Sean's club was the reason we went to see that nut Toner in the first place. You see Sean loves dance music and he has this dream of opening his own club. He's got the name and everything. It's going to be a club in an old Orange hall so he's calling it the Clockwork Orange ...

The trouble was Sean has no cash, so he rang me and said that Toner had offered him a business opportunity, 'a doddle' he said. Now I know there's no such thing, especially if it involves that spacer Sean, but I went with him anyway, just for support.

We were told to meet Toner in the Bradbury, he runs a night there or something. Neither of us had met Toner before but we knew him by reputation, and what a reputation. We arrived at about ten and the place was stuffed, everybody was dancing like mad things. No wonder Toner's so loaded. I grabbed a quick double brandy at the bar and necked it back while Sean went off to find Toner. It wasn't my scene, a bit too mainstream, but there were some right wee honeys in there all the same. So, back came Sean with this big guy that works for Toner. This guy was huge, I mean *massive*. So, we followed Godzilla through the bottle store and up the back stairs into this wee room. Toner's office I suppose. All very

301

hi-tech, portable, you know? Ready to be shifted in a hurry I suppose.

A guy in a black fleece was sitting with his back to us, working on a lap-top.

'Toner?' Sean asked. The guy stopped what he was doing stood up, turned to face us and nodded.

He was about thirty, tall, fit and tanned, not what I was expecting at all. Except for the broken nose, those sort of guys always have a broken nose.

'So what's this business opportunity you're offering us?'

Us! Since when was it *us*? I threw Sean this look but he was just standing there staring Toner out, cool as anything.

'This is Justin,' Sean nods to me. Toner nods at me, I nod at Toner, everybody's nodding at everybody else. It was looking like a fucking nodding dog puppy farm.

'I need someone to deliver some merchandise for me.' Toner spoke with quite a posh accent, Bangor or Lisburn or some hole of a place like that.

'What is it?' Sean asked.

Toner picked up the *Belfast Telegraph* lying on his desk and threw it at Sean. It was open at the farming pages. Pictures of big thick culchies and cows and stuff. One of the pictures was circled in black biro.

'That's Harry Mitchell,' said Toner. Yeah, like we didn't know who he was, the big Orange bastard. 'And that's his pig.' Well I nearly burst myself laughing. Here was this big-time dealer giving us this whole big French Connection routine about a stolen fucking pig!

Mitchell's ugly mug has been plastered over every newspaper all week, it even reached the '*and finally . . .*' spot on *News at Ten*. Nobody here gives a shit about Mitchell's pig except Mitchell, even other Orangemen thought it was a bit of a laugh. They wouldn't say it to his face though. I'd thought it was some sort of stunt to do with Mitchell being involved in the stand-off, you know to make him look even more stupid.

'What's so fucking funny, specky?' I stopped laughing immediately. Toner's staring me out now.

'So did *you* kidnap his pig then?' I asked all innocent.

'None of your business.' Toner was talking to Sean but still glaring at me. 'The only thing that you need to be concerned with is getting rid of it.'

Well as soon as I heard this I turned on my heels and headed for the door. Sean caught me at the top of the stairs.

'What's up?'

'There's no fucking way I'm doing that.'

'Aw come on, hear him out. It's the only way I'm going to get enough money together.' I didn't answer. 'Look we'll be partners. You saw how bunged it was downstairs, well that could be ours.'

I picked at the woodchip wallpaper by the bannister.

'Fifty-fifty.' I said.

'Sixty-forty.'

'Sixty-forty and *I* get to choose the name of the club.'

'Okay big brother, deal.'

I followed Sean back into the room.

'No problem,' says Sean 'Just tell us how, when and where. You can rely on us.'

'Why can't you use one of your own fellas?' I asked,

'The cops know them. In fact, they know some of them too well, if you know what I mean, specky.'

There were all sorts of rumours going around about Toner having a tout in the camp. I nodded again. Enough said. 'How do you know you can trust us?'

'Sean here has a dream. He needs the money to make that dream come true. I hear you want to open a place of you own.'

'The Clockwork Orange ... you see it's in an old Orange hall ...'

'Very clever,' says Toner. 'Not that I'm interested, it could have been anyone. I find it's better being in the company of strangers and all that. It was just a fluke that Sean contacted one of my associates when he did. By the way that gear you ordered, it's in the glove compartment.' Toner chucked over a set of car keys to Sean. 'Red Isuzu in the back entry. The pig's in the boot.'

I giggled again, Toner just ignored us. 'Drive to Belvoir forest. Take a right at the main gate. Drive along that track and take the first left you come to. Drive as far as you can. When you can't drive any further go to the boot. Take out the pig and the shovels. Walk into the forest. Do not use the path. When you are far enough from the road dig a deep hole and bury the pig. Simple.'

'Why don't you eat it?' I said. I think the brandy must have gone to my head. Toner just stared at me for ages, his eyes boring into my skull.

'It's rotten, it's been lying dead in a garage for days. Stinking, apparently.'

The next thing Toner started to scrabble in this bag. After a minute he took out a Lucozade bottle with some creamy coloured stuff in the bottom and he handed it to Sean.

'There'll be a guy expecting this at the SeaCat terminal. Deliver it at four, be back here by closing at five and you get your money.'

Sean looked at the bottle and asked what was in it. Do you know what it was? Semen. Pig jiz. I really wanted to laugh but I wasn't going to push my luck.

'It's worth a lot of money, lads. Be careful.'

Old Mitchell's pig was a bit of a stud apparently, and this scouser'd paid a lot of cash for a sample. I guess that was why Toner had nicked the pig in the first place. Apparently there's a big trade in this type of thing, it's all done on the Internet, did you know that? All Sean cared about was getting the cash to start his club.

We headed out into the entry and found the jeep. Sean threw me the keys and told me to drive. Look, I wasn't going to get involved, I just went along for support, but by this stage Toner thought that I was involved, and if I'd pulled out I'd have been in big shit.

I opened the door and this unbelievable stench hit us. Rotten I mean *stinking*. I nearly heaved on the spot. Sean said it'd be fine once we rolled down the windows and got moving.

I held my breath and got in, almost drowning before I could get the thing going. We drove about two hundred yards up the Dublin road with our heads out the windows and stopped at the Winemarket. I needed a drink. I ran in and bought a half-bottle of brandy and twenty smokes. As I got back into the car Sean was wiping white powder from his nose and Sonic Youth was blaring from the tape deck.

He'd obviously found the glove compartment.

I said nothing. He knows what I think of him taking that shite. I turned off the music.

The smell had eased by this stage and as soon as I'd downed a mouthful of the brandy it was almost undetectable. So, off we went into the night.

We got about another two hundred yards and no further. A pile of Orangemen and a band had blocked the road. There was no way we were getting through. So we turned back on ourselves and went down Great Victoria Street. No problem.

As we turned right into Bruce Street some wee shite, with a Rangers scarf for a mask, came tearing out into the road in front of us and stood there with his arms raised. I slammed on the brakes and skided to a halt inches from the wee bollocks.

As we stopped another older guy with a huge beer gut ran up to the passenger door punched Sean through the open window and tried to open the door but Sean hung on and managed to lock it in time. The bastards were trying to hijack the jeep. I put the boot down, hit the wee lad at the front and kept going. A brick hit the roof as we headed towards Ormeau Avenue. Sean's nose was bleeding, so I give him some brandy and a fag.

It was starting to get very dark as we headed up the Ormeau Road.

I turned around and Sean's trying to snort more coke up his bloody nose.

'Would you get rid of that shit. There's a fucking check-point.' Sean sniffed and whimpered a bit and I tried to look calm. The cop eyed us as we approached, put up his hand and we stopped.

'Evening, officer,' I said, not too friendly like, you don't want to look suspicious.

'Where are you coming from lads?'

'The Bradbury.' I did the talking while Sean hid his nose and looked out the passenger window.

The cop leaned in a bit and sniffed. I just looked blankly at him. I'm good at that.

'Sorry about that,' Sean said and wafted his hand under his nose, 'Kebab.'

'I know what you mean,' said the cop, 'On you go.' Brilliant. I had another snifter to celebrate.

Things went okay for the next ten minutes as we drove along the river up to the Malone Road. Posh people don't tend to riot, what's the point of burning nice things. We got onto the dual carriageway to Belvoir, turned the bend and almost drove into a burning bus and more mental Rangers supporters. So a quick U-turn and back into town.

Sean suggested going back to the Ormeau Road and going around the long way by Sainsbury's. Well it was worth a try, so we did. No use. By the time we got back down to the bridge there were cops and rioters everywhere. The only way out was through the Holyland and down Botanic. At Bradbury place the Orangemen had gone and the place was deserted, except for a few die hard drinkers heading for Lavery's. So we drove at high speed down Great Victoria Street again. We passed the wee bollocks from before limping up the road waving a Union Jack.

The middle of town was empty too, except for the small groups of news crews trying to film the deserted city centre but there were so many of them it wasn't really deserted.

We decided to avoid protestant areas, but by now we were being forced into north Belfast, completely the wrong direction. I was starting to panic, Sean seemed totally together.

'Look, what does it matter where we get rid of the pig, as long as we get rid of it?' he said.

I thought about it for a while and he had a point. But where? We drove on hoping that the police or the Orangemen would decide for us. After twenty minutes of diversions and U-turns we ended up in Glengormley facing yet another blocked road.

'Where to now?' I asked. 'We're as far as we can go, the only way is back the way we came.'

It was approaching one in the morning and according to the radio the rioting was getting worse all over town.

'*The Zoo*,' Sean said and pointed to a brown sign-post. 'Let's feed the fucker to the animals.'

He was serious. I thought he was messing but he was serious. Look I was desperate and it was the best, well, *only* suggestion so far. I turned the jeep round and went up the driveway and stopped by the picnic area at the main gate. The view at the top was amazing. You could see all over the lough and most of Belfast. You could see the flickering light of the burning cars and buses dotted around town. It was beautiful.

I took a slug of brandy, Sean took a toot of coke and we opened the boot. By now we were used to what smell there was, so we just got on with it.

The pig was wrapped in a blanket and bin liners tied up with sellotape and string. It was bigger than I'd imagined. We tried to lift it out but it was a lot heavier than we thought, so it took a few attempts, but eventually we bounced it out onto the tarmac and trailed it the few feet over to the gate.

I was knackered and the sweat was lashing off us. Sean was breathless, he couldn't breathe through his nose very well by this stage.

I took another slug of brandy and offered some to Sean but he didn't take any, he just lit a fag and sat down on the pig.

The gate was about seven or eight foot high. There was no way we were going to be able to lift the pig up that height, it was far too heavy. We dragged it over to a picnic table and bundled it up onto the seat, then up onto the table top. My legs were like jelly, and my heart was pounding in my head. We must have sat there wheezing for about half an hour, looking at the view with the pig lying between us.

'Have you ever noticed the lights reflecting off the flats in Newtownabbey?'

'No, what about them?' I said.

'They look like those old black and white pictures of Diana Ross and the Supremes in their spangley silver dresses.'

Sean was obviously out of it by now.

I reversed the jeep over to the picnic table. Sean climbed onto the roof. I leaned the pig against the side of the jeep. Sean pulled and I pushed the big dead lump up onto the roof of the jeep. Eventually it was there. We collapsed again. It was almost two thirty.

I drove back over to the gate and reversed the jeep as close as I could to the gate. I braked a bit too suddenly and Sean slid off the roof and onto the bonnet. He didn't seem to notice. I was tired and getting very pissed off by now.

The pig was only a few inches away from the top of the gate, now that it was on the roof of the jeep, so we heaved it over and it landed with a splat on the other side. Then the two of us lowered ourselves down. I landed awkwardly on my ankle. Sean, meanwhile, got his fucking trendy jeans caught on the latch of the gate and fell backwards waving his arms about for something to grab onto. As he did, the Lucozade bottle in his jacket pocket started to slide out. I made a lunge for it and caught it just as Sean's arms locked around my neck.

After a few minutes of Laurel and fucking Hardy we're sorted.

'Which animals do we feed?' I asked.

'What?'

'Which ones eat meat?'

'I don't fucking know.'

'It was your idea.'

Sean's no David Attenborough so we found a map on a grubby information board.

'Chimpanzees?'

'No.'

'Bears?'

'Eat fish.'

'Red Pandas?'

'Haven't got a fucking clue.'

'Lions?'

'Lions!' We dragged the pig towards the lion enclosure. The noise of the dragging woke the parrots as we passed. After ten minutes Sean's legs buckled and he collapsed on the pig.

'I'm wrecked.'

I gave him a kick but he didn't move. We were only a few feet from the lions, we were almost there and with an hour to spare. I sat down beside him, had a fag and talked about the Clockwork Orange. It bored me to tears but it seemed to do the trick for Sean. He lit another fag rubbed some shit on his gums and he was ready for action.

'It's too big, we need to cut it up,' I said.

I thought about it for a moment and then sent Sean to get the shovel from the boot. I'm dead organised when I want to be.

'Right, you cut,' I said. 'I've done enough.'

'I can't. I'm squeamish.'

I couldn't be arsed arguing so I grabbed the shovel, aimed the side of the blade near the top of the bag and raised my arms ready to strike. As I did, the Lucozade bottle slipped out of my pocket and fell. Before we could do anything, it had smashed on the path.

'Holy god, you complete prick! We are fucking dead men!'

I swung the shovel at Sean as hard as I could, but he ducked out of the way. We just stood and stared at the broken glass and the sticky liquid as it seeped into the tarmac.

'Maybe we could get another bottle of Lucozade and fill it ourselves, eh?'

'Can you smell coconut?' I asked. There was this overpowering smell, like Malibu. I bent down sniffing. Meanwhile Sean was pacing around like a dervish talking ninety to the dozen, holding his head.

I ignored him. I put my finger into the gloop on the path and sniffed. I dabbed it on my tongue. Sean freaked out.

'You mingeing bastard!'

It was shampoo, Bodyshop coconut shampoo, we have it at home. What were we doing delivering shampoo to a guy at four in the morning? My head turned to ice. I went over to the pig and ripped at the black plastic. There were three or four layers but eventually I got to the pig's pink flesh. There was a blue mark on the flesh. I tore some more of the plastic away. I jumped back four feet.

'FUCK! IT'S HUMAN!'

Sean took a peak.

'It's a tattoo. Pigs get tattooed as well you know, for id and stuff.'

'How many pigs have a FOR GOD AND ULSTER tattoo?! This must be the tout.' I didn't know what to do. Sean was shaking like mad and drinking my brandy.

'If we don't get rid of the body then Toner will get rid of us.'

'And if we do get rid of it then we're involved. The whole thing was probably a set up anyway, the jeep was probably stolen and there's nothing to connect us with Toner. I knew this was a fucking stupid idea, you bastard.' I punched Sean and he fell back and lay crying by the corpse.

I grabbed the shovel and ran to the gate, smashed the padlock off and drove the jeep up to where Sean and the body were both lying. We bundled the body into the boot and drove off at high speed.

I didn't know where we were going or what we were going to do I just knew we had to go.

It was four o'clock. I stuck on the radio. Most of the rioting had died down. We passed the SeaCat terminal. There was no-one waiting, we drove on. There were police and army patrols everywhere, too tired to deal with us though. We passed small groups of dancers from The Bradbury who looked just as tired.

I was driving in a daze, my mind was blank as we headed up Great Victoria Street. Then from nowhere a face masked in a Rangers scarf hit the windscreen. I slammed on the brakes and we both jumped out. We already had one dead body on our hands, we didn't want another.

It was that wee bollocks from earlier. He was lying flat out on the road, he was alright, just a bit dazed. Then from behind us I felt this great surge of heat and rush of hot air as somebody threw a petrol bomb into the jeep. More Rangers fans cheered and whooped as the jeep took light ...

... that's when you lot came along. If we'd had the energy to run and Sean was more together we might have got away.

'Look son you were lifted by a half burnt out car registered in your brothers name ...'

'It's not his! Toner ...'

'... registered in his name with a body in the boot and twenty thousand in cash stuffed under the driver's seat ...'

'What twenty thousand?'

'Look don't play the innocent, I don't know who you were working for ...'

'Toner, I told you ...'

'That bloke you described isn't Toner son. The body in the boot, *that's Toner*. Interview terminated at zero six forty, Thursday ninth of July.' The sergeant leaned over, switched off the tape and gathered his papers together. 'Your solicitor's on her way.'

Contributors

BRIDGET O'CONNOR

Bridget O'Connor lives in London and is the author of two short story collections *Tell Her You Love Her* and *Here Comes John* published by Picador. She is working on another collection and a novel.

MIKE McCORMACK

Mike McCormack was born in 1965 and now lives in the west of Ireland. His anthology *Getting It In The Head* won the 1995 Rooney Prize.

JULIAN GOUGH

Conceived in Spain, born in England '66, grew up in Tipperary, lives in Galway. Made four Toasted Heretic albums with his childhood friends. Top 10 hit at home, Melody Maker SOTW, played New York, Paris, blah blah. Wrote two novels, laserprinted limited editions of ten, for his friends' amusement. Co-wrote successful musical comedy, *Peig – The Musical!* Music editor of Galway's *List*. Currently working on first feature film, a comedy about unemployed terrorists. Villa fan.

JO BAKER

Born in 1973, Jo Baker is a graduate of Somerville College,

Oxford and the Queen's University of Belfast. She lives and works in Belfast.

EMER MARTIN

Emer Martin is a Dubliner who fled the country at seventeen and has since been causing havoc in various disreputable corners of the globe. Her first novel *Breakfast In Babylon* won the prestigious Listowel award for Book Of The Year 1996. It was released in the US in October 1997.

Emer's novella *Teeth Shall Be Provided* was published in Britain by Rebel Inc in *The Rovers Return* collection. Her second novel *More Bread Or I'll Appear* came out in the US in January 1999.

Emer currently resides in New York and does all her after-hour drinking at Frankie Splits – check your guns at the door.

COLIN CARBERRY

Colin Carberry was born in Belfast in 1975, has lived there all his life, but was in Blackpool when Elvis died.

HELENA MULKERNS

Helena Mulkerns is a writer and freelance journalist whose fiction has appeared in *Hot Press, Here's Me Bus, Irish Tatler* and in the anthologies *Ireland in Exile, Wee Girls* and *Cabbage And Bones.* Nominated for the *Sunday Tribune*/Hennessy Cognac Literary Awards and the American Pushcart Prize, she is also a founder of BANSHEE (www.banshee.cnchost.com). She has a particular fondness for computers, platform shoes, good Tequila and motorbikes.

CASPAR WALSH

Caspar (Walsh) is not a ghost, acrobat, cross-breed dog or aspiring chemical writer. He is the winner of the first Portobello Film Festival. He has written the first of a charged stream of bass-driven books. Has set up The Tall Geezer, short story live readings for the masses. Likes: extra virgin oil, Dingle, drum 'n' bass, stoned spiders, Bristol, indefinable smells and Mary Ellen Walton.

OLAF TYARANSEN

Olaf Tyaransen was born in Dublin in 1971. His first book *The Consequences Of Slaughtering Butterflies* was published in 1992. He makes regular appearances on Irish radio and television and contributes to a wide range of newspapers and magazines including *Hot Press, Magill, Mojo, Himself, The Sunday Times* and *The Sunday Independent*. A collection of his journalism will be published in 1999.

In 1997 Tyaransen ran in the general election on a cannabis legalisation ticket. Nobody can understand why he's never been arrested.

JOE AMBROSE

Joe Ambrose is a DJ and member of hip-hop group Islamic Diggers. He co-produced the album *10% File Under Burroughs* featuring Marianne Faithful, William Burroughs and Bomb The Bass. In Morocco, he works with the Sufi musical brotherhoods The Master Muscians of Joujouka and The Gnoua od Marrakech. He has performed with Lydia Lunch, John Cale and Anita Pallenburg.

His rap novel *Serious Time* (Pulp books) came out in October 1998.

DEX.357

DEX.357 was born in Dublin in the mid-sixties. He was educated by the Christian Brothers who beat the shit out of him and told him he would never be anything but a corner boy. Like many great Irish artists before him, he felt restricted by the society he grew up in, so he travelled to other countries, to become an even better corner boy. In 1996 he changed his ways, but he still yearns for the corner.

LANA CITRON

Lana Citron, a native of Dublin, now lives in London. Previous work includes the short story 'Lapdog Days', a radio short *Now And Forever* and her first novel *Sucker* published as a Vintage paperback in April 1999. Her story 'The Scoreboard' will appear in *New Writing 8*.

IMELDA O'REILLY

Imelda O'Reilly dreamed herself out of Kildare. Although spotted in New York, Paris, London and Edinburgh, no place would house her permanently. As a playwright works include: *CoooooLouds* (Dublin, Source Theatre, 1998), *Twilight Cafe* (New York, Ensemble Studio Theatre, 1992) and *Faz In Ate*, which she recently completed. Imelda just finished carousing Eastern Canada, performing her poetry combined with music which she calls loems. The tour featured her album *In People's Heads*, a collaborative project with composer Joel Diamond (*Welcome To The Dollhouse* – soundtrack, *Four Ballets* for the Cuban National Ballet.) *Stovepipe* is her first published story. You can e-mail Imelda at: www.banshee.cnchost.com

ROBERT CREMINS

Robert Cremins was born in Dublin in 1968. He now lives in

Houston, Texas with his wife Melanie Danburg, also a writer, and their son, David. His debut novel *A Sort Of Homecoming* was published by Sceptre in 1998; the paperback is due out in early 1999. The Times called it 'an exceptional novel', and *The Observer* critic said it was 'the funniest book I've read all year'. You can e-mail Robert at danburg@flash.net

P-P HARTNETT

P-P Hartnett is the author of *Call Me, I Want To Fuck You* and *Mmm Yeah* all published by Pulp Books. The potent combination of a mother from Dublin and a father from Cork, he grew up in a residential home for the elderly.

Hartnett's club and street style photography has been widely published, from *The Sunday Times Magazine* and *The Independent* to *The Face* and *i-D*.

P-P Hartnett lives alone in a little house on a hill in Colne, Lancashire.

COLUM McCANN

Colum McCann is author of *Fishing the Sloe-Black River, Songdogs* and *This Side of Brightness* (all published by Phoenix House). He currently lives in New York.

GAVIN PATRICK CARVILLE

Gavin Patrick Carville was born in Armagh in 1975. At Queen's University, Belfast, he studied English, Politics and Buckfast Wine. 'Hanratty's Time Capsule' was written to the soundtrack of Fatima

Mansions, Divine Comedy and Scott Walker. He would like to thank Jesus Christ and, the guvnor, David Vine.

NICHOLAS KELLY

Nicholas Kelly lives in Dublin and works mainly as a playwright and teacher. Work to date includes: *United Colours of Domino* (Dublin Youth Theatre, 1998), *The Black Rider* (RTE Radio Drama, 1998), *The Future Is Betamax* (Royal Court, London, 1996) and *Blameless* (RTE Radio Drama, 1996). He received a bursary in Literature from the Irish Arts Council in 1997.

COLIN MURPHY

Colin Murphy is a stand-up comedian and lives in Belfast with Paddy and Pepsi. He has performed at, amongst others, the *Cat Laughs Comedy Festival* and the 1998 Edinburgh festival in the sell-out show *Young, Gifted And Green*. This is his first short story though he has written for television and radio, most recently writing and acting in Comedy Nation for BBC2 and @last tv for RTE. He has had his own comedy show on BBC Northern Ireland and UTV and stars in the feature film *Divorcing Jack*.

Sarah Champion

A Manchester 'wild child', now grown up and living in London, Sarah Champion likes drinking, dancing, reading and holidays in Cambodia. She edited the best-selling fiction anthologies *Disco Biscuits* and *Disco 2000*, as well as writing about pop culture and compiling CDs. Forthcoming projects include *Southside Stories*, a CD of Brixton electro, and *Fortune Hotel*, a travel collection for Penguin.

Her ambition is to become a digital nomad, travelling the world with just a Powerbook and a mobile phone.

Donal Scannell

Donal Scannell spends the money he makes working on various television, radio, Internet and writing projects on the Dublin-based Quadraphonic and Stereophonic Records, which release, encourage and promote a varied diet of electronic squiggles for enlightened portions of the world to enjoy. His ambition is to do Tokyo on expenses.

Acknowledgements

Acknowledgements

'Red Isuzu' copyright Colin Murphy 1998

The words of 'Safe from Harm' by Massive Attack appear in Caspar Walsh's story 'N52' courtesy of Music Sales Ltd, Warner Chappell and Island Music.

Words and music by Robert Del Naja, Grantley Marshall, Andrew Vowles, Shara Nelson and Billy Cobham.

© Copyright 1991 Chippewa Music Incorporated and Neue Welt Musikverlag, GMBH. Warner Chappell Music Limited, Griffin House, 161 Hammersmith Road, London W6 (90%) and Island Music Limited, 47 British Grove, London W4 (10%).

Collect The Set

Disco Biscuits (Sceptre)
ISBN 0 340-682655

i-D called it a 'phenomenon'. The first and best-selling collection of its kind. Nineteen stories about drugs, sex, dancefloors, dealers, police and DJs. Featuring Britain's finest contemporary writing from Irvine Welsh, Jeff Noon, Nicholas Blincoe, Q, Alan Warner, Martin Millar, Charlie Hall, Alex Garland, Douglas Rushkoff and more. see: www.discobiscuits.org

Disco 2000 (Sceptre)
ISBN 0 340-707721 2

Nineteen stories set in the last hours of 31 December 1999, encompassing religious mania, suicide cults, future technology, time travel, chemical excess and media conspiracy. Features exclusive stories from some of the world's top cult writers including Douglas Coupland, Neal Stephenson, Poppy Z Brite, Grant Morrison, Douglas Rushkoff, Bill Drummond, Courttia Newland, Robert Anton Wilson, Nicholas Blincoe, Pat Cadigan, Martin Millar and more.

Disco 2000: various artists (bokå) bokå 2

The incendiary soundtrack album that captures the apocalyptic vibe of electronic music at the end of the 21st century – a vibrant selection that defies categorisation, fusing twisted funk, hip hop, big beat and disco with spacey drum 'n' bass. Features specially recorded tracks from Alabama 3, Conemelt, Witchman, Blame, Plug, Jimi Tenor, Glamorous Hooligan and U-ziq plus exclusive mixes of Coldcut, Bentley Rhythm Ace and 2K's 'Fuck The Millennium'.

Disco Biscuits: various artists (Coalition) 0630-181924

The companion CD with nineteen classic anthems including: 808 State 'Pacific State'; Future Sound Of London 'Papua New Guinea'; Underworld 'Rez'; LTJ Bukem 'Horizons'; Goldie 'Inner City Life'; Green Velvet 'Preacher Man'; Orbital 'Halcyon'; Leftfield 'Not Forgotten'; Sueno Latino 'Sueno Latino'; Hardfloor 'Acperience' and The Beloved 'Sunrising'.

Respect Due

Donal would like to thank Sarah Champion for starting this ball rolling and Simon Prosser and Michael McLoughlin for rolling this ball in my direction; Susan for being a flatmate, sister, reader and advisor; Mark, Dor and Donal for the constant reminders; Biggie and all who played Quadraphonic for the good times; Donal D and the Kerry posse for being gits; and Adriana for saying 'sí'.

Sarah would also like to thank Neil Taylor, Katie Collins and all at Hodder for their patience. Also, Glenn Patterson, Kevin and Jamie at Rebel Inc, Elaine Plamer of Pulp Faction, Hot Press, the Banshees of New York and Roxy Walsh for their help. Thanks also to Denise Moore, fire-starting soulmate from Belfast to the Mekong Delta.